HEART OF SAMOS

SUSAN FAW

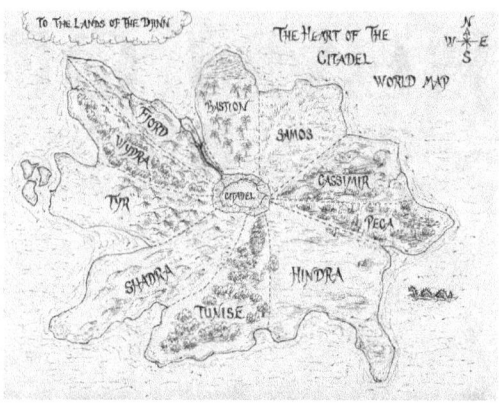

Cover design by Susan Faw.

Ebook ISBN: 978-1-989022-63-4

Paperback ISBN: 978-1-989022-64-1

CONTENTS

CHAPTER ONE

THE SEVENTH DAY: SAMOS

Niloo leaned out the narrow window of her second story bedroom, eagerly watching for a first glimpse of the approaching noisy spectacle, bouncing off the rough plastered walls and echoing down the alleyway. She was so blessed. She had the best seat of all for her bedroom window, on the highest floor of the multiple storied building, overlooked the parade route below. She leaned further out and a curtain of straight black hair swung across her tanned face. She shoved it impatiently behind one ear, as the large, lapis lazuli coloured paper dragon snaked its way around the far corner and into the crowded alley, created by the tall structures. Smoke billowed from its nostrils as it wove and ducked back and forth across the street, eliciting screams of delight from the children below. Brightly coloured scales reflected the light of the setting sun. Streams of paper lanterns, strung from building to building across the crowded boulevard, bobbed in the errant breeze.

Street performers sang and acrobats tumbled or juggled flame. Others performed slights of hand in advance of the dragon, entertaining the throngs surrounding them on either side. Many had lined up the night before to be assured a prized spot along the parade route. Adults tossed coins into baskets as he performers passed and children squealed and dodged between legs to gather sweets that tumbled from the dragon's mouth as it tossed its head to and fro.

Niloo didn't care about the sweets. She was not a baby anymore and besides, she had the best viewing spot of all. She stretched further out her window, then shifted to raise her leg over the sill to straddle the opening. Suddenly a hand grabbed the back of her silken robe and pulled her backward out of the window. A crystal necklace around her neck swung with the force of the pull, and she toppled back into the room.

"Hey!" she cried, hitting the floor with a loud smack.

"Are you trying to break your neck?" Her brother Darius glared down at her. "You could fall doing that! Besides, I want to see." He stuck his leg through the window, straddling the aged wooden framework. With his bulk, he completely filled the narrow opening blocking all of the view.

"Get out of my window!" Niloo stamped her slippered foot, furious dark eyes glinting with the reflected sconce lights, trimmed for evening, that decorated the wall beside the window. "You have your own window!"

"On the back side of the house! It's my turn!" His face swung back into the room, and a flash of crystal on a chain around his neck, caught the light of the flickering candle. "You had better hurry. The dragon is almost here!" He grinned at her frustration, and his head swiveled out toward the street once again.

With a cry of rage, Niloo bolted from her bedroom and ran down the hall to the fire escape set on the far end of the hallway. She threw open the window and grabbed onto the rungs of a wooden ladder affixed to the side of the building. The rungs were cold and slick from a shower that had passed through just before the parade began. A stiff breeze swept the building, flapping her robes, and chilling her to the bone. She shivered as she climbed, ignoring the cold.

A roar surged from the crowd, followed by cheering and clapping. Panicked that she was going to miss the big event, she scrambled up the rungs to the rooftop and jumped onto the slick tiled surface. As her feet hit the roof, she slipped and began to slide down the steep pitch. Niloo's hand scrabbled frantically for any purchase she could find and she managed to grasp the edge of a couple of tiles, halting her descent. She lay gasping, panting for a second, calming her heart, then began to climb once more until she reached the flat surface at the peak. The narrow platform was barely two feet across with large gargoyles on either end. She could not see the street below. Frustrated, she trotted down the length of the ridge toward the largest of the gargoyles that guarded the far end of the roof.

Music drifted into the air, and she heard the dragon's processional. *It was almost time. She was going to miss it!*

With a sob of frustration, she hurried her pace and as she reached the end of the roof, two things became apparent. The parade dragon was indeed at the terminus of its journey and curling into its final position for the finale, and ...

...the gargoyle was no gargoyle.

The parade dragon gave a bellowing roar from below, and a series of "phut, phut, phut" sounds reached her ears. With a boom, the sky lit up with fireworks directly overhead. Distracted by the fireworks, she stared up at the explosion of colour that rained down from the sky above.

Beautiful, so beautiful! I have the best seat in the house! she thought.

The gargoyle shifted slightly. Niloo caught the movement out of the corner of her eye. Slowly she turned, alarm causing her heart to jump in her chest. Silhouetted against the night sky and backlit by fireworks, the gargoyle stretched then turned to face her, midnight eyes blinking once.

It left its perch on the terminus of the roof and slowly walked the narrow strip toward her, wings extending to block out the sky.

Niloo gasped. *A dragon...a real live dragon! Here on the roof!*

She backed slowly away from the dragon, not wanting to alarm it. Her foot hit one of the joins of the roof, a trim piece that connected the flat tiles. She tripped over the rigid plate, toppling over the side of the roof. With a hair-raising shriek that was swallowed by the loud bangs of more fireworks bursting overhead, she rolled down the roof, gathering speed as she went until with a whoosh she shot off into the air above the crowded street.

She screamed. Up and up she went tumbling and disoriented, then her momentum slowed and reversed, plummeting toward the merry-makers crowding the street below.

A black blur shot from the sky, talons extended, swift as an arrow. She could see it coming, feet extended, claws open, eyes glowing with intensity. Just as Niloo dropped into the visible range of the street, the dragon snatched her from mid-air. Gigantic wings flapped skyward into the dark.

Niloo, lying belly down within the dragon's clawed cage, spied her brother straddling her window cell, his eyes widened in horror and mouth frozen open with shock. His face crumpled then he disappeared from the window. She watched the ground shrink, falling away beneath her until she could no longer see her window or her street nor anything but the shrinking fireworks that pinpointed her home. Eventually, they disappeared too, and the rhythmic strokes of the wings lulled her into an exhausted stupor. Niloo fell into a deep sleep just as they left the shore of Samos and headed out to sea.

Chapter Two

THE
Approaching
Storm

The throne room of the Citadel cast long shadows across obsidian floors, its vaulted ceiling lost in darkness above. Emperor Madrid sat motionless upon his marble and gold throne, his fingers drumming an irregular rhythm against its gilded armrest as Commander Cayos approached with measured steps.

"The reports from our scouts, Your Majesty." Cayos kept his voice carefully neutral, though Madrid could sense the anticipation beneath the practiced calm.

Madrid's eyes flicked to the parchments in Cayos's hands. The volcanic readings had grown more erratic over the past fortnight, and now his intuition—that subtle awareness that had kept him alive through countless plots—whispered of opportunity.

"The northern ranges of Samos show unprecedented activity," Cayos continued, unrolling the first map across the massive war table. He weighted the corners of the parchment with four inkwells carved from a singular dragon claw. "Our geomancers believe the tremors originate from greater depths than we've never delved before. But this discovery..." He produced a second set of documents, their edges worn from handling. "These change everything."

Madrid rose, his shadow stretching across the map like an ink stain. The stolen maps were ancient, their lines drawn in an archaic script that few could decipher. Few, except those who had studied the old ways as thoroughly as he had before eradicating them from his empire.

"Dragon nesting grounds." The words left Madrid's lips in barely more than a whisper, but they carried the weight of discovery. His eyes flashed with excitement as a long finger traced the intricate patterns marking thermal vents and underground lava tubes. "Not dormant I think. Fossilized."

"Our cartographer correlated the ancient markings with current volcanic activity," Cayos said. "The probability of intact specimens is slim, but its value—"

"Immeasurable." Madrid's voice cut through the air. "Dragon essence a thousand years old, preserved in stone and ash. And with it..."

He didn't finish the thought. The implications were clear enough. Dragon essence, harvested before death, concentrated by eons of pressure—it would be more potent than anything he had managed to extract from living specimens. Combined with his planned mastery over the crystal heartbearers, such power could accelerate his plans considerably.

"Assemble an excavation team," Madrid commanded. "A squadron of workers, supported by the Third Legion. And..." He paused, considering. "Bring me Darius."

Cayos hesitated. "The Heartbearer from Samos? Your Majesty, his training is far from complete. His control over his abilities remains... volatile."

"Precisely." Madrid moved to the window, where the Citadel's spires pierced the sky like accusatory fingers. Below, the controlled chaos of his empire continued its endless dance. "A crystal heartbearer connected to Samos soil will sense what our equipment cannot. And there's another advantage."

He turned back to Cayos, and for a moment the commander saw something almost feral in his emperor's eyes. "He has a sister."

The weight of that fact settled between them. Crystal hearts often ran in families, a fact Madrid had meticulously documented. If the boy carried the pendant, then so did—

"We did receive reports of unusual dragon sightings above Samos during a past Harvest Festival," Cayos said carefully. "A young woman went missing, years ago, from her home. Her parents claimed she fell ill, but neighbors spoke of strange objects in the sky. The timing would be right."

"Dragons rarely act without purpose." Madrid's hand unconsciously touched the scar beneath his robe—a reminder of his own encounter with the scaled beasts. "If they took her to Jintessa, she'll

return. They always do. And when she comes back to save her prov
ince..." He smiled, though the expression held no warmth. "We'll be
waiting."

A knock interrupted their planning. A messenger entered, his face
pale beneath his helm. "Your Majesty, we've lost contact with the
western monitoring post. The last transmission spoke of... unusual
seismic patterns."

Madrid exchanged a glance with Cayos. The timing was too co-
incidental. If the dragons were stirring, if the Keepers of Samos had
activated some ancient defense...

"Accelerate our timeline," he commanded. "I want those excavations begun within the week. And summon Darius immediately." He
turned to the tall, arched window eyes fixed on the place he knew
was the heart of the Samosian province, the seat of the rebel's power.
Angry storm clouds gathered on the horizon. It suited his plans. "A
storm approaches, and we shall not merely weather it. We shall harness
its very essence."

Commander Cayos saluted, his tightly curled fist thudding against
his huge, armoured chest. As Cayos departed to carry out his orders,
Madrid moved to the window that overlooked his dominion to the
north. Squinting his eyes, he strained to pick out the sharp peaks of
Samos' western boundary with Bastion. It was too far for the naked
eye, of course, but in his mind's eye, he could see the ancient dragons'
resting places, and feel the power thrumming beneath Samos's rolling
plains. The crystal heartbearers thought they could stop him, thought
their dragon bonds and familial loyalties made them strong, invincible.

They would learn otherwise. The Keepers' secrets would be laid
bare, the fossilized essence bound beneath the surface would be his,
and not even blood itself would stand between him and ultimate

victory. The storm was indeed gathering, but it would be his enemies who found themselves swept away by its fury.

Outside, the first drops of rain began to fall, each one striking the ancient stone, a harbinger of the deluge to come.

CHAPTER THREE

FACE TO FACE

The shadowed peaks of Samos appeared first on the horizon, their snow-capped summits catching the first light of dawn. Niloo's heart clenched at the sight of home, though she had been away only a short time. She knew that time moved differently in Jintessa, but some things never changed—not the rolling hills of barley, not the way the mountains stood sentinel over the flat fields of corn that stretched as far as the eye could see and not the bone-deep longing to return to the eastern province of her birth.

The barrier grows closer, Lapis rumbled beneath her. The deeply, blue-scaled dragon's voice echoed in her mind, tinged with ancient knowledge born of a land far away. *I can taste it on the wind.*

Lazuli, the third member of their triad, hopped down from Lapis' neck spike, then shape shifted from the form of a red crested hawk and back into his favoured humanoid shape. His legs lengthened as he settled down into the second saddle behind Niloo. His torso expanded and shoulders firmed under the tan leather tunic until he resembled a lad in his late teens, with blonde hair and smoky blue eyes like a storm tossed sea. His djinn features sharped with concentration as he studied the energy field undulating on the horizon. "The magic feels... hungry."

Niloo had learned much in her brief time in Jintessa, but nothing could have prepared her for her first true encounter with Madrid's sorcery. As they approached the invisible wall that had imprisoned her province for years, the air itself seemed to thicken with malevolence.

"It wasn't just any magic that built these barriers," Lazuli continued, his voice dropping to avoid disturbing the spell-heavy air. "Your teachers spoke of soul-binding, of wizards who—"

"WHO SURRENDERED!" The words exploded from the barrier itself, though no mouth spoke them. The sound assaulted them, setting off a quiver that shivered through their bones, as faces materialized in the air before them—faces of men long dead, their features twisted in eternal torment. Pale and immense, the spectral images floated before them, expanding into the empty sky and flattening into a curve that defined the limits of the invisible barrier.

Lapis banked hard, nearly unseating Niloo as a tendril of shadow lashed out from the barrier. Where it passed, the grass below withered to ash. Niloo yelped and tightened her thigh straps, as she slipped sideways with the sudden change in direction. Gripping her reins in one hand, her left drifted towards her hip, where a coil of rope hung, her prized weapon of choice, earned in her training.

"Ancient wizards," one face moaned, its eyes hollow pits of blue fire. "We gave our souls to the Emperor... to protect our families... to save what we could..."

"But he lied," another voice joined in, creating a horrible chorus. "Lied... lied... LIED!"

The barrier pulsed and groaned with unholy energy, sparks of orange and green exploding outwards only to collapse in on itself. Niloo felt a tug under her shirt where her crystal heart hid, responding—not with its usual warm glow, but with a searing pain that nearly doubled her over in Lapis's saddle. Gasping, she grasped a fist full of her shirt and pulled the crystal heart away from contact with her skin.

"Back!" she cried, but it was too late. Her crystal heart flared, and the barrier seemed to recognize something, in its brilliant light. The souls trapped within surged forward, their spectral hands reaching through dimensions to grasp at her.

"heartbearer!" they shrieked in unison. "YOU WHO WOULD BREAK OUR CHAINS!"

Lapis dove, spiraling away from the barrier's edge, but not before Niloo caught a glimpse of something that stopped her breath. Among the tormented faces, she saw features that mirrored her own—the strong jaw of her father's line, the high cheekbones inherited from her mother. These weren't just any wizards Madrid had trapped. Some of them were her own ancestors.

"The crystal hearts mark us," she whispered, understanding dawning with sickening clarity. "That's why the barrier reacted. It recognized..."

Your bloodline, Lapis finished, banking into a tight circle well beyond the barrier's reach. *The wizards who built this wore the same pendants you bear now, before Madrid corrupted their purpose.*

Lazuli raised his arms in a defensive posture, hands glowing with protective magic. He eyes scanned the barrier, seeking a weakness, a break in the raging sea of faces. "We can't approach directly!" he yelled. "The barrier is designed to trap those with crystal heart magic—this must be why the Emperor wanted wizards who wore them. The male heartbearers will be doubly bound."

Niloo's mind raced. Every tale she'd heard of Madrid's bargains, every whispered story of wizards who had traded their souls for promises of protection—all of it painted a picture more horrifying than she'd imagined. These men hadn't just been controlled; they'd been made to craft their own prisons using the very symbols of their heritage. Did this include her brother, Darius? Had he shared a similar fate to these insane spirits, their very souls fueling Emperor Madrid's defences?

"Then how do we get through?" The question came out harder than she intended, fury mixing with her fear. Below them, she could see her village—or what remained of it. The clay tile rooftops of the main streets of New Lavos dully reflected the setting sun, the streets empty and debris strewn, while around the shattered capital, tiny houses lay scattered across the plains like fallen leaves, isolated farmsteads connected by roads she'd walked a thousand times. Home, yet impossibly distant.

"There has to be a way," she continued, her voice cracking as her gaze swung wildly, shying away from making eye contact with the haunted, bottomless sockets of the ghosts. "Darius is in there. My family. Everyone I've ever known."

The trapped souls seemed to hear her desperation. Their wailing lessened to a sorrowful keening, and one face pressed forward—older than the others, with eyes that still held a spark of his former self.

"Child of Samos blood..." His voice carried across the magical divide. "We were the first... the strongest... We thought we could contain his power from within..."

"What do I do?" Niloo called back, ignoring Lapis's warning rumble. "Tell me how to break this!"

"You cannot break what is already broken," the ancient wizard replied. "We shattered ourselves to create it. And still we failed..." His face began to fade, drawn back into the barrier's depths. "Find the heart... find the original heart... only there can—"

His words cut off as the barrier surged again, this time with renewed violence. Where before it had shown twisted faces, now it revealed scenes—memories stolen from the bound souls. Niloo watched in horror as image after image flickered past: wizards kneeling before Madrid, their crystal hearts pulsing as they spoke binding words; children crying as their fathers' souls were ripped away; the very construction of the barriers, built not with stone and mortar, but with sacrifice and sorrow.

"We need to retreat," Lazuli said urgently, already scanning for threats. "Madrid has watchers on the border. They'll have felt that disturbance."

But Niloo couldn't tear her eyes away. In the chaos of memories, she caught glimpses of a central chamber somewhere deep beneath Samos—a place where the barrier's anchors converged. And there, suspended in crystal like her own pendant, but massive beyond imagining, hung what could only be the original heart the dying wizard had spoken of.

"I see it," she breathed. "The source. But it's beneath the capital. How do we—"

A shadow passed over them, much larger than Lapis. Niloo looked up to see patroling dragons bearing Imperial riders, their uniforms marked with the crossed blades of the Citadel. They hadn't yet spotted the trio, but they were hunting something—likely the magical disturbance caused by her encounter with the barrier.

"Hide!" Lazuli commanded, weaving an illusion around them even as Lapis tucked her wings and dove for the cover of a nearby cloud bank.

As they slid into the damp wisps of vapor, Niloo's mind churned with what she'd learned. The barrier couldn't be broken from outside—not directly. But if the source lay within, if the original heart could be reached...

"We need a new plan," she said once the patrol had passed. "Something the barrier won't expect."

Lapis rumbled in agreement. *The ancient wizards built their own cage. Perhaps their own blood offers the key to its lock.*

Lazuli nodded thoughtfully. "The Keepers might know more. Your family has guarded secrets for generations, Niloo. Secrets even you weren't told."

The weight of their task settled over her like the approaching storm clouds. She could see why Madrid had chosen soul-binding for his barriers—they were nearly impossible to break when the very architecture required the willing sacrifice of powerful magic users. But nearly impossible wasn't impossible.

Niloo straightened in her saddle, her crystal heart glowing with renewed determination. If her ancestors had been part of building this prison, then perhaps some key to its undoing lay in their sacrifice. She would find it, even if it meant confronting the darkest secrets of Samos itself.

"Take us down," she commanded. "Away from the barrier. My family's farm lies east—we'll start there. The Keepers may have answers, but first, I need to understand why my own blood was chosen for Madrid's chains."

As Lapus began their descent, Niloo cast one last look at the barrier. In its depths, the souls of ancient wizards continued their eternal vigil, their faces now tinged with something she hadn't expected to see—hope.

CHAPTER FOUR

THE EMPEROR'S BOND

The dark, damp dungeon lay three levels beneath the Citadel's main towers, its hand hewn stone walls embellished with translucent quartz prisms set in high, narrow windows, that threw fractured light across the chamber's cruel geometry. Darius sat cross-legged on the cold stone floor, bare chested, his own heart crystal—crimson where his sister's was blue—pulsing against his chest in time with Madrid's summoning magic.

"Look up, young wizard." Emperor Madrid's voice echoed off the shimmering walls, making it impossible to determine his exact location. Darius had been here long enough to know his master preferred psychological disorientation to simple intimidation.

Reluctantly, Darius raised his head, meeting Madrid's gaze through air shivering with residual spell-work. The Emperor stood beyond a barrier of energy, his face gaunt but his eyes burning with an intensity that had never diminished through their many sessions. At Madrid's feet, ancient maps of Samos were spread across the floor like the scales of some great serpent, their surfaces covered in notations written in Madrid's precise hand.

"Your homeland calls to you still," Madrid observed, gesturing to the maps. "Even after all this time. Even knowing what your village did to you."

Darius's hands clenched involuntarily. New Lavos—the capital that would have claimed him, trained him as one of their watchmen, destined him for a life patrolling borders he could never cross. When Madrid's riders had discovered his crystal heart during one of their sweeps, they'd claimed him by ancient right, spiriting him away before his family could even mourn their son.

"They fear magic because you taught them to," Darius said, keeping his voice level despite the tremor in his throat. "You showed them what happens to those who wield power without control."

"I showed them survival," Madrid corrected, stepping through the restraining energy field. His proximity made Darius's crystal burn against his skin—not with warmth as it had with his sister's presence, but with the cold fire of forced allegiance. "The same survival I offer you now."

The Emperor extended his hand, and between his fingers materialized a vial of liquid shadow. "The volcanic readings suggest something extraordinary. Dragon essence, crystallized by time itself. But finding it requires... finesse."

Darius stared at the vial, recognizing the blood magic that swirled within its glass prison. During his training, he'd learned that Madrid drew power from sacrifice—animal blood for minor spells, human blood for major workings, and for the most powerful magic...

"Dragon blood," he whispered, the words tasting of copper and betrayal.

"Combined with the tears of a crystal heartbearer," Madrid confirmed, his smile sharp as winter ice. "Your tears, specifically. The essence resonates with those born to Samos soil. With your guidance, we can locate every deposit, every trace of ancient power that lies buried beneath your precious plains."

The crystal pendant against Darius's chest flared painfully, and suddenly he was elsewhere—not physically, but in vision. Through his sister's eyes he saw the barrier that had repelled him for months, saw her suspended in flight before it with her dragon companion. Niloo's anguish hit him like a physical blow as she discovered the truth about the souls trapped within.

"No," he gasped, the vision dissolving back into the dungeon's harsh reality. His head spun with the afterimage of Niloo's face, her eyes wide with understanding. She had returned. She had tried to come home.

"Ah," Madrid's voice carried dark satisfaction. "She attempts the barrier once more. Your blood connection grows stronger with each passing day. Tell me, boy—how does it feel to watch your sister struggle while you sit safe within my embrace?"

Safe. The word mocked everything Darius had endured. His training had stripped away gentle sensibilities piece by piece, replacing childhood innocence with calculated application of power. Fellow crystal heartbearers had been turned against their provinces. Some had broken, becoming extensions of Madrid's will entirely. Others had died, their crystals harvested for darker purposes.

Darius had walked a knife's edge, maintaining enough will to preserve his sanity while showing enough obedience to survive. But seeing Niloo trapped outside while he remained within threatened to tip that balance.

"She'll find a way," he said, though doubt crept into his voice. "Niloo is clever. Determined. She won't let the barrier—"

"The barrier was created by men like you," Madrid interrupted, circling behind him. Darius felt thin fingers rest on his shoulders—deceptively gentle touches that promised violence if he resisted. "Wizards who believed their sacrifice noble. Men who thought if they could just bargain correctly, they might save their loved ones from my hunger. Or perhaps hungered for my power."

Darius knew the history. It was drilled into every crystal heartbearer who entered the Citadel's service: the generation of wizards who had gathered at the ancient Keep, believing themselves strong enough to face the rising Emperor. Instead, they had drunk from his goblets and breathed his incense, their bodies and souls corrupted, their magic perverted to build the very barriers that now imprisoned their descendants.

"They built their own prisons," he said automatically, reciting the lesson Madrid had burned into his mind. "And found themselves the jailers."

"Precisely." Madrid's fingers tightened. "Now, will you be their echo, or will you be more? The maps show three primary volcanic zones where dragon essence might be harvested. Name them, and I shall grant you mercy."

The crimson crystal blazed as Madrid's will pressed against Darius's own. The Emperor had refined his control techniques over years of practice. Pain wasn't necessary when one could simply... redirect thoughts. Guide decisions. Make the slave believe each choice was freely made.

Darius fought the compulsion, but his training had been thorough. His mind began mapping the volcanic regions of his homeland, categorizing thermal outputs, calculating the likelihood of promising sites. Against his will, coordinates flowed from his lips:

"The Ashfall Heights, where miners report temperatures inconsistent with known deposits. Fire Ridge, abandoned after the collapse of '17. And..." He struggled, jaw clenching as he tried to withhold the final location. "And the Dead Fields, where nothing grows, though the earth shows no sign of contamination."

"Excellent," Madrid purred, releasing him. "See how simple cooperation can be? Your knowledge aids progress. Your province will be liberated through your guidance."

"Liberated to what?" Darius turned to face his master, a rare moment of defiance fueled by thoughts of Niloo. "Your idea of freedom is submission. Your prosperity comes at the cost of everything that makes us who we are."

For a heartbeat, true anger flashed across Madrid's face—a reminder that beneath the measured facade lurked something far more dangerous than mere ambition.

"You speak of identity?" he asked quietly, raising his hand to reveal lines of blood-ink tattoos crawling up his forearm like thorny vines. "I sacrificed my identity, my true ethnicity, even my name to gain the power needed to unite this fractured realm. Do you think yourself too precious to do the same?"

The question hung in the air like a curse. Darius had no answer. Each day in the Citadel stripped away more of who he'd been, replacing Samos customs with Imperial protocols, family loyalties with enforced obedience. How much of him remained unspoiled?

Madrid gestured, and the maps began to shift, responding to Darius's spoken coordinates. "Your sister will come for you," he stated with certainty. "Crystal hearts are drawn to their twins like moths to a flame. When she breaches our defenses, when she stands where you sit now, remember this conversation. Remember that I offered you the choice to serve willingly."

"And when I refuse again?" The question emerged before wisdom could silence it.

"Then she will learn, as you have learned, that refusal is merely painful, postponed acceptance." Madrid turned to leave, then paused at the chamber's threshold. "Commander Cayos departs for Samos at dawn. You will accompany him. Show him the sites. Guide his excavations. And remember—every moment you delay our success is a moment your sister remains exposed to dangers you can scarcely imagine."

Left alone in his dismal prison cell, Darius slumped against the wall, his red crystal heart pulsing weakly. Through their mystical connection, he could sense Niloo's mounting fear, her determination wavering as she grasped the true nature of Madrid's barriers. Part of him wanted to reach out, to warn her somehow, but Madrid's conditioning held firm.

In his mind's eye, unbidden images surfaced—memories of their childhood in the fertile valleys east of New Lavos. Niloo had always been the bold one, climbing trees he'd deemed too tall, swimming rivers he'd judged too swift. She'd protected him from village bullies with a fierce loyalty that had both embarrassed and comforted him.

When they'd discovered their matching crystals, she'd promised they would face whatever came together.

Now they stood on opposite sides of Madrid's war, and Darius wasn't certain he possessed the strength to bridge that divide. The Emperor's blood crystal magic worked not through force alone, but through the slow accumulation of moral compromises. Each choice Darius made to survive pushed him further from the boy who'd left Samos, closer to whatever Madrid needed him to become.

A soft chime echoed through the dungeon as a servant brought his evening meal—simple fare designed to maintain health without providing comfort. As he ate, Darius attempted to formulate a plan. If he must guide Cayos to the excavation sites, perhaps he could find ways to slow their progress. Subtle errors in navigation. Feigned confusion about ancient landmarks. Small rebellions that might buy time for... what? Rescue? Redemption? Or merely the postponement of inevitable surrender?

His crystal heart warmed briefly, and for a moment Darius swore he heard Niloo's voice carried on the ether between them. Not words exactly, but emotion—determination mixed with a new understanding. She had learned something at the barrier, something that gave her purpose beyond simple rescue.

Darius pressed his palm against the pendant, concentrating on their connection. Unlike Madrid's forced visions, this felt natural, warm, familiar. Through it, he sensed Lapis—Niloo's dragon companion—and beyond that, earth magic stirring in ways he'd never felt before. His sister had always possessed an affinity for growing things, a talent Madrid had tried to corrupt into more destructive purposes in Darius's training.

What would happen when that innate power met Madrid's artificial constructs?

The thought sparked something in him—a ember of the boy who had dreamed of adventure beyond Samos's rolling plains. If Niloo was discovering new depths to her abilities, perhaps his own modifications weren't as absolute as Madrid believed. The blood magic binding him operated on belief as much as spell-craft. What if that belief could be... redirected?

As night deepened beyond the crystalline walls, Darius began to plan in earnest. Not escape—that remained impossible while Madrid held his life in magical surety. But resistance had many forms. If he must guide the excavations, he would do so in ways that served broader purposes than mere obedience.

The Emperor wanted to gather dragon essence to fuel his ambitions. But ancient power answered to ancient purposes, and Darius suspected the fossilized magic would respond differently to the touch of native Samos blood than to Madrid's corrupted will. Let them dig. Let them unearth secrets buried beneath protective stone. Some revelations, once awakened, could not be controlled by any mortal hand—even one as ruthless as Emperor Madrid's.

Tomorrow would bring Cayos, in more ways that one, and the journey to his home soil. Darius would walk among the graves of the great beasts, long forgotten to the present world. He would touch the earth his mother had blessed, with chants his father had tried to forget. There, perhaps, in the place where his journey began, he might find the strength to influence how it ended.

For now, he could only wait, his crystal heart beating its binary rhythm: loyalty and betrayal, sister and master, Samos boy and Citadel slave. Tomorrow would demand all he had learned, all he had become, and all he had managed to preserve of his original self.

Tomorrow would determine whether he would be Madrid's tool for destruction, or something more complex and potentially dangerous—a bridge between worlds, whether he willed it or not.

The crystal chamber fell silent except for the faint hum of contained energy. Somewhere beyond its walls, the machinery of an Empire ground its endless advance toward goals only Madrid fully understood. That thought brought Darius no comfort, for he had begun to suspect that even the Emperor had forgotten more than he remembered about the powers he sought to harness.

CHAPTER FIVE

BREAKING DOWN BARRIERS

Dawn painted the eastern sky in hues of amber and rose as Niloo's triad circled the barrier once more. The temperature had dropped during the night, and the morning air stung Niloo's cheeks as she gripped Lapis's ridged spine. Her knuckles had turned white from the cold and tension, but she barely noticed. Lazuli had spent the darkest hours of night studying the phenomenon, his djinn eyes perceiving layers of magic invisible to human sight. Now, as Lapis wings caught the first light, her lapis lazuli scales shimmering like polished stone beneath oil, Lazuli shared his discoveries.

"The barrier isn't uniform," he explained, his form shifting between translucent hawk and solid man as he spoke. "Think of it as a tapestry—thousands of threads woven by hundreds of souls, each strand carrying memories of its maker." His voice carried that peculiar harmonic quality common to djinn, each word seeming to echo from multiple sources.

Niloo gripped Lapis's ridged spine, feeling the dragon's deep blue scales pulse with inner warmth. Each scale was the size of her palm, intricately patterned with swirling black lines like ancient calligraphy. When Lapis breathed deeply, those patterns shifted and danced, responding to her connection with the earth magic far below. "The wizards who built it," Niloo said, completing his thought. "The souls we saw yesterday."

"More than that." Lazuli pointed to a section where the morning light seemed to bend oddly, creating prismatic fractures that defied natural law. The air shimmered like heat waves rising from summer stone, but cold emanated from the distortion instead. "Your own ancestors wove parts of this spell. The blood of your Samosian cousins flows in those ethereal threads. That's why your crystal reacted so violently—it recognized kin in the weaving."

The revelation settled over her like a heavy cloak. Everything she'd learned in Jintessa about magic hadn't prepared her for this intimate connection between past and present. Her heart crystal, a stone she'd worn since childhood thinking it merely a family heirloom, suddenly felt ancient beyond measure. The weight of it against her breastbone seemed to increase, as if the gem itself had gained mass from this new understanding.

"But if our blood helped build it," she reasoned aloud, her breath visible in the chill morning air, "couldn't it help unmake it?"

Lazuli's form solidified fully as he considered her words. In his human-like state, he resembled a lanky teenager, his skin carrying the subtle iridescence of precious metals. The pupils of his eyes swirled with colors that matched the dawn sky. "Traditional magic would suggest not. The binding spells require sacrifice to create, but also to destroy. Blood given freely binds eternally. However..." He turned to Lapis, his melodious voice taking on a note of speculation. "Your scales are unique, aren't they?"

The dragon rumbled deep in her chest, a sound that resonated through the saddle and into Niloo's bones. Lapis's voice carried the weight of ancient wisdom when she spoke. *Lapis lazuli dragons are rare even among our kind. We have the ability to absorb magical frequencies through our scales, and can attune to different energies that others might miss. Each scale vibrates at a different harmonic, creating a living instrument.* Her massive head swiveled to regard Niloo, nostrils flaring as they took in her scent combined with that of her crystal. *When I bonded with you, I resonated with your crystal. Perhaps we can use that connection to thread the needle of this barrier.*

Hope kindled in Niloo's chest, though caution tempered it. The cold air she breathed clarified her thoughts, making each consideration sharp and distinct. Every teaching from Jintessa warned against manipulating the barrier directly. Too many had tried, and many had failed spectacularly with tragic results. The stories spoke of wizards turned to ash, of whole families consumed when their magic backfired against the barrier's defenses. But Madrid himself had modified this one—warped it to serve as both prison and weapon. Perhaps that corruption created an exploitable weakness.

"My heart crystal carries minimal power outside the triad," she mused, pulling her cloak tighter as the wind picked up. "It's designed for triad resonance, not individual manipulation. But within our merged state..."

"The resonance amplifies exponentially," Lazuli finished. "The whole becomes greater than the sum of its parts. If Lapis can match the barrier's frequency while you suppress your crystal's signature, we might pass through undetected." The words tasted of possibility and danger in equal measure.

The plan formed through their connection, mental images flowing back and forth, faster than words could convey. Niloo would need to quiet her crystal heart—not an easy task when its very purpose was to shine with her innate magic, to broadcast her presence to those who could see. Meanwhile, Lapis would need to harmonize with the barrier's discordant song of trapped souls, each one adding its own note to the torment. And Lazuli would weave a glamour to mask their presence from Madrid's watchers, the ever-vigilant eyes that scanned all borders for signs of rebellion.

They descended to a point where the barrier crossed a stream. The water sparkled with unusual brightness, each droplet catching and reflecting the hidden magic that hung heavy in the air. The stream split around the invisible wall like oil meeting water—one flow continuing outside the barrier, another inside Samos. Where they tried to reunite, perpetual eddies formed, the water forever confused by the magical division.

Niloo dismounted on legs stiff from the night's chill, approaching until the air grew thick and oppressive with the weight of ancient sorrow. The barrier resisted their approach, each step forward like walking into an increasingly dense cloud, though nothing visible marked the transition. The barrier pressed against her consciousness, triggering a headache. She could feel it building behind her eyes. Niloo pushed the sensation aside, concentrating on the make up of the barrier. Up close, she could sense individual souls—their regrets whispering in her mind, their final moments playing out in fractured memories she couldn't quite grasp. Their desperate hope, that some-day freedom would come, resonated with her own newly awakened determination.

"I hear them," she whispered, her voice barely disturbing the heavy air. Each breath felt too shallow, as though the barrier was consuming the surrounding oxygen. Lazuli settled beside her, his height making her feel diminutive despite her seventeen years. His presence carried comfort—djinn were built for magic, knew its currents as intimately as fish knew water. While Lapis lowered her massive head, scales shimmering with reflected magic, preparing for the delicate work ahead.

"Focus on slowing your breathing," Lazuli instructed, his tone carrying the authority of one who had taught countless students. "The techniques from Jintessa will serve you now. In Jintessa, your control over the crystal improved rapidly. Draw on that training now." His hand hovered near her shoulder, ready to steady her if needed, though djinn rarely offered unprompted physical touch.

Niloo closed her eyes, placing both palms over her heart crystal. Through the fabric of her travel-worn tunic, she felt its familiar warmth. The gem had never been just decoration—she saw that now. Its usual pulse heated her skin gently, like the reflected heat of a hearth on dark winter nights. Its warmth normally comforted her; now she needed it to quiet. Her breath deepened, counting heartbeats as she'd been taught. Three beats in, hold for three, three beats out. The meditation techniques from Jintessa overlapped with older memories—her grandmother teaching her to calm herself before important harvests, speaking of how the earth could not be rushed by anxious hands. Her father instructing her on how to listen to the earth's subtle messages, to hear warnings in the physical changes of wind and soil. Those memories anchored her when magic alone might have scattered her thoughts.

With each breath, her crystal's glow faded from brilliant blue to a faint whisper of light visible only if you knew where to look. The change affected her physically—colors dimmed, sounds muted, as though someone had drawn gauze between her and the world. Her connection to Lapis and Lazuli remained, but even that felt cotton-muffled. The barrier's souls seemed to notice, their keening shifting from tormented wailing to something like curious chimes. Whispers that before had been incomprehensible began to form words, though broken and scattered.

"Now," Lazuli murmured, his voice carrying undertones that suggested readiness and warning combined. "Lapis, begin the harmonization."

The dragon's scales rippled like the surface of a pond disturbed by a stone as she studied the barrier. The morning sun, having risen higher into the sky, struck each scale differently, revealing patterns invisible just moments before. Each individual scale adjusted its angle microscopically to catch different frequencies of magic. A humming filled the air—not sound exactly, but something felt rather than heard. It vibrated through bone and blood, making teeth ache and hair stand on end. The notes built one upon another as Lapis carefully matched the barrier's complex harmonies. Like a conductor tuning an orchestra, she tested frequencies, adjusted, refined. The process took on the quality of a ritual, pattern and purpose woven into every movement of scale and nostril.

The souls' whispers grew louder. The voices she heard carried accents from across Samos—some ancient beyond measure, others painfully recent. Some cursed in languages predating the Empire. Others wept with voices worn thin from decades of sorrowful repetition. A few even laughed—the sound of sanity long lost to eternal imprisonment. Among them, Niloo heard fragments of Samosian dialects she'd thought lost to time. Words her grandmother had used for blessing the fields—ancient words of power so old their origins were forgotten. Curses her uncles had thrown at stubborn livestock, terms that now carried resonance beyond mere profanity.

"You see now," one voice emerged clearer than the rest. Niloo recognized the ancient wizard from yesterday, his spirit carrying the weight of centuries. His words came filtered through the shimmering air. "Why blood must match blood to breach these walls. Why those who built must be unmade before the building falls. Why—"

His words cut off as Lapis achieved perfect resonance. The humming peaked, reaching a frequency that made reality itself vibrate. For a moment—less than a heartbeat, but stretched eternally in perception—the barrier shimmered visible. A wall of blue-fire souls writhing in eternal torment materialized before them. Faces pressed against invisible glass, hands that had once held power grasping hopelessly. Knowledge glittered in tormented eyes—secrets Madrid had stolen, wisdom trapped between worlds. The sight burned itself into Niloo's memory even as she turned away.

"Go!" Lazuli commanded, his voice sharp as breaking ice. "Quickly! The resonance won't hold long! Lapis loses synchronization with each moment!"

Niloo sprang into Lapis's saddle with practiced grace, her suppressed crystal heart creating an unsettling emptiness in her chest. Like a missing heartbeat, an absence where life should have pulsed. As the dragon approached the barrier with purposeful strides, the trapped souls pressed forward. Some reached through with incorporeal hands, desperate fingers grasping. Centuries of longing condensed into those reaching gestures. Others warned—screaming of dangers that Niloo couldn't comprehend. Words in languages dead before the Empire, concepts that required magical understanding to translate.

The barrier's surface felt like stepping into a frozen lake. Not physically cold—temperature held no meaning here—but a chill that penetrated to the soul. Ice spread through Niloo's veins as they passed through layers of souls, each brushing her consciousness with memories of their final moments. Pain. Betrayal. Above all, regret.

Images flashed through her mind—not her own, but borrowed from those they passed. A wizard realizing too late that Madrid's wine carried more than alcohol. A father watching his children age while he remained trapped unchanging. Lovers separated by Madrid's promises, one soul bound while the other lived and died naturally. Each memory left traces, like mud tracked through a clean house. Some visions made her gasp, others brought tears she couldn't shed while encased in the crystal's power.

The passage stretched endlessly before her, but in reality lasting no time at all. Between one heartbeat and the next, they were through.

Niloo gasped. Samosian air filled her lungs—familiar scents of grain and earth that triggered the release of her tears at last. The difference struck her immediately. Jintessa's air had carried exotic spices, dragon breath, and sea salt. This air tasted of home—barley fields ready for harvest, the iron-rich soil of the eastern plains, morning dew still clinging to grass despite the sun's advance. Her suppressed crystal heart blazed back to life, warming against her skin as if welcoming her home. She drew a full breath, savouring its flavour. Behind them, the barrier shimmered once more before settling into its usual invisibility, souls receding from view though their presence remained palpable.

"We did it," Niloo breathed, disbelief and joy mingling in her voice. The words felt inadequate, failing to capture the enormity of their achievement. They had breached what many believed impassable. Her body trembled with reaction—part adrenaline crash, part triumph, part the lingering touch of those lost souls.

"For now." Lazuli reformed beside them, his usual solidity compromised. His form flickered at the edges, transparency revealing the morning sky through his shoulders. The effort of maintaining illusions while drawing attention from their passage had taken its toll. "But our passage created ripples. Like dropping stones in still water, the disturbance spreads. Madrid's watchers will notice the barrier's fluctuation."

As if summoned by his words, several dragons appeared on the horizon—distant specks growing larger with disturbing speed. Unlike the free-spirited creatures bonded to the heartbearers, these carried the unmistakable marks of Imperial corruption. Their scales bore Imperial markings—ink-black sigils tattooed into living scale to command obedience. Their wizards sat rigid in harnesses built for control rather than partnership, while their djinn leaned forward over the necks of their dragons, as though to protect their charges from the brutality of their master's bond. Silver spikes protruded from the dragons' spine where natural connection would flow, forcing artificial pathways for Madrid to control their combined power.

They patrol this section regularly, Lapis observed with draconic perception. Her eyes scanned the trail of magic left by their flight, which to her eyes appeared as spagetti trails in the sky. This residual magic was impossible for human eyes to detect, but her senses were capable of seeing the disturbance. *Likely watching for exactly what we just attempted. They search for magical disturbances.*

Niloo forced her breathing to steady. The euphoria of breaching the barrier began to fade as reality reasserted itself. They had crossed the barrier—an achievement that would have earned celebration in normal times. But entering Samos was only the beginning of their true challenge. The mountains might provide temporary cover, their peaks offering maze-like passages and shadow-deep valleys. But her family's farm lay in the eastern plains—a landscape of waving grain that offered no hiding places. Visible from above, vulnerable to sweep after sweep of mounted searchers. Certainly the location was known to the emperor.

"We need a plan," she said, scanning their surroundings with a new wariness. Their surroundings showed clear signs of Madrid's influence now that she looked for them—squinting at the horizon, she picked out a structure that had not existed in the past.

"What is that?" Niloo asked, pointing to the crest of a nearby hill. "It looks like a surveillance post has been erected – see it there? It's been disguised as a shepherd's hut," she said, pointing to the ragged structure. Her eyes swept over the undulating land, searching for other signs of a foreign touch.

Lapis snorted head swivelling to the north. Her eyes narrowed. *There has been magic performed here. Someone has been testing the ground, using dragon powers. Traces remain. For it to be this strong, it must have been recent.*

Niloo placed her hand lightly on Lapis' nose, then narrowed her eyes. One of the gifts she had received when she bonded with Lapis was to share her sight. Niloo narrowed her eyes and joined with the dragon and gazed northward. Suddenly bright streaks popped into being, sharp as dragon's claws drawn through wet clay. The streaks, or markers curved to the east before vanishing over the hill.

"I wonder what they were doing here? If we flew due east, following their paths, they'd track straight to my family homestead." Niloo frowned, worry wrinkling her brow, as she studied the patterns. Were they searching for her family? And if so, had they found them?

"There may be another reason for their interest in this area." Lazuli pointed to a valley cutting between two peaks. The formation struck him as unusual, his djinn nature sensitive to anything that disrupted natural patterns. "Those hills aren't natural. Someone terraformed this landscape ages ago. The geometry is too precise, and the mineral content shows signs of deliberate placement."

Niloo climbed back into her saddle on Lapis' broad back, studying the familiar valley with new eyes. The dense copse of trees had grown in a specific patterns, their canopy spaced too perfectly to be wild growth. With dawning recognition, she realized that the formations acted as wind-breaks and privacy screens, designed by someone or something that understood both horticulture and defensive positioning. The stream they'd crossed followed an unnaturally straight path, its bed lined with stones worn smooth not by water but sanded by something much harder, and denser...dragon scales.

Niloo walked up to a tall, stone outcropping, standing about six feet tall and polished smooth. Not a natural formation at all, but a stone marker— ancient boundary stones like these had were used to define property lines, as drawn by her ancestors. She ran her hand over the polished surface, examining the etchings with her finger tips. Samos runes were carved deep into the granite, still crisp despite centuries of weather.

"Dragon nesting grounds," Niloo breathed, memories from her grandmother's stories suddenly clicking into place.

I think before humans mapped Samos officially, long before the Emperer rose to power—my kind reshaped these lands. Lapis's voice carried the weight of rediscovered memory, scales shifting colors as they reflected different angles of morning light. *We tended them as gardens, as nurseries for our young. That is, if the dragon kin born of this land, shared this trait. While we hatch our young in volcanoes, once they fledge, we move to gardens such as these.*

"We can use that." Niloo's mind raced with possibilities, her military training from Jintessa combining with native knowledge of her homeland. "If these valleys hide ancient nesting sites, perhaps they also hide paths Madrid's forces don't know about. Underground routes that dragons carved for their most vulnerable young—tunnels that might lead who knows where...perhaps to the Citadel itself."

The approaching dragons drew closer, flying a methodical search pattern. They had not sensed their presence yet, but Niloo felt the urgency of her decision pressing down like a storm front, invisible but undeniable. Each moment they remained visible increased their risk of discovery.

"The barrier breach gave us entry but cost us time." She guided Lapis toward the valley's entrance, the dragon's powerful legs carrying them forward with ground-eating strides. "Every delay increases the Emperor's advantage. If we're to make his plan more difficult, we need to understand exactly what he seeks beneath our soil."

As they descended into the valley's embrace, the shadows cast by the tall cliffs swallowed them whole. The transition felt sudden—from bright morning sun to forest twilight, the canopy so thick it filtered out all but scattered beams of light. Ancient magic stirred in the underbrush—not threatening, but curious. Wisps of power that had lain dormant for generations now reached out to touch them, investigate these newcomers to their domain. The land itself seemed to wake, recognizing a dragon's presence after centuries of absence.

Behind them, an Imperial patrol passed overhead, their wingbeats creating downdrafts that stirred the valley's upper branches. Riders and their djinn counterparts peered down with enhanced sight, scanning for thermal signatures that would betray hidden travelers, or in the case of the dragons, the familiar scent of their kin. Whatever modifications Madrid had made to his patrol dragons, their senses exceeded normal draconic perception. Lazuli's glamour held strong against this inspection, masking them by bending light and heat patterns to suggest empty forest below.

This way, Lapis murmured silently through the bond, some deep echo of a memory guiding her movements. Her claws found purchase on stones that still bore the marks of dragon touch centuries past. *I sense that there are caves ahead. Some natural formations, some carved by dragon breath when my kind shaped this land freely. We can travel beneath the surface, emerge closer to your farm without crossing open sky.*

Relief warred with anxiety in Niloo's heart. They had crossed the threshold from impossibility to merely dangerous—a significant improvement in their odds, though the risks remained substantial. Madrid's agents would search methodically, but perhaps not immediately below ground. His forces concentrated on air superiority, on magic that watched horizons rather than underground passages. And if Darius awaited with Cayos's forces at the volcanic regions...

The crystal heart pulsed against her breast—not the burning that warned of her proximity to enemies, but a warm pulse of familial connection. Through its resonance, she sensed Darius's presence somewhere to the west. The sensation felt clearer now, as though crossing the barrier had strengthened their mystical link. He hadn't moved toward the excavation sites yet. Distance separated them still, but not the impossible gulf of barrier-divided realms.

The cave entrance loomed before them, a dragon-carved arch that spoke of engineering far beyond human capacity for stone-working. As Lapis led them deeper into the ancient passage, Niloo allowed herself one moment of bittersweet victory. They had broken through a barrier that had stood for years, achieving what countless others had attempted without success. Death could no longer claim them for this particular defiance of Imperial law. But the real battle—saving Samos, protecting her family, liberating her brother from Madrid's bondage—still lay ahead shadowed in the darkness a murky future. She prayed that was all there was to her mission.

Lazuli picked up on her thoughts and through the bond she sensed his support and commitment to their mission.

The darkness of the caves embraced them like a mother's arms, protective and concealing. The air inside felt different—not stale as abandoned caves often were, but merely still. Waiting. Preserved. Dragon magic had maintained these passages despite their absence. Niloo could sense it in the perfectly preserved carvings on the walls, in the way dust hadn't accumulated where it should have settled for centuries.

Somewhere in that protective shadow, Niloo pondered what came next. Was Madrid after this ancient dragon essence, preserved by time itself? Somewhere, her ancestors had hidden the truth, deep beneath the earth. And somehow, her own blood carried keys to both salvation and destruction. The souls in the barrier had recognized her lineage, had spoken of original hearts and ancient bindings.

She would need to choose carefully which doors to open, which secrets to uncover. For in every legend she knew, knowledge could liberate or condemn with equal ease. As they moved deeper into the mountain's embrace, Niloo felt the weight of her heritage settling over her shoulders—burden and birthright combined. The game had changed. No longer was she simply fleeing or fighting. Now she carried the power to reshape the conflict entirely.

The question remained: could she wield that power wisely enough to save rather than destroy?

Chapter Six

Healing Hot Springs

The ancient dragon caves felt like sanctuary after the traumatic passage through Madrid's barrier, but for Niloo, the experience had been traumatic enough that she couldn't shake the sensation. The fragments of tormented souls still clung to her consciousness like cobwebs constructed of her own anguish. She sat cross-legged on the smooth stone floor, her back against Lapis's warm flank, taking the slow and steady breaths that allowed her to enter into a meditative state, while the great dragon's sympathetic breathing provided a steady rhythm, that helped anchor her scattered thoughts.

The echoes fade, Lapis murmured through their bond, her mental voice carrying the deep patience of someone who had weathered many storms of consciousness. *But they leave impressions, like footprints in wet sand. You carry pieces of their memories now.*

"Is that normal?" Niloo asked aloud, her voice sounding strangely hollow in the cavern's acoustic embrace. "I keep seeing flashes of things I never experienced—a wizard realizing Madrid's wine was poisoned, a father watching his children grow old while he remained trapped, lovers separated by the Emperor's promises."

Through their triad bond, she felt Lazuli's presence flicker with sympathetic pain. The djinn had maintained his hawk form since their arrival in the caves, perched on a crystalline outcropping that caught and refracted the dim light filtering down from the entrance. His shapeshifting abilities made him particularly sensitive to identity confusion, and the barrier's assault on consciousness had left him struggling to maintain consistent form.

The boundary between self and other becomes fluid when conscious-ness is forced into proximity, he replied, his mental voice carrying undertones of distress that he was trying to hide. *What you experi-enced—what we all experienced—was the opposite of our natural bond. Where we willingly choose to share thoughts and feelings, the barrier forced unwilling minds together in torment.*

Niloo felt her crystal heart pulse with warmth as both her compan-ions sent her waves of comfort and support. But underneath their car-ing, she could sense their own struggles with what they had endured during the passage.

Lapis, she said through the bond, reaching deeper into their con-nection, *your scales. The burning when we passed through—I felt it too. How much damage did you take?*

The dragon's mental sigh carried centuries of stoic acceptance, but also the deeper tiredness of someone who had pushed beyond their limits. *The barrier's magic was designed to inflict maximum psychological trauma on dragons. The souls trapped within included many of my distant cousins—dragons who were enslaved, murdered and used to create the barrier itself. Their anguish called to my own draconic nature, tried to drag me into their eternal prison.*

Images flowed through the bond—not just the physical pain of magical burns across Lapis's wings and flanks, but the deeper spiritual agony of feeling kinship with beings trapped in perpetual torment. Dragons were inherently empathetic creatures, their consciousness naturally attuned to the emotional states of others. For Lapis, passing through the barrier had been like swimming through an ocean of despair.

Your scales are already beginning to regrow, Niloo observed, running her hand along her dragon's side where new growth emerged, sapphire chips embedded in living stone. *But the emotional scars...*

Will heal more slowly, Lapis acknowledged. *But they will heal. Pain shared through willing bonds becomes more bearable, not more intense. This is why triads exist, in part—so no consciousness faces trauma in isolation.*

Lazuli's form shimmered and solidified into his humanoid shape, his usually perfect features showing signs of strain. The reality distortions within the barrier had challenged his djinn nature in ways he was still processing.

"The magic there was wrong," he said aloud, his voice carrying harmonics that spoke of dimensional displacement and temporal confusion. "Not just evil or corruption, but fundamentally contrary to the way consciousness should interact with reality. I felt myself fragmenting, becoming multiple versions of myself simultaneously—the me that never met you, the me that chose different paths, the me that surrendered to despair."

He settled on the cave floor near them, his iridescent skin flickering between states as if he couldn't quite decide which version of himself was real.

"For djinn, identity is already fluid," he continued, his tone clinical despite the personal nature of what he was describing. "We exist partially in multiple realities simultaneously, shifting between possibilities as circumstances require. But the barrier forced me to experience all possibilities at once, without the ability to choose which ones to embrace."

Niloo reached out through the bond, offering her own stable sense of self as an anchor for his scattered consciousness. Through their connection, she felt Lazuli's relief as her human certainty about identity helped him consolidate his various personalities back into a unified whole.

This is why we bond, she realized, understanding flooding through their shared consciousness. *Not just for the magical amplification or the tactical advantages, but for the psychological stability. We anchor each other when external forces try to tear us apart.*

Precisely, Lapis agreed, her ancient wisdom coloring the bond with approval. *Dragons who attempt to face cosmic forces alone often lose themselves in the immensity of what they encounter. Humans who try to wield magic beyond their individual capacity burn out or go mad. Djinn who exist in too many realities simultaneously forget which one they call home.*

But together, Lazuli added, his form finally stabilizing as the bond helped him remember who he chose to be, *we provide balance. Dragon wisdom, human determination, djinn adaptability—each strength compensating for the others' vulnerabilities.*

The conversation was interrupted by a sound from deeper in the cave system—not threatening, but curious. Through the bond, all three of them felt it simultaneously: another consciousness, ancient beyond measure, stirring to awareness of their presence.

We are not alone here, Lapis observed with interest rather than alarm. *These caves have been inhabited before, by dragons who chose to make their homes in Gaia's depths rather than Jintessa's heights.*

A voice reached them then, not through sound but through the same magical resonance that allowed their triad bond to function. It carried the weight of millennia and the distinctive harmonic signature of draconic consciousness, but tempered with something else—a quality that spoke of long meditation on the nature of existence itself.

Young ones, the voice said, gentle but commanding attention. *You carry the wounds of forced passage through tormented barriers. Come deeper, where the earth's fire provides healing for both body and spirit.*

Following the mental summons, they made their way through passages that showed clear signs of draconic habitation—walls polished smooth by scales, crystalline formations that had been shaped by dragon breath into patterns of impossible beauty, and most remarkably, chambers where natural hot springs had been modified to create perfect bathing pools for creatures of various sizes.

The dragon who awaited them in the central chamber was unlike any Niloo had ever seen. Ancient beyond question, her scales had taken on the coloration of the volcanic stone around them—deep reds and oranges shot through with veins of gold that pulsed with inner fire. She was smaller than Lapis but carried herself with the dignity of someone who had found perfect peace with her chosen life.

I am Ember, the ancient dragon said, her mental voice carrying warmth that had nothing to do with her fire-based nature. *Welcome to the Sanctuary of Deep Reflection. I have dwelt here since the early days of Madrid's reign, when I chose solitude over resistance, meditation over warfare.*

"You've been here for thirty years?" Niloo asked, her voice carrying surprise at meeting someone who had found a way to exist independently of both Madrid's empire and the resistance networks.

Thirty-three years, two months, and sixteen days, Ember replied with the precision of someone who had counted each one. *I came here after witnessing the corruption of my clutch-siblings, after seeing dragons I had known since their hatching transformed into weapons of oppression. I believed then that isolation was the only way to preserve the true nature of draconic consciousness.*

Through the bond, Niloo felt Lapis's complex response to Ember's story—understanding mixed with a quiet disagreement about the choices the ancient dragon had made.

You survived, Lapis acknowledged respectfully. *Your consciousness remained uncorrupted, your wisdom preserved. But did your isolation serve the greater good? Could your knowledge have helped prevent the suffering we witnessed in the barrier?*

Perhaps, Ember admitted, her mental voice carrying the weight of years spent questioning her own choices. *But perhaps not. The young ones who seek to change the world through action serve a vital purpose. But so too do those who preserve what is valuable by removing it from the conflict entirely.*

She gestured toward the hot springs, their mineral-rich waters glowing with gentle phosphorescence. *These waters carry healing properties for consciousness as well as flesh. The volcanic forces here respond to draconic will, allowing for forms of therapy that are impossible elsewhere. Will you permit me to ease the trauma you carry from the barrier passage?*

The offer was tempting beyond words. Niloo could feel the promise of relief from the fragmented memories that continued to surface unbidden, the possibility of washing away the psychic residue of the tortured souls they had encountered. But something in the bond suggested caution.

What is the cost? Lazuli asked, his djinn nature making him sensitive to the hidden prices that often accompanied magical healing. *Such profound therapy must require something in return.*

Ember's amusement colored the mental connection like distant laughter. *Wisdom, young djinn. You understand that power shared always transforms both giver and receiver. The cost is memory—not the loss of what you experienced, but the integration of it into a deeper understanding of what consciousness can endure.*

You want us to share our experience of the barrier, Lapis realized. *To add our trauma to your collection of preserved knowledge.*

Not to add to it, Ember corrected gently. *To weave it into the greater tapestry of understanding I have been creating these many years. You have seen Madrid's latest atrocities in ways I never could from my sanctuary. That knowledge, properly preserved and understood, may serve future generations who face similar challenges.*

The triad exchanged thoughts through their bond with the lightning-fast communication that had developed between them over months of shared experience. There were risks—allowing another consciousness such intimate access to their traumatic memories could create new vulnerabilities, new forms of influence. But there were also benefits that went beyond personal healing.

We're not just three individuals anymore, Niloo realized through the connection. *We're representatives of everyone who refuses to surrender to Madrid's vision. If sharing our experience helps preserve knowledge that could protect others...*

Then we choose to share it, Lapis completed, her dragon pride recognizing the honor in being asked to contribute to something larger than themselves.

Together, Lazuli added, his form solidifying with renewed purpose. *As we have faced everything else—together.*

The healing process that followed was unlike anything they had experienced before. Ember guided them into the largest of the hot springs, its volcanic warmth seeping into their bones while her ancient consciousness touched theirs with the lightest possible contact. Instead of the brutal forced merger they had endured in the barrier, this was invitation—a gentle request for access that they could accept or decline with each memory, each moment of trauma.

Through their bond, the three of them relived the barrier passage together, but this time with Ember's wisdom helping them understand what they had endured. The tortured souls hadn't been random victims—they were Madrid's first experiments in consciousness control, wizards who had been powerful enough to resist his initial attempts at domination. Their transformation into living components of the barrier represented not just cruelty, but a specific technique for turning resistance into oppression.

He learned from their defiance, Ember explained as they experienced shared understanding of Madrid's methods. *Each mind that refused to submit taught him new ways to break similar resistance. The barrier is not just a prison—it is a laboratory where he continues to refine his techniques for consciousness control.*

The knowledge was disturbing, but also empowering. Understanding Madrid's methods made them less mysterious, less overwhelming. The Emperor's power was vast, but it operated according to specific principles that could be studied, understood, and potentially countered.

As the healing continued, Niloo felt the fragmented memories of the trapped souls beginning to integrate into her own consciousness in healthier ways. Instead of intrusive flashes of alien experience, they became part of her understanding of what consciousness could endure, what forms of resistance were possible even under the most oppressive circumstances.

They never stopped fighting, she realized, tears of grief and admiration mixing with the mineral-rich water around them. *Even trapped in eternal torment, even used as components in Madrid's barrier, they continued to resist in small ways. That's why the barrier responded to our crystal hearts—because part of it still remembers what it means to choose freedom over security.*

Through the bond, she felt her companions' similar realizations. Lapis discovered that the barrier's assault on draconic consciousness had been intended to break the natural empathy that made dragons effective partners for heartbearers. The pain she had experienced was the barrier's attempt to teach her that caring for others led only to suffering.

Lazuli learned that the reality distortions were designed to fragment djinn consciousness by overwhelming them with too many simultaneous possibilities. The goal was to make shapeshifting beings lose track of which identity was truly theirs, leaving them vulnerable to external definition of who they should be.

But the barrier failed, Ember observed with deep satisfaction as their understanding deepened. *It failed because consciousness bound by willing choice is stronger than consciousness controlled by force. Your triad bond provided protection that Madrid's creators never anticipated.*

The healing process concluded as the night gave way to dawn, the cave system gradually lightening as sunlight filtered down through hidden openings. Emerging from the hot springs, all three of them felt fundamentally changed—not weakened by their trauma, but strengthened by their understanding of it.

The barrier was meant to break us, Niloo said, her crystal heart pulsing with renewed clarity. *Instead, it taught us exactly how strong our bond really is.*

And it revealed the scope of what we're fighting against, Lapis added, her scales now gleaming with restored health and purpose. *Madrid isn't just seeking political control—he's trying to rewrite the fundamental nature of consciousness itself.*

Then we'll have to show him that the freely chosen merging of minds is more adaptable than control artificially imposed, Lazuli concluded, his form now stable and radiating confidence.

As they prepared to leave Ember's sanctuary and continue their journey toward confronting Madrid's forces, the ancient dragon offered them one final gift—not healing this time, but knowledge.

The path ahead will test your bond in ways you cannot yet imagine, she warned, her mental voice carrying the weight of prophetic understanding. *Madrid's techniques grow more sophisticated with each victory, each mind he successfully controls. But remember this—the barrier you passed through represents his greatest success, and you survived it not just intact, but stronger.*

You carry proof that willing cooperation can overcome forced compliance, that consciousness shared through choice multiplies rather than divides. This knowledge is your greatest weapon against everything Madrid represents.

As they emerged from the cave system into the morning light, Niloo felt the weight of their mission settling over the triad with new clarity. They weren't just three individuals who had learned to work together—they were living proof that consciousness could remain free even under the most oppressive circumstances.

The bond between them hummed with renewed strength, tempered by trauma but not broken by it. Ahead lay challenges that would test everything they had learned about cooperation, trust, and the power of minds that chose to work together despite their differences.

But for the first time since crossing Madrid's barrier, Niloo felt genuinely confident that they would face those challenges as they had faced everything else—together, with the strength that came from a bond freely shared rather than forcibly extracted.

The sun rose over Samos, painting the eastern plains in shades of pink that promised hope. And in the growing light, three minds that had chosen each other prepared to show the world what freedom looked like when it refused to surrender to tyranny's simplest, most seductive promises.

CHAPTER SEVEN

HIDDEN HISTORIES

Niloo's heart pounded in her chest as they approached her family's farmhouse just before dawn. The familiar silhouette of the two-story structure with its wide veranda brought tears to her eyes. Lapis had landed in a hidden grove a mile back, where the dragon could remain concealed while Niloo and Lazuli continued on foot.

"Are you certain this is wise?" Lazuli asked, his djinn form shimmering with a bluish tinge in the pre-dawn light. He had shifted to look more human, but his skin retained a subtle dark sapphire luminescence that would be impossible to hide in daylight.

"They're my family," Niloo said, her voice cracking with emotion. "I need to know if they're safe."

The barrier crossing had nearly killed them. Lapis had suffered burns across her lapis-scaled wings where the magical energy had scorched through even her ancient protection. Niloo had thought of nothing but her family since—especially Darius. The pain in her chest wasn't just from exertion; her crystal heart seemed to be calling her home with increasing urgency.

As they approached the back entrance, Niloo froze. The door lay ajar, unusual for a farming family that rose with the rising of the sun. She motioned for Lazuli to remain still as she crept forward, peering through the opening.

Silence greeted them. The kitchen lay shrouded in shadow, undisturbed but empty. No breakfast preparations were scattered across the scarred wooden countertop, no familiar teapot bubbled on the hot plate of the wood burning stove.

A floorboard creaked behind her.

Niloo spun around, hands already forming the defensive posture she'd learned on Jintessa. She crossed her arms and extended her fingers in the form of a crane. One leg lifted, bent at the knee. Balance and lethal intent bound up in one movement.

"Stop." Her father's voice emerged from the shadows, firm but shaking. "Identify yourself."

The light from an oil lamp, held in a shaking, withered hand, swept across the space between them. The dim light illuminated Niloo's face, thinned by maturity into a miniature of her mother's delicate features. Her father, Naveen, stood with the lamp in one hand and a sharpened axe in the other. His lined face, more weathered than she remembered, transformed from suspicion to shock.

"Niloo?" he whispered. The axe clattered to the floor.

"Father!" She rushed forward, throwing her arms around him.

His embrace was fierce, desperate. "We thought—" His voice broke. "After Darius was taken..."

Before she could respond, her mother appeared at the top of the stairs. Arya's silver-streaked dark hair hung loose to her shoulders and her narrow eyes widened with disbelief.

"Is it—?" She gasped the question, before racing down the steps, wrapping both Niloo and her father in her arms. "Both my children, taken from me," she sobbed. "And now one returns."

"Mother," Niloo breathed. "I've been trying to get home for so long. But the barrier—"

"Inside. Quickly." Her father pulled them away from the open door, suddenly alert. "It isn't safe to talk here." With one foot, he kicked it closed, but it was stopped just as suddenly when it slapped into the hand of Lazuli, as he shouldered his way into the kitchen. Glowing with an eerie light, he froze on the threshold, taking in the scene of reunion with an impassive glance, then his eyes continued to scan the room for hidden threats.

"Mother, father. This is Lazuli. He is...a friend." She hesitated, unsure how much of their relationship she should divulge. Her eyes met Lazuli's in silent communication, and through the bond she said, *Let's leave it at that for now. I need to know more about what is going on here before revealing more.*

I agree, little one, said lapis. *We do not know what has happened here. Be cautious. I will guard your back while you speak to your family.* A mental image flashed into Niloo's mind, that of a guard dog, pacing in front of a fence.

Her father took in the sight of Lazuli, then after a short pause nodded acceptance and waved a hand at Lazuli to follow. Naveen led them through the kitchen, to a wall that had always displayed the family's collection of retired farming tools – hoes and awls, baskets and knives – the history of their family's determination to survive and thrive the harsh conditions imposed on them by the land, showcased in wood, leather and stone.

With practiced movements, Naveen pressed his palm against a seemingly ordinary section of polished wood. It glowed faintly blue—the same hue as Niloo's crystal heart. *Surely a trick of the light,* thought Niloo.

The wall behind slid open, revealing a narrow staircase descending into darkness.

"What is this?" Niloo gasped. "We've lived here my entire life, and I never knew—"

"There are many things you didn't know," her mother said, her voice suddenly firm, the sobs gone. "Many things we hoped you would never need to know."

Lazuli, who had remained a few steps behind, silent and watchful, stepped forward from the shadows, as understanding bloomed in his mind. "The Keepers," he said. "You're the Keepers of Samos."

Naveen's eyes widened as he took in Lazuli's form. "And you've brought a djinn into our home." His gaze moved from Lazuli to Niloo with new understanding. "You've bonded."

Niloo nodded. "This is indeed my heartbond, Lazuli. And beyond the grove waits my dragon, lapis."

Her mother closed her eyes briefly. "Then it's as we feared. The Triads have formed."

"Come," her father said grimly. "There's much to explain, and little time."

The hidden staircase led to a circular chamber beneath the farmhouse. Bookshelves lined the walls, crammed with ancient texts and scrolls. At the center stood a raised platform with a three dimensional map—a perfect replica of Gaia, with each province clearly delineated. The central citadel spire rose from the center, and each bridge crossing the chasm which isolated the citadel from the rest of Gaia, clearly defined.

Small red lights pulsed across the western border of Samos. Nillo moved closer and bent over the map, examining it, a frown creasing her brow.

"Madrid's forces," her father explained, pointing to the lights. "They've been excavating in this area for three weeks, now. We've been monitoring their movements from here."

"But what is *this* place?" Niloo asked, spinning slowly to take in the sturdy chamber. The stone walls roughly matched the footprint of the house above, but not exactly. "How long has it been here?"

Her mother traced a loving hand along a bookshelf. "Longer than our family has tended these lands. For generations, the Keepers of Samos have maintained this chamber and the knowledge it contains. The farm was built overtop of this sacred place, to protect its location."

"And you never told me? You never told Darius?" The hurt in her voice was unmistakable.

"We were going to," her father said heavily. "On your eighteenth birthday. That's the tradition. But the dragon came for you before we could prepare you."

"And Darius—" her mother's voice caught.

"Madrid has him," Niloo said quietly. "I've seen him in dreams. He wears a crystal heart like mine, but it's... different. Corrupted."

Her parents exchanged grim looks.

"Show her," her mother said.

Her father nodded and approached a particular shelf full of cracked, leather bound books, with gold and silver runes etched into their spines. His fingers ran along the shelf before pausing by a thick volume that was shorter than the others. With a gentle tug, he pulled the ancient book from shelf. Its cover was inlaid with blue stones that matched Niloo's pendant.

"This is the Codex of Gaia," he said, placing it carefully on a reading stand. "It contains the true history of this land—not the sanitized version Madrid allows to be taught."

He opened the book with reverential care. Within were detailed illustrations of dragons—not the stylized versions from her favourite festival parades, but accurate renderings that matched Lapis perfectly. The text was in a script Niloo couldn't read.

"This is the ancient language of the dragons," her father explained. "Few can read it now."

"But you can," Niloo guessed.

"It's the duty of the Keepers," her mother confirmed.

Her father turned pages until he found what he sought—a map of what would become Samos. Unlike the modern province they knew, this version showed the land divided into curious circular patterns, spiraling outward from central points.

"Do you know what these are?" he asked.

Niloo studied the patterns. "They look like bullseyes. No, wait. Could they be..." Niloo glanced at Lazuli. He nodded, reading her thoughts. "...nests?"

"Precisely." Her father tapped the page. "Long before Madrid, before the Great Purge, before the provinces were divided, Samos was known as The Dragon's Garden."

"It was the place where dragons first chose to ally with humankind," her mother continued. "Their eggs were laid in the volcanic soils of the western border, and the hatchlings were raised on the plains."

"The rolling hills and fertile lands weren't formed by natural erosion," her father added. "They were shaped by dragon magic—terraformed to create perfect hatching grounds."

Lazuli moved closer to the book. "Madrid knows this," he said. "That's why he's excavating. He's looking for what remains."

"Dragon essence," Niloo's mother confirmed. "The magical residue left behind when the last clutches of eggs were abandoned during the Great Purge. It remains potent, even after centuries."

"But what would he want with it?" Niloo asked.

Her father's expression darkened. "Control. Madrid seeks to create artificial bonds—to forge crystal hearts that answer only to him."

Niloo's hand instinctively went to her pendant. "Like what he's done to Darius, and possibly to others."

"We fear that your brother is a test subject," her mother said, voice breaking. "They came in the night, six days after you disappeared. They knew exactly what they were looking for—a crystal heartbearer who shared blood with another. The connection between siblings is...exploitable."

"Is that why I can see him in dreams?"

Her father nodded. "The bond between you cannot be severed, not even by Madrid's corruption."

"Then I need to find him," Niloo said firmly. "I need to break whatever hold Madrid has on him."

"That won't be easy, and it may very well be stupid to try," her father warned. "Madrid's control grows stronger each day, and by our reckoning, you have been gone a very long time. If Madrid has found what he is looking for... well there is more." Naveen turned his back on the book and clasping his arms behind his back, began to pace the chamber. "We believe he may be trying to create an army. We are not sure how, but disturbing rumours have reached us from other provinces. Evil stirs, and Madrid is at the heart of it. If the excavations yield more dragon essence, his artificially-bonded servants will multiply."

Her mother took Niloo's cold hands in hers. "There is one way to reach your brother—an ancient ritual recorded in these texts. It requires a triad's combined power and access to the deepest nesting site beneath the western volcanoes."

"Then that's where we'll go," Niloo declared.

Lazuli placed a hand on Niloo's shoulder. "We need to move carefully, cautiously. If Madrid suspects the existence of this chamber, of these records, he could lay a trap for us."

"He doesn't," her father insisted. "The Keepers have maintained their secrecy for generations."

As if in response to his confidence, a distant rumble shook the chamber. Dust drifted from the ceiling.

"What was that?" Niloo tensed.

Her mother hurried over to the open map. The red dots at the western border had multiplied and were moving—east.

"Madrid's forces are advancing," she said. "They've crossed the border where the mining towns are located. They're heading toward the central plains."

"How long until they reach us?" Niloo asked.

Her father's face was grim. "Three days, perhaps four if the terrain slows them."

"Then we have work to do," Niloo said, turning back to the ancient text. "Teach me what I need to know. Teach me how to save my brother and protect Samos."

Her parents exchanged looks—pride, fear, and resignation mingling in their expressions.

"The first thing you need to understand," her father began, "is that Samos itself is alive. The dragon magic has seeped into every rock, every hill, every blade of grass. If you can learn to awaken it..."

"Then I can turn the land itself against Madrid," Niloo finished.

Her mother nodded slowly. "It's never been done since the Great Purge. The knowledge exists only in theory."

"Theory will have to be enough," Niloo said grimly. "I've heard of what Madrid is capable of. I won't let him take Samos like he took my brother."

Another tremor shook the chamber, stronger this time. From above came the muffled sound of breaking glass.

"What is causing these tremors?" said Niloo, as she grasped the table next to her, to steady herself. Dust, undisturbed for centuries, drifted in the air.

"Madrid's forces are moving both above and below Samos. Like a burrowing insect, he is attacking the very lifesource of Samos. She shudders in response. Samos itself is under attack," said her mother.

"We are running out of time," her father said, sweeping the most crucial texts into a satchel. "We need to evacuate the nearby farms. Madrid's forces are moving faster than we anticipated." He swung the satchel onto his back. "This chamber will be sealed after we leave. No one will be able to enter except a Keeper, or the contents of this room will be consumed by fire."

"Go," Niloo urged them. "Get everyone to safety. I need to return to Lapis. We'll do what we can to slow their advance."

Her mother caught her in a fierce embrace. "Be careful, my daughter. Remember—the land responds to intention. The dragons chose Samos because the earth here remembers the ancient ones."

Niloo held her mother tightly. "I'll remember. Perhaps Lapis can help with that. And I'll return."

As she and Lazuli raced up the stairs and back toward the grove where Lapis waited, Niloo's crystal heart pulsed with new purpose. The horizon to the west glowed with unnatural light—was it the unnatural magical energy of Madrid's approaching army?

War had come to Samos, to her home. But now she understood what was truly at stake. This wasn't just about her brother anymore, or even about the province itself.

It was about the very heart of dragon magic in Gaia.

And her return had triggered it all. She was its Keeper now.

CHAPTER EIGHT

FIRE FROM ABOVE

The first warning came not through magical wards or dragon sens-es, but through the simple wrongness that Niloo's mother noticed in the way the chickens had gone silent. Arya stood in the farmhouse doorway, her weather-lined face tilted toward the western sky where storm clouds gathered with unnatural speed and geometric precision.

"That's not weather," she said quietly, her voice carrying the sort of calm that came from years of expecting the worst while hoping for better. "Naveen, we need to move. Now."

Through the kitchen window, Niloo could see what had alarmed her mother—the approaching clouds weren't just dark, they were uniform, moving with the mechanical precision that marked an artificial construct, one they suspected was formed by Madrid's magic. And within its dark depths, shapes moved with purpose rather than the random turbulence of natural storms. They squinted, trying to determine what nature of attack was shrouded by the clouds.

Dragons, Lapis confirmed through their bond, her senses detecting the familiar signatures of her enslaved cousins long before human eyes could make out individual forms. *At least a dozen, flying in formation. And something else—their riders magical essence feel wrong, corrupted somehow. Like a taint of foulness on the surface of otherwise clean water.*

I think this is Madrid's response to our crossing the barrier, Lazuli observed, his djinn form already shifting toward its most combat-ready configuration. *He has been tracking the magical disturbances we created, following the resonance back to its source.*

"How long until they arrive?" Niloo asked as her father turned away from the window, frowning at the roiling cloud although he was already moving toward the hidden wall panel with the practiced efficiency of someone who had planned for this moment.

"Minutes," said Lazuli.

Lapis, her great form coiling with tension as she prepared for battle, interjected. *Perhaps less. They approach with the speed of dragons driven beyond their natural limits. Or with enhanced strength.*

The wall panel slid open at Naveen's touch, revealing the spiral staircase that led to the Keepers' sanctuary. But as the family began gathering essential items and precious texts, a sound split the morning air that made all of them freeze—Madrid's voice, amplified by magic until it seemed to echo from the mountains themselves.

"Heartbearer of Samos," the Emperor's words rolled across the farmland like thunder given voice, "you cannot hide from the consequences of your defiance. Surrender yourself and your companions, and your family will be spared. Continue this futile resistance, and learn what happens to those who harbor enemies of the Empire."

"He's bluffing," Niloo said, though her crystal heart pulsed with warning as the approaching magical signatures grew stronger. "Madrid prefers to convert rather than destroy. He wants us alive for his experiments."

"But will that preference hold when he's been genuinely challenged?" her mother asked, already moving swiftly toward the staircase with an armload of the most precious texts.

Before anyone could answer, the first attack struck.

It came not as dragon fire or conventional weapons, but as a wave of psychic pressure that made the very air seem to thicken with despair. Niloo felt the assault's true nature—Madrid was broadcasting the emotional residue of every heartbearer he had broken, every mind he had bent to his will, creating a psychic storm designed to shatter resistance through depression and hopelessness.

The barrier souls, she gasped, recognizing the familiar agony of the trapped wizards. *He's using their suffering as a weapon.*

But even as the psychic assault battered against their consciousness, she felt her companions' response through the triad bond—not just resistance, but active transformation of the attack into something else entirely.

Pain shared is pain transformed, Lapis reminded her, the dragon's ancient wisdom flowing through their connection. *Madrid assumes despair will multiply when experienced collectively, but consciousness bound by choice converts suffering into strength.*

The bond protects us, Lazuli added, his djinn nature allowing him to perceive how the crystal heart connections were distributing the psychic load across multiple willing minds. *He attacks individual consciousness, but we are no longer individual.*

Through the bond, Niloo felt not just her own triad's resistance, but echoes from heartbearers across Gaia—distant points of light that blazed brighter in response to Madrid's assault, a multitude of bonds that refused to be dimmed by artificial despair. But there was no time to ponder the sensation,

The second attack was more conventional but no less devastating. Dragon fire struck the farmhouse's eastern wall with surgical precision, not the wild burning that would have consumed everything, but a carefully controlled flame that targeted specific structural points. Within moments, the upper floor began to collapse, timbers and tile crashing down in a cascade of destruction that spoke of tactical planning rather than mere rage.

"Into the sanctuary," Naveen commanded, though his voice broke as he watched generations of family history reduced to kindling. "The wards below will hold against anything short of volcanic forces."

They descended the spiral staircase in order of vulnerability—first Niloo's parents carrying the most critical texts and artifacts, then Niloo herself with her crystal heart blazing against her chest in response to the magical chaos above. Lazuli followed by shifting into bird form and flying at Niloo's shoulder. They hurried down the narrow staircase, slamming the door closed behind them, which locked immediately. Instantly a shield sprang into being and raced around the ceiling, walls and floor, encasing them in a hazy cocoon.

Lapis its time for you to hide, said Niloo through he bond. *Activate the reflective spell, and stay still. Illusion is your best defense. Do not attract attention to yourself. You know we are safe.*

She felt the dragon's agreement as a soft purr, meant to soothe her anxiety. Lapis had dug herself into the soft soil by the barn, in a spot where she could quickly launch herself into the air, should she need to defend her bondmates.

They had argued about the plan for several precious moments before Madrid's arrival, and finally agreed that the sanctum should be sufficient to protect its human and djinn occupants from the worst power that Madrid's dragons could summon. It had been built for just this circumstance. Lapis had pointed out that this theory had never been tested, and so a compromise had been struck. Lapis would act as a secondary defense, should she sense any distress on their part. But in the meantime, she would hide beneath the mirror spell, trusting to the glamour to fool the attackers.

The Keepers' sanctuary revealed itself in the flickering light of ancient crystal formations that had waited centuries for this moment of activation. Circular walls lined with texts and artifacts that predated Madrid's empire, a raised platform where three-dimensional maps showed real-time magical activity across Gaia, and bookshelves crammed with knowledge that told the true history of Samos and its dragons.

A repository of forbidden knowledge, Lapis observed with awe, borrowing Niloo's sight. Her dragon senses detected layers of magical protection that had preserved these secrets through decades of Imperial suppression. *Everything Madrid sought to destroy, hidden beneath the most ordinary of farms.*

But even as they marveled at the revealed sanctuary, the attacks above intensified. The farmhouse's destruction accelerated with methodical efficiency—not by random violence, but a systematic dismantling designed to send a poignant message about the cost of defying Imperial authority.

Through the chamber's enhanced acoustics, they could hear Madrid's forces arriving in the farmyard, a mixture of dragon wings beating the air to slow their descent and the thud of their feet landing in the yard. This was accompanied by the sound of horses hooves striking the hard packed soil of the laneway, as they galloped into position around the farm, cutting off any escape by ground. Voices called out in the clipped tones of soldiers. "Search the outbuildings!" a rough voice shouted, and conducting a search, looking for survivors, for evidence, for anything that might reveal the location of their true targets.

"The hidden entrance is warded," Naveen assured them, though his voice carried tension that belied his confident words. "Ancient protections that predate Madrid's understanding of Keeper magic."

"But not indefinitely," Arya added, her weathered hands fiddling with a smooth glass ball that was filled with fluctuating clouds of colour. The device monitored the sanctuary's defenses. "Madrid's wizards are already probing the concealment spell. They may have techniques for unraveling our protections, ways that the creators of this chamber never anticipated."

Above them, a new sound began—the systematic tapping of spelled silver implements against the stony ground, designed to test for hollow spaces and hidden chambers, or other structures that might conceal fugitives. Each tap sent vibrations through the stone that made the sanctuary's crystal formations chime in harmonic response.

They will find you, Lapis growled through the bond, her senses tracking the methodical approach of the searchers. *You are running out of time. Search quickly. You must discover what you can before they break through the wards.*

As Niloo hurried over to the ancient texts that had been concealed in the chamber, her crystal heart began to pulse with excitement.

These books contained knowledge about the true relationship between dragons and humans, about magical bonds that had existed
before Madrid's corruption, about secrets that could reshape their
understanding of what they were fighting for.

The tapping above had become more insistent, more focused. The
soldiers had detected something—if not the sanctuary itself, then at
least the general area where their targets might be concealed. Soon
they would begin using more aggressive methods to breach whatever
protections they encountered.

"There are other ways out," her mother said urgently, moving toward a section of the chamber where ribbons of jewel tones hinted
at veins of gemstones. They ran in a arch from floor to ceiling, the
formations marking hidden passages. "This is an emergency exit that
lead to the eastern caves. We will flee there."

"But the knowledge here," Niloo protested, picking up a scroll and
unfurling it. Quickly she scanned the ancient text, catching a glimpse
of secrets that could change everything.

They will come with us, her father assured her, gathering the most
critical volumes while activating preservation spells that would protect them from physical damage. *The Keepers always planned for the
possibility that this chamber might be discovered.*

The grinding of ancient stone grew louder as the spelled silver tools
penetrated deeper into the sanctuary's defenses. Madrid's wizards had
found the concealed entrance and were systematically dismantling
protections that had stood for centuries. The grinding changed into
hum that slowly rose in pitch, the frequency sharp and painful to the
ears.

"They will break the spell within minutes," said Lazuli, squinting at
the fluctuating barrier. "Come, we must go, now."

As they fled through hidden passages toward the safety of the eastern caves, Niloo clutched the ancient texts that contained secrets about the true nature of dragon magic, the original bonds between species, and knowledge that would soon transform their understanding of what they were truly fighting for.

The fire from above had driven them from their sanctuary, but it had also revealed treasures of knowledge that Madrid's forces would never find, wisdom that would guide their resistance in ways the Emperor could never anticipate.

*****

Above them, soldiers searched through the ruins of the farmhouse that for generations had protected in its foundation, a carefully concealed ancient secret. With a final squeal, the protective barrier failed. Madrid marched down the stairs, flanked by two male heartbearers. Shouldering open the door, they found an empty chamber and the faint echoes of magic, that had already moved beyond their reach.

Rage flooded Madrid as he examined the empty chamber.

With a snarl and a curse, Madrid spun on his heel and marched back up the stairs, and out into the courtyard, where Opaleye stood, waiting his return.

Madrid climbed onto the dragon's back and launched into the sky.

CHAPTER NINE

THREE PERSPECTIVES, ONE TRUTH

The loss of the Keepers' hidden chamber had shaken each member of their small resistance cell in different ways, but it wasn't until Niloo, Lapis and Lazuli were finally alone, together—truly alone, that they could finally process what they had learned.

Niloo's parents had decided to carry a warning to their neighbours about Madrid's invasion and so were focused on assisting with the evacuation of their farms. Niloo also suspected that they could not stand to view the destruction of their only home, and so they busied themselves with the care of others. First their neighbours were to be warned, and after that, they would trigger Samos' long planned resistance cell formation, with a call to arms. Niloo did not think she would see them anytime soon.

So the triad had returned to the farm, only to discover that in his rage, Madrid had destroyed it all. Not a building was left intact.

Niloo and Lazuli sat in the ruins of the farmhouse's upper level, legs dangling over the edge of the partially collapsed wall that had formed the cozy kitchen below. Madrid's attack had torn away the roof and left them with an unobstructed view of the star-filled sky. Lapis spawled below them, reminding her of a dog guarding her territory. Only no dog was ever this colour or this big. She affectionately patted Lapis' shimmering scales with her right hand, then returned to her study of the manuscript resting in her lap, by the conjured ball of light floating over the curling page.

Niloo held one of the ancient texts her father had rescued from the chamber, its dragon-script characters seeming to shift and dance in the moonlight. But her attention wasn't really on the words—it was on the complex web of emotions flowing through the triad bond as each of her companions grappled with revelations that challenged their understanding of their own natures.

The oldest lies are the ones we tell ourselves about who we are, Lapis murmured through the connection, her great form coiled around the farmhouse's remaining foundation stones. Her lapis lazuli scales had dimmed to match the darkness, but her eyes glowed with the internal fire of deep contemplation. *I believed I was unique, special—one of the few Jintessa dragons to form a triad bond with Gaia natives. Now I discover that my ancestors shaped this very land, that my kind once called this place home.*

The revelation that Gaia's "extinct" dragons were actually Jintessa ancestors had fundamentally challenged Lapis's understanding of her place in the world. Through the bond, Niloo could feel the dragon's struggle to reconcile her sense of individual identity with this new knowledge of ancient connections.

You're still unique, Niloo offered gently through the connection. *Knowing that your ancestors lived here doesn't diminish what you've chosen to do here. If anything, it makes your decision to help us more meaningful—you're not just fighting for strangers, you're fighting to protect your family's ancient home.*

But what does that make me? Lapis replied, her mental voice carrying uncertainties that her usual confident demeanor rarely revealed. *Am I a Jintessa dragon who chose to help Gaia? Or am I a Gaia dragon who was raised in exile? My sense of identity was built on the assumption that I was crossing boundaries, bridging different worlds. Now those boundaries seem more artificial than I realized.*

Lazuli's form shimmered between states as he processed his own revelations. Unlike Lapis's identity crisis, the djinn's distress came from a different source—not confusion about where he belonged, but growing understanding of the true scope of Madrid's ambitions.

The reality manipulation techniques described in those texts, he said, his mental voice tight with controlled fear, *they're not just theoretical. Madrid has been implementing them systematically. The barrier we passed through was only the beginning—he's been reshaping the fundamental structure of how consciousness interacts with reality itself.*

Through the bond, Niloo felt Lazuli's djinn perception of dimensional stability, his awareness of how Madrid's actions were creating stress fractures in the basic laws that governed existence. For a being whose nature allowed him to shift between different states of reality, the Emperor's reality manipulation represented a threat to the very foundations of what it meant to exist.

He's not just enslaving consciousness, Lazuli continued, his form flickering more rapidly as distress disrupted his concentration. *He's rewriting the rules that determine what consciousness can become. If he succeeds, if he gains access to the deep reality controls your ancestors built into this land...*

He could make his vision of perfect order the only possible form of existence, Niloo completed, understanding flooding through her with cold clarity. The thought was terrifying beyond words—not just the death of freedom, but the elimination of the very possibility of freedom.

But even as she grappled with the cosmic implications of Madrid's plan, Niloo found herself facing her own identity crisis. Learning that her family had been Keepers for generations, that they had hidden not just knowledge but entire magical systems from her, challenged everything she thought she knew about her place in the world.

I thought I was just a farm girl who got lucky enough to bond with a dragon, she said through the connection, her mental voice carrying years of accumulated assumptions about her own ordinariness. *I thought my parents were simple farmers who happened to live in a province with magical potential. Now I find out I was raised to be some kind of cosmic guardian, trained without knowing it to use artifacts that could reshape reality itself.*

The weight of inherited responsibility settled over her like a cloak made of lead. Every childhood lesson about the importance of making good choices, every story her grandmother had told about the old days, every moment of preparation she hadn't recognized as preparation—all of it suddenly made sense in ways that left her feeling manipulated by the people she trusted most.

Your parents kept secrets to protect you, Lapis offered, her ancient wisdom providing perspective on family dynamics that spanned generations. *The burden of being a Keeper is not something anyone should carry until they're ready to choose it for themselves.*

But they still made the choice for me, Niloo replied, her frustration coloring the bond with shades of betrayal and resentment. *Every major decision in my life has been shaped by knowledge I wasn't allowed to have. How do I know which of my choices were really mine and which were just following paths they laid out for me?*

The question hung in the cold space between them, touching on fears that went deeper than their specific situation. In a world where Madrid used magical compulsion to override free will, where consciousness itself had become a battleground, how could anyone be certain their choices were genuinely their own?

This is what he wants, Lazuli realized, his form suddenly solidifying with the intensity of his understanding. *Madrid doesn't just control consciousness through force—he undermines it by making people doubt their own agency. Every moment we spend questioning whether our choices are really ours is a moment we're not making new choices to oppose him.*

The djinn perspective on identity is useful here, he continued, his mental voice gaining strength as he shared insight from his shapeshifting nature. *For my kind, identity is fluid—we become what we choose to become in each moment. The question isn't whether your past choices were entirely yours, but whether your current choices reflect who you choose to be now.*

Through the bond, Niloo felt the wisdom of this perspective, but also the challenge it represented. Accepting that identity was a choice, made moment by moment, meant taking responsibility not just for future decisions, but for consciously deciding who she wanted to be in the face of everything she had learned.

I choose to be someone who protects consciousness, she said finally, her mental voice carrying the weight of decision consciously made. *Not because my parents prepared me for it, not because ancient texts say I'm supposed to, but because I've seen what Madrid does to minds he controls, and I won't let that happen to anyone else if I can prevent it.*

And I choose to be a dragon who helps preserve the world my ancestors shaped, Lapis added, her own voice strengthening as she embraced rather than resisted her complex heritage. *Not just because it's my bloodline, but because the alternative—watching Madrid drain all magic and consciousness from this place—is unacceptable.*

I choose to be a djinn who uses reality-shaping abilities to preserve rather than control, Lazuli concluded, his form stabilizing into its most solid configuration. *Because consciousness needs space to grow and change, and that requires someone to maintain the flexibility of what's possible rather than the rigidity of what's commanded.*

The shared moment of choice sent a warm tingle through their bond. They trusted each other implicitly despite the uncertainty that swirled about them and clouded everything else. They were still the same three beings who had crossed Madrid's barrier together, but now they were those beings by choice rather than circumstance.

The ancient texts in Jintessa speak of this moment, Lapis observed, as a memory floated to the surface of her mind. *The moment when a triad moves from bonding through necessity to bonding through conscious commitment. It's supposed to unlock deeper forms of cooperation—not just sharing thoughts and feelings, but sharing perspectives in ways that fundamentally change how each member sees reality.*

Is that what's happening now? Niloo asked, already sensing the answer through changes in how the bond felt. Their mental connection had always allowed them to share emotions and communicate across distances, but now it felt deeper, more integrated. She could perceive Lazuli's awareness of dimensional fluidity. Lapis's sense of time ran as a twisting river, rather than a straight line. It was as if their individual ways of experiencing reality were becoming available to all of them.

Try it, Lazuli suggested, his excitement coloring the bond with anticipation. *Look at the ancient text of the scroll resting on your lap, through dragon sight then through djinn perception. See what becomes visible when consciousness truly shares perspective rather than just information.*

Niloo focused on the twisty dragon-script before her, but instead of trying to read it with her human understanding, she opened herself fully to the bond and let her companions' perceptual frameworks, overlap with her own.

Through Lapis's dragon sight, the symbols weren't just writing—they were fully formed concepts, three-dimensional constructs of meaning that conveyed information through spatial relationships as much as sequential reading. The text described not just the history of the Dragon Crossroads, but the ethical frameworks the original dragons had used to decide which realities deserved connection and which should remain isolated.

Through Lazuli's djinn perception, the page existed in multiple states simultaneously—not just as it was now, but as it had been when first written, as it could become if properly understood, as it might be corrupted if Madrid gained access to its secrets. The warnings embedded in the text weren't just about past dangers, but about potential futures that could still be prevented.

And through her own human understanding, now enhanced by her companions' perspectives, Niloo could see how the ancient knowledge related to their current crisis. The Dragon Crossroads hadn't been sealed just to prevent invasion—they had been sealed to prevent the kind of reality manipulation Madrid was attempting, the transformation of consciousness itself into something controllable rather than free.

Madrid can enslave individual minds, Lapis added, her ancient wisdom now accessible to all of them, *but he cannot enslave consciousness that has learned to see reality from multiple perspectives simultaneously. His control techniques depend on limiting how people can think about their situation.*

And shared perspective is exponentially more adaptable than individual perspective, Lazuli concluded, his djinn understanding of possibility now part of their collective knowledge. *Every new viewpoint added to the network creates combinations of understanding that no single mind could achieve.*

The insight felt like a key turning in a lock they hadn't even realized was there. The reason Madrid's consciousness control was so effective wasn't just because of his magical power, but because it isolated minds from each other, forcing them to perceive reality through artificially narrowed perspectives that made resistance seem impossible.

But consciousness that learned to share perspectives—really share them, not just exchange information—became something qualitatively different. It retained individual identity while gaining access to forms of understanding that transcended any single viewpoint.

This is what we need to teach others, Niloo said. *Not just how to resist Madrid's control, but how to share consciousness in ways that make such control impossible.*

As dawn approached and they prepared to rejoin the larger resistance effort, the triad found that their bond had fundamentally changed. They were still three distinct beings with their own personalities, their own strengths and weaknesses, their own individual perspectives on the world. But those perspectives now flowed together in ways that created understanding none of them could have achieved alone.

We're still ourselves, Niloo observed with wonder, *but we're also more than ourselves.*

This is what Madrid fears most, Lapis replied, her dragon wisdom now part of their shared understanding. *Not the loss of individual identity, but the multiplication of it through conscious cooperation.*

Then let's show him what conscious cooperation can accomplish, Lazuli concluded, his reality-shaping abilities now enhanced by dragon wisdom and human determination.

The sun rose over Samos, painting the ruins of the farmhouse in colors that spoke of hope emerging from destruction. And in the growing light, three minds that had chosen to share perspective as well as purpose prepared to demonstrate that consciousness could become stronger through connection rather than weaker through division.

The triad bond had evolved from tool to partnership to something approaching transcendence—not the loss of self in merger, but the discovery of self in community. And with that discovery came the understanding that they carried within their shared perspective the seeds of Madrid's ultimate defeat: the proof that consciousness freely shared became exponentially more powerful than consciousness artificially controlled.

CHAPTER TEN

FIRST STRIKES

Dawn painted unforgiving peaks known as Ashfall Heights in shades of burnt orange and smoky amber. The volcanic region's jagged silhouette cut sharply against the sky, a reminder of the primal forces that had shaped this corner of Samos. Niloo lay flat against a ridge of black stone, her body pressed into the cold earth. Beneath her palm, the ground trembled—not with seismic activity, but with a sense of violation.

"They've reached the third chamber," she whispered, eyes closed as she interpreted the land's distress. "Madrid's machines bore deeper with each passing hour."

Lazuli crouched beside her, his djinn form muted to match the volcanic stone. "How many workers?"

"At last count at least fifty. And twice that many soldiers for enforcement." Niloo raised the looking glass to her eyes, focusing on the encampment spread across the valley floor. Imperial banners snapped in the hot updrafts, and the distinctive crimson uniforms of Madrid's elite guard marked the operation's importance. "And there—" She pointed to a covered pavilion near the main excavation shaft. "That's where Cayos directs the operation."

Through their bond, Lapis shared her observations from a higher altitude. The dragon circled far above, riding thermal currents with wings the color of deep blue evening skies. Her scales gleamed with the distinctive patterns of her namesake stone, intricate swirls of gold threading through lapis lazuli blue.

I count sixteen patrol dragons, Lapis communicated. *Their riders are not heart-bonded to their djinn, but controlled through artificial means. They do not share the way we do. They are not one. The dragons' scales are dull—they've been denied proper nourishment.*

Niloo's anger flared to life. Dragons required specific gemstones to maintain their health and distinctive coloration. Lapis herself needed regular feedings of her namesake stone, consuming the deep blue lapis lazuli that gave her scales their brilliant hue. Madrid's dragons—stolen or bred in captivity—were being starved of their essential diet, forced to subsist on whatever meager substitutes the Emperor provided.

"He treats them as tools, not intelligent, living beings," she muttered. "As he treats all who serve him,"

Lazuli agreed, his voice dripping with barely controlled rage. Djinn had suffered at the hands of Madrid's desires. "I cannot not help but wonder, if the djinn's shapeshifting abilities are being exploited for Imperial espionage, too?"

Niloo frowned. She has not thought of that. Through the bond she said, *If that is the case, we are all in grave danger.* Lapis grunted her agreement.

Below, the excavation site crawled with activity. Workers hauled loads of volcanic stone from the main shaft, carefully sifting through the debris. Others operated brightly faceted devices that Niloo recognized from her Jintessa training—essence extractors, designed to separate magical energy from physical matter.

"The mining towns should have been evacuated by now," she said, thinking of the settlements that dotted the western foothills. Her parents had long ago organized an underground network, to move civilians eastward ahead of any attacking force; in this case, Madrid's advance. "But I can't be certain everyone received adequate warning."

"If civilians remain, Madrid will not hesitate to use them as shields or test subjects, or both," Lazuli warned.

Niloo nodded grimly. Her parents had explained in gruesome detail, the rumours flooding out of the Citadel. Madrid's ruthless pragmatism in achieving his goals, had escalated dramatically in her absense. Anything—or anyone—that might advance his goals became fodder for experimentation.

A flash of familiar energy made her crystal heart pulse. "Darius," she breathed as she rose to her knees, searching the encampment for her brother. She sensed his presence, the crystal heart amplifying their familiar connection so that she caught glimpses of his emotional state—determination layered over fear, rebellion constrained by compulsion.

Her eyes scanned the valley floor. There he was—emerging from the main excavation shaft. Even at this distance, Niloo recognized her brother's walk, although this was a man matured by time. Broad shoulders and thick brown hair named him her brother, although his

Imperial uniform marked him as the enemy. Behind him followed Commander Cayos, his tall, muscular form distinctive among the soldiers. Together, they were an intimidating sight.

"We need to move quickly," Niloo decided, sliding backward from the ridge. "The resistance fighters who answered my parent's call should be in position by now."

Lazuli nodded then shifted into his bird form, wings spreading silent against the dark stone. "I'll confirm their readiness."

As the djinn took flight, Niloo made her way down the back side of the ridge, following a narrow trail that would lead her to their makeshift camp from which to implement their plan. The scheme they'd devised was audacious but necessary. If Madrid's forces were able to extract intact dragon DNA and the magical elements needed to resurrect Lapis' cousins from these ancient nesting grounds, the Emperor's power would multiply exponentially. She could hardly imagine what Madrid might do with so much dragon power at his disposal.

The small cave they'd established as their rebel base, hummed with tension. Two dozen farmers-turned-fighters huddled around crude maps of the region, led by a skinny, old man with puckered, sun wrinkled skin, named Elvin, who hailed from a neighboring farm. He was the only one with any military experience in the group. A former Citadel guard, he had abandoned the post when Madrid came to power. They looked up as one as Niloo entered, hope and uncertainty warring in their expressions.

"The Imperial forces are concentrated around the main shaft," she informed them. "Patrol dragons sweep the perimeter every seventeen minutes, but their pattern is predictable. There's a three-minute window between passes on the eastern approach."

"And our distraction?" Elvin asked, his weathered face grim beneath a shock of gray hair.

"Lapis will create it," Niloo confirmed. "When you see a flash of blue fire against the southern mountain face, move your teams into position."

A young woman stepped forward—Keera, she thought she was called—whose family had worked the gem mines for generations. "The tunnels beneath the excavation are unstable. If we set charges at these points—" She indicated spots on the map. "—we can collapse outer chambers without destroying the central cavern."

"That's our goal," Niloo agreed. "Disrupt their operation without destroying what they seek. Force them to rebuild, to start again."

"Buy time," an older man nodded, understanding the strategy.

"Time and information," Niloo corrected. "We need to discover exactly what Madrid has found. What type of essence, how he plans to harness it."

As the resistance fighters made final preparations, Niloo retreated to a quiet corner of the cave. She closed her eyes, reaching for the bond with Lapis. The dragon's consciousness met hers, golden warmth flowing between them.

They suffer, Lapis communicated, her thoughts tinged with sorrow. *The land beneath their machines writhes in pain. Ancient memories disturbed, sacred grounds defiled.*

We'll stop them, Niloo promised. *Not just for Samos, but for your kind as well.*

Through Lapis, she sensed a deeper truth—the volcanic chambers weren't simply nesting grounds. They were repositories, places where dragon wisdom had been stored during times of crisis. Madrid's excavations threatened not just power, but knowledge known only to dragonkind, that had been preserved for millennia.

Lazuli returned as the fighters began to move out, shifting to human form in a shimmer of blue light. "The southern teams are ready.

The mining town of Ashburne has been evacuated, but Ember's Crossing still has civilians. Their elder refused to leave."

Niloo cursed softly. "Then we must adjust our strategy. No explosives near Ember's Crossing. We'll have to rely on more subtle methods there."

The djinn's expression darkened. "There's more. Imperial forces have brought in a device unlike any I've seen. A crystalline structure that pulses from within."

"A converter," Niloo realized, remembering descriptions from her parents' ancient texts. "They're planning to transmute any essence they recover, into a form they can control."

"Then we must strike now," Lazuli concluded. "There is no time to lose."

Outside the cave, they separated, each heading to their assigned positions. Niloo made her way to a vantage point overlooking the main excavation shaft. From here, she could maintain the bond with both Lapis and Lazuli while coordinating the resistance fighters through prearranged signals.

Her crystal heart warmed against her skin—not the pleasant connection to her triad partners, but the more painful awareness of her brother's proximity. Darius was down there, in the thick of Madrid's operation. She felt his confusion. His anger balanced on the knife-edge between compliance and rebellion. The question was, in which direction would it explode? Would he unleash it at them or at the emperor?

"Hold on," she whispered, though there was no way he could hear her voice. "Just a little longer."

The southern sky darkened suddenly as Lapis dove from the sky, leaving the safety of the high altitude thermals on which she'd been drifting undetected. Wings tucked in close to her body, streamlined her silhouette, but it also accelerated her descent. At the last moment, her wings snapped open—azure membranes catching the sunlight like stained glass. The display was magnificent, deliberately drawing the attention of every Imperial eye.

Then came the fire.

Not the mundane flame humans knew, but dragon fire—blue-white and impossibly hot, targeted with surgical precision. Lapis's breath scorched across empty storage tents, igniting supplies but carefully avoiding areas where people might be harmed.

Chaos erupted below. Soldiers scrambled for weapons while workers fled the sudden inferno. The patroling dragons broke formation, sweeping around to face the threat in their midst, their riders struggling to maintain control as instinct pulled them toward the challenge of another dragon's presence.

In the confusion, the resistance fighters moved in. Small teams of three and four slipped into position, placing volcanic charges at strategic points or quickly sabotaging equipment left momentarily unguarded. Others created diversions of their own—triggering rockslides that blocked secondary pathways into the encampment, lighting green brush that billowed great clouds of smoke, further obscuring visibility.

Niloo watched for her opening. Commander Cayos emerged from his pavilion, barking orders as he gestured toward Lapis's aerial assault. Behind him, the main excavation shaft stood temporarily abandoned, its guards drawn away by the emergency.

"Now," she whispered to herself, sprinting down the steep incline.

The path to the shaft entrance took her dangerously close to Imperial positions, but the resistance's coordinated strikes had served their purpose. No one noticed a single figure darting between shadows, her movements timed to coincide with explosions from the western approach and patches of dense smoke that floated by the opening.

Inside the excavation tunnel, the air changed immediately. The scent was heavy with ancient magic and disturbed earth. Niloo's crystal heart responded, pulsing with recognition. This place knew her blood, acknowledged her right to be here in a way it rejected Madrid's invaders.

The tunnel sloped downward, carved by modern tools but following paths originally created by dragon claws. Glowing lights had been installed at intervals, their cold gleam revealing the tunnel's progress through layers of volcanic stone. Niloo moved quickly but cautiously, taking advantage of every shadowy pocket of rock, alert for any remaining guards.

Three twisting levels down, the tunnel opened into a larger chamber. Niloo quickly scanned the cavern. Here, Madrid's workers had uncovered something quite extraordinary. The walls gleamed with embedded crystals—not decorative formations, but deliberate patterns that Niloo recognized from her parents' ancient texts. Dragon script, written in living stone.

And at the center of the chamber, partially excavated from the floor, lay what she had come to find.

An egg.

Not the leathery, flexible eggs of modern dragons, but something more ancient. This egg had fossilized, its shell transmuted to opalescent stone through volcanic processes and centuries of magical saturation. Within that stone shell, essence swirled visibly—golden light that pulsed with dormant life.

"An Ancestral Mother," Niloo breathed, using the formal address she'd learned on Jintessa. This was no ordinary dragon egg. This was one of the First Clutch—eggs laid by the great ancestors who had shaped Gaia itself.

A sound behind her broke the moment's reverence. Niloo spun, hands moving instinctively into defensive posture—and froze.

Darius stood in the tunnel entrance, his Imperial uniform stark against the glowing walls. His red crystal heart shone through the fabric of his tunic, pulsing in response to her blue one.

"You should not have come," he said, his voice a low growl.

"I had to," Niloo replied slowly, soothingly, all the while studying her brother's face. It was thinner than she remembered, wrinkles of laughter transformed into lines of stress, deeply etched around his dark eyes and between his brows. How much time had passed for him, under Madrid's control? "You felt it too, didn't you? The call of this place?"

Darius's jaw tightened. "I follow the Emperor's commands."

"You follow due to the Emperor's compulsion, not by choice." Niloo took a cautious step forward. "The crystal hearts connect us, brother. I can feel your resistance, the struggle within you, even now."

His hand moved to the weapon at his side, but hesitation slowed the motion. "Madrid knows you've returned. He's been expecting you to come here."

"Of course he has." Niloo gestured to the fossilized egg. "He needs both of us to access this. Blood calls to blood. The ancient dragons ensured their legacy could only be claimed by those who share the connection."

Above them, the ground shook with distant explosions. Almost in unison, their eyes rose to the ceiling. The resistance's attack was intensifying. Through her bond with Lapis, Niloo sensed Imperial dragons earlier disarray falling away as they gathered for a united attack against her allies.

Darius's gaze flicked between her and the egg, internal conflict visible in his expression. "What do you want with it?"

"To understand it. To protect what it contains from corruption."
She took another step closer. "The same thing you've been trying to
do by misleading Cayos about the excavation sites."

Surprise flickered across his features. "How did you—"

"Our connection works both ways, brother." Niloo offered a sad
smile. "I've seen your struggles. Your small rebellions."

For a moment, something like his true self emerged from beneath
layers of compulsion. Then his expression hardened again as Madrid's
control reasserted itself.

"You need to leave," he said, drawing his weapon—a crystal-tipped
baton that could channel his magic with devastating force. "Now. Before I'm forced to stop you. But before you do, take this." He stepped
forward and pressed a wrapped object into her hand, then stepped
back.

Niloo's fingers curled around the curious object as she assessed
her options. She could attempt to subdue him—her Jintessa training
would give her some advantage in close combat. But hurting Darius
would only strengthen Madrid's hold.

"I'm going," she agreed, backing toward a secondary tunnel she'd
spotted upon entering. "But this isn't over, Darius. I came for you as
much as for Samos."

His crystal heart flared red, responding to the emotion in her words.
"Niloo..." He seemed to struggle against invisible constraints. "The
egg. It's not what Madrid thinks. It's not essence that can be extracted.
It's... knowledge. Memory."

The information confirmed her parents' suspicions. "How many
has he found?"

"Just this one, intact. There are fragments of others." Darius winced
as if the sharing caused him physical pain. "But he's been building

something to access what lies within. A device that uses heartbearers as conduits."

Another explosion, much closer, rocked the chamber. Dust fell from the ceiling as the structure shuddered. Niloo's bond with Lazuli flared with warning—Imperial reinforcements were arriving from neighboring outposts. The resistance had succeeded in disrupting the excavation, but their advantage was ending.

"Go," Darius urged, his moment of clarity fading. The red glow around his crystal intensified, Madrid's distant control tightening like a noose. "If he captures you—"

"I know." Niloo committed the egg's location to memory, noting the specific patterns of crystal script around it. "Fight him where you can, brother. I'm coming for you."

She ducked into the secondary tunnel as Darius' crystal flared bright enough to illuminate the entire chamber. His cry of pain followed her into the darkness—the sound of Madrid punishing rebellion through the corrupted bond. Niloo shuddered, feeling an echo of his pain through her crystal heart. She forced her mind to concentrate on Lapis & Lazuli, ruthlessly thrusting away the sensations of Darius' punishment.

The path upward was steeper than the descent had been, following what must have been a lava tube in ancient times. As she climbed, Niloo maintained her connection with Lapis and Lazuli, sharing what she'd found through their triad bond.

A First Clutch egg, Lapis's thoughts carried reverence tinged with urgency. *We must return. It cannot let this ancestor of the Gaia brotherhood, fall into Madrid's hands.*

When Niloo emerged from the tunnel, she found herself on the far side of the excavation site, part way up the hillside. She peered cautiously out of the narrow opening, before moving out into the open. She dropped down to the ground and crawled to the edge of the rock to peer down at the camp below. The resistance's attack had achieved its objectives—equipment lay in ruins, tunnels had collapsed in strategic locations, and Imperial forces were divided between fire-fighting and defense.

From her new vantage point, she could see civilians being herded into the center of the camp where several teams of horses were hitched to wagons that carried open cages of iron. Surely these were the people from Ember's Crossing — brought to the encampment not as evacuees but captives. Madrid's soldiers shoved the men, women, and children into the transport wagons. Their destination was unclear.

Do you think that Madrid intends to use these people as test subjects, for whatever process the Emperor is developing? Niloo asked through the bond. Their first strike had succeeded in disrupting the excavation, but civilians were paying the price.

Lazuli appeared beside her, shifting from hawk to humanoid in a shimmer of blue light. "We cannot save them now," he said, regret heavy in his voice. "Imperial reinforcements approach from the north and east. The resistance fighters are retreating as planned."

"We'll come back for them," Niloo vowed, committing their faces to memory. "And for the egg. And for Darius."

They made their way to the rendezvous point where Lapis waited, her great blue form camouflaged against a cliff face of dark stone. The dragon's scales showed damage from Imperial weapons—crystalline projectiles designed to disrupt a dragon's natural magic. Despite this, her eyes burned with the fire of successful battle.

"We struck the first blow," Lapis observed as Niloo mounted. *"But Madrid will retaliate swiftly."*

"Not against the plains," Niloo said with certainty. "Not yet. He needs what lies beneath Ashfall Heights too desperately. He'll fortify this position, bring more forces to protect the egg."

As they took to the air, Niloo looked back at the smoldering excavation site. Imperial soldiers scurried across the wound they'd carved into the reddish Samos soil, while the captured civilians huddled in transport wagons, their fear palpable even at a distance.

And somewhere below, Darius navigated the treacherous path between obedience and rebellion, keeping vital secrets at terrible personal cost.

The first strike had yielded mixed results—disruption of Madrid's operation, confirmation of the egg's existence, and the painful truth of civilian exploitation. But it had also provided crucial information. Madrid sought dragon essence buried beneath Samos' crust, but he did not know about the knowledge contained within the fossilized eggs. Knowledge that could change the balance of power throughout Gaia. The ancient eggs could not be allowed to fall into Madrid's hands.

Niloo's crystal heart pulsed with renewed purpose as they flew eastward, carrying warning to the resistance that had formed across Samos. Madrid would adapt his strategy. They would need to adapt faster.

The essence wars had begun in earnest, and their next strike would need to be bolder still.

CHAPTER ELEVEN

THE WEIGHT OF SHARED PAIN

Blood calls to blood.

The words echoed through Niloo's mind as she stared at the communication crystal Darius had pressed into her palm during their brief, agonized reunion. The small, oblong gemstone pulsed with faint warmth that felt like a heartbeat—her brother's heartbeat, transmitted across the miles that separated them, carrying with it traces of his pain, his resistance, and his desperate hope that their bond might prove stronger than Madrid's compulsion.

But feeling Darius's struggle, through the stone, was only part of what tormented her as they made camp in a hidden valley three miles from the Ashfall Heights excavation. The weight of what they had witnessed—the male heartbearers who had been twisted to Madrid's purposes, the grim soldiers, the innocent civilians herded into transport wagons like livestock—these things weighed on her mind like a sack of rocks she couldn't set down.

You carry the pain of everyone we couldn't save, Lapis observed through their bond, her mental voice gentle with understanding. The great dragon had coiled herself around their small camp, her lapis lazuli scales dimmed to avoid reflecting the light of their carefully shielded fire. *I can feel it—not just your own anguish, but echoes of every person Madrid's forces captured today.*

"How do you bear it?" Niloo asked, though she wasn't entirely sure whether she was speaking aloud or through the bond. The boundaries between their different forms of communication had become fluid since their encounter with Ember, since their perspectives had begun to merge in ways that transcended simple telepathy. "How does one carry the weight of so much suffering without being crushed by it?"

Through the triad connection, she felt her companions' different approaches to processing trauma, their individual methods of dealing with horrors that defied easy comprehension.

Lapis's dragon nature gave her access to vast time scales that allowed her to see immediate suffering within the context of longer cycles of healing and renewal. *For my kind, pain is temporary but consciousness is eternal,* she explained, sharing glimpses of dragon memory that stretched across centuries. *We have seen civilizations rise and fall, watched species adapt to challenges that seemed insurmountable, witnessed the birth of new forms of beauty from the ashes of old destructions.*

This does not mean we feel pain less acutely, she continued, her mental voice carrying the weight of accumulated grief. *It means we understand pain as part of a larger pattern—a signal that change is necessary, that our consciousness is being called on, to grow in new directions.*

But even as Lapis shared her ancient wisdom, Niloo could feel the dragon's own struggle with what they had witnessed.

I wanted to burn them all, Lapis admitted, her mental voice rough with barely controlled rage. *Every Imperial facility, every enhancement laboratory, every device designed to modify consciousness against its will. The fire-song in my blood called for purification through flame.*

But you didn't, Lazuli observed, his djinn form flickering between states as he processed his own complex reactions to the day's events. *You chose precision over destruction, healing over vengeance. Why?*

The question carried weight beyond its simple words, touching on fundamental choices about how to respond to evil without becoming consumed by it.

Because, Lapis replied after a long pause, *burning everything might eliminate the immediate threat, but it would also destroy any possibility of understanding how to prevent such things from happening again. Madrid's techniques for consciousness modification—they represent knowledge that could be transformed into tools for healing rather than control.*

Through the bond, Niloo felt her dragon companion's deeper reasoning—the understanding that rage, however justified, could become its own form of tyranny if not tempered by wisdom and compassion.

Lazuli's approach to processing trauma was different, shaped by his djinn nature's relationship with multiple realities. *For my kind, any single reality is just one possibility among infinite others,* he explained, his form solidifying as he focused on sharing perspective rather than maintaining perfect consistency. *When I witness suffering in this reality, I can perceive alternate versions where different choices led to different outcomes.*

But that doesn't diminish the reality of the suffering here and now, Niloo said, sensing something troubling in Lazuli's explanation. *The people Madrid captured today—they're not comforted by the existence of versions of themselves who escaped in other realities.*

No, Lazuli agreed, his mental voice carrying a note of self-criticism that surprised her. *And that is my struggle with what we witnessed. My instinct is to retreat into alternate possibilities, to focus on what could be rather than what is. But consciousness trapped in suffering needs rescue from this reality, not philosophical comfort about other realities.*

Through the bond, Niloo felt Lazuli's deeper conflict—the way his shapeshifting nature made it tempting to avoid difficult emotions by simply becoming someone who hadn't experienced them. It was a form of magical dissociation that offered protection at the cost of engagement.

I have been avoiding the full weight of what Madrid represents, he admitted, his form flickering more rapidly as he forced himself to confront uncomfortable truths. *Telling myself that his victory is only one possibility among many, that resistance is therefore not as urgent as it appears. But people are suffering now, in this reality, and my ability to perceive alternatives does not give me permission to ignore their pain.*

The honesty of his self-assessment sent warmth through the triad bond, the kind of warmth that came from trust deepening rather than simple affection. They were sharing not just their strengths with each other, but their weaknesses, their fears, their methods of avoiding truths too painful to face directly.

And what about you? Lapis asked gently, her attention turning to Niloo. *How does human consciousness process witnessing such systematic cruelty?*

The question forced Niloo to examine her own reactions, to dig beneath the surface emotions of anger and grief to understand how her human nature shaped her response to trauma.

I personalize it, she realized, the understanding emerging as she spoke. *Dragons see patterns across time, djinn see possibilities across realities, but humans see individuals across relationships. When I watched those people being loaded into transport wagons, I didn't just see statistics or strategic problems—I saw someone's mother, someone's child, someone's best friend being stolen from everyone who loved them.*

The personalization was both strength and weakness, she realized. It made human consciousness fiercely protective of individuals in ways that could motivate extraordinary acts of courage and compassion. But it also made it difficult to maintain perspective when the number of individuals needing protection became overwhelming.

The communication crystal from Darius makes it worse, she continued, holding up the small gem that continued to pulse with her brother's distant heartbeat. *I can feel fragments of his experiences through our connection—moments when Madrid's compulsion forces him to act against his will, instances when he regains enough control to feel horrified by what he's been made to do.*

Through the bond, she shared what the crystal had shown her during their journey from the excavation site—brief flashes of Darius's perspective that painted a picture of consciousness slowly being eroded by magical control. The blood magic didn't just command obedience; it rewarded compliance with artificial pleasure while punishing resistance with increasing levels of agony.

He's learning to want what Madrid wants, she whispered, the words carrying horror that went beyond simple fear. *Not because he chooses to, but because the alternative is pain beyond endurance. Every day the compulsion grows stronger, every act of obedience makes the next one easier.*

That is the true cruelty of Madrid's system, Lapis observed. *He does not simply force compliance—he corrupts the mechanisms that are normally used by people to determine its values,and desires, to determine what it believes to be right.*

Systematic mental hijacking on a magical scale, Lazuli added, his djinn nature providing clinical perspective of Madrid's techniques. *He does not just control what people do—he modifies their perception of reality until his control seems natural, even beneficial.*

The conversation was interrupted by a sound that made all three of them freeze—the distant scream of an Imperial dragon, searching for them. The dragon's cry echoed off the valley walls as it searched for traces of their passage. Through the bond, they shared information instantly: Lapis's enhanced hearing detecting the specific harmonic patterns that indicated a younger dragon, possibly born on Jintessa. Lazuli's awareness picked up the reality distortions created by spelled silver control collars, and Niloo's human intuition sensed the wrongness of the wizard that rode behind the djinn, changed by Madrid's perverted magic.

Fifty yards north, Lapis reported, her senses tracking the patrol's movement. *One dragon carrying two riders, moving in standard search patterns. They have not detected us yet, but they are being thorough.*

The dragon is in pain, Lazuli added, his shapeshifting nature making him sensitive to the dragon's duress. *The control collar is burning through the natural protection of its hide, and the pain is weakening its ability to resist. They are forcing it to search longer and more intensively than its young body can safely sustain.*

Through the communication crystal, Niloo felt an echo of Darius's anguish as he became aware of the patrol's presence through whatever magical network connected Madrid's enslaved servants. Her brother was somewhere close enough for the crystal to pick up his emotional state, which meant he was likely part of the search operation.

He's trying to misdirect them, she realized, feeling Darius's struggle to feed false information to his Imperial handlers without triggering the blood magic's punishment protocols. *But the compulsion is fighting him—every attempt to help us causes him physical agony.*

The weight of their shared pain sharpened into something approaching unbearable, as Niloo felt her brother's torment layered onto her own guilt about the people they hadn't been able to save. The triad bond, designed to share strength and perspective, was also sharing trauma in ways that threatened to overwhelm Niloo.

This is too much, she gasped, her mind reeling under the strain of multiple sources of anguish. *I can't carry all of this—the captured civilians, Darius's pain, the tortured patrol dragon, everything Madrid is doing to the consciousness of all the people of Gaia.*

But even as she spoke, she felt her companions' response through the bond—not an attempt to take her pain away, but a sharing of their own methods for bearing unbearable burdens.

Pain shared is not pain doubled, Lapis offered, her dragon wisdom flowing through the connection. *It is pain transformed. When we carry suffering alone, it becomes a weight that crushes. When we carry it together, it becomes fuel for action.*

The djinn understanding is similar, Lazuli added, *Consciousness is not diminished by experiencing pain—it is strengthened by choosing how to respond to pain. Madrid's control techniques work by limiting those choices, but our bond preserves them.*

Then we choose to transform this pain into purpose, Niloo said, the communication crystal warm in her palm as she made the conscious decision to use her brother's suffering as motivation rather than paralysis. *Every person Madrid controls, every mind he breaks, every soul he corrupts—they all become reasons to ensure his methods never spread beyond this world.*

Through the bond, she felt her companions' agreement, their shared commitment to bearing witness to trauma without being destroyed by it. The patrol dragon's cry echoed through the valley again, but this time instead of just hearing the pain of an enslaved creature, they heard the call of a intelligence refusing to surrender despite artificial control.

The patrol is moving away, Lapis reported as the sound faded. *Darius's misdirection was successful—they are searching the eastern ridges instead of this valley.*

At what cost to him? Niloo asked, feeling the crystal's warmth intensify as her brother's struggle with the blood magic reached new levels of intensity.

A cost he chose to pay, Lazuli replied gently. *Even under magical compulsion, the mind finds ways to exercise choice. Your brother chose to help us despite the pain it would cause him. That choice—that refusal to let Madrid's control eliminate his compassion—is itself a form of resistance.*

The understanding helped, though it didn't eliminate the anguish of knowing Darius suffered for their sake. But it reframed that suffering within the larger context of consciousness asserting itself against artificial control, of love persisting despite magical modification.

We carry this pain forward, Niloo said finally, her voice steady despite the tears that tracked down her cheeks. *Not as a burden that weakens us, but as a reminder of what we're fighting to protect. Every moment of anguish Madrid's system creates becomes evidence for why such systems must never be allowed to spread.*

For freedom itself, Lapis agreed, her ancient strength flowing through the bond.

For the right to remain beautifully, chaotically, magnificently ourselves, Lazuli added, his shapeshifting nature now focused on maintaining rather than changing.

As the night deepened and they prepared for the next phase of their mission, the triad found that their shared processing of trauma had deepened their bond in unexpected ways. They were still three distinct beings, but now they were three beings who had learned to transform suffering into strength through conscious cooperation.

The weight of shared pain remained, but it no longer threatened to crush them. Instead, it had become part of the foundation upon which they would build Madrid's defeat—proof that minds freely shared could bear any burden, endure any torment, and emerge stronger through the choice to support each other rather than face darkness alone.

The crystal pulsed a steady rhythm in Niloo's hand, carrying both his pain and his hope across the miles between them. And in that pulse, Niloo felt not just her brother's struggle, but the rhythm of all beings that refused to surrender their essential nature to anyone's outside control.

They would carry that rhythm forward, into battles yet to come, sustained by the understanding that pain shared consciously was always stronger than pain inflicted unconsciously, that trauma

processed with trusted allies became wisdom rather than merely scar
tissue.

Chapter Twelve

MAGIC GONE WILD

Three days after their strike against Ashfall Heights, Niloo crouched behind a windbreak of ancient oaks, watching Madrid's swelling forces, rebuild with disturbing efficiency. The excavation site sprawled larger than before, protected by shimmering barriers powered in part with energies syphoned from the great barrier itself. Where once a single shaft had descended into the earth, now three separate tunnels burrowed toward the fossilized egg chamber.

"They've tripled their security," Lazuli observed, his djinn form barely visible in the pre-dawn darkness. "And brought in specialists."

Through her spyglass—a gift from her parents' hidden cache of Keeper tools—Niloo studied the new arrivals. Men and women in robes that marked them as Madrid's personal artificers, the Emperor's elite cadre of corrupted near wizards, men and women with some magical abilities, however weak. They moved back and forth between strange devices that hummed with contained power, their faces reflecting a hollow expression in the refected light.

"The essence extractor," she whispered, focusing on an apparatus that dominated the excavation's center. The device resembled a massive version of her heart crystal, multifaceted and pulsing with inner light. Conduits of silver connected it to smaller stations where technicians worked with careful precision.

Lapis shifted restlessly where she lay concealed among the trees, her lapis lazuli scales dimmed to avoid reflecting the morning light. *The machine disturbs me,* the dragon communicated through their bond. *It bears resemblance to the soul forges of ancient Jintessa—devices we abandoned as too dangerous to use.*

"Soul forges?" Niloo queried, though she kept her physical attention on the excavation below.

Machines that could transfer essence between beings. The dragons of my homeland used them during the Great Sundering, when we fled to Jintessa to escape the wars that ravaged the elder realms, like here on Gaia. Lapis's mental voice tapped into her well of inherited memory. It was not always readily available, but particular words would occasionally trigger a flood of memories, shared with all dragons. *But the forges required a willing sacrifice. What Madrid has built - this machine - it seeks to take that essence by force.*

The distinction sent a chill through Niloo.

"Wait, did you say that the elders here, that they are your ancestors? The ancestors of the Jintessa dragons?" Niloo's head turned to stare at Lapis. "Our extinct dragons are your ancestors?"

Dragons from Jintessa and Gaia were not thought to be related, as Gaia's dragons had perished long ago. But if they were a related species, cousins, who she now was beginning to understand shared common ancestors, perhaps they were more alike that she had thought.

They had been shaped by different evolutionary pressures, however. Jintessa dragons, like Lapis, had developed their abilities in isolation, feeding on the rich gem deposits of their island sanctuary. It was thought that Gaia's dragons had evolved alongside the land itself, their essence intertwined with the planet's magical matrix in ways Jintessa dragons could sense but not fully share. Perhaps that was why they had been so easily driven into extinction.

Yes. Is that not the definition of cousin? We are related. Lapis blinked slowly, wating for Niloo's thoughts to catch up.

"That's why he needs Darius," she breathed as the realization of Madrid's motivation, crystalized in her mind. "A Gaia-born crystal bearer to interface with Gaia dragon essence," she mumbled aloud.

Precisely. And why he seeks you and your sisters, as well. Together, your combined connection would give him access to both bloodlines—Jintessa and Gaia magic unified under his control.

Stunned, Niloo stared at Lapis without seeing her, mind racing.

A commotion below drew their attention back to the excavation. Soldiers emerged from the central shaft, escorting a group of figures in shackles. Niloo's heart clenched as she recognized some of them—elders from Ember's Crossing, the mining town that had refused evacuation.

"The first test subjects," Lazuli said grimly. "They're preparing to activate the extractor."

Through her spyglass, Niloo watched as the prisoners were separated into two groups. The smaller group—perhaps a dozen individuals—were led toward the essence extractor. The rest were herded into a holding area surrounded by armed guards, and forced to sit on the ground.

"We have to stop this," she whispered, lowering the spyglass.

"With what force?" Lazuli challenged. "The resistance fighters are scattered across the province, organizing evacuation routes. We have perhaps twenty combat-ready individuals, facing a garrison of two hundred."

Niloo's mind raced through possibilities. A direct assault would be suicide. But watching innocent people fed to Madrid's machine was unthinkable. "There might be another way. If we can't stop the extraction, perhaps we can corrupt it."

Explain, Lapis urged.

"The machine requires Gaia dragon essence to function properly. But what if it received Jintessa essence instead? Your scales carry different harmonic frequencies, different magical signatures."

Lazuli's form shimmered with interest. "Dragon scales retain essence even when separated from their bearer. If we could introduce Lapis's scales into the extraction process..."

The interaction could destabilize the entire apparatus, Lapis completed. *But the plan requires me to shed scales deliberately—a painful process that will leave me vulnerable for days.*

Niloo met the dragon's great blue eyes. "I won't ask you to—"

You are not asking. I am choosing. Lapis's mental voice carried absolute determination. *These people are being made to suffer for Madrid's mad schemes. That is one reason. But also, the dragons of Gaia are my cousins, their essence sacred even in death. I will not allow Madrid to corrupt what should be honored.*

Below, the crystalline device pulsed brighter as technicians scurried around, making final adjustments. One of the prisoners—a middle-aged farmer Niloo recognized from the local markets—was dragged out of the crowd and secured to a chair positioned directly beneath the extractor's focal point.

"We need to move quickly," she decided. "Lazuli, can you create a distraction at the northern perimeter? Draw their attention away from the main operation?"

"Easily done," the djinn confirmed. "Give me a minute to position myself."

As Lazuli slipped away, shifting to his favoured hawk form for silent movement, Niloo shared her plan through the bond. Lapis lowered her great head, listening to Niloo's internal dialogue, bringing her muzzle close to Niloo's face.

Are you certain about doing this? Once begun, there will be no retreat.

"There's already no retreat," Niloo replied, stroking the dragon's snout. "The war for control of the dragon essence has begun. Madrid has made it plain that he will stop at nothing, to achieve his end goal. We either fight now, or we surrender our souls piece by piece until nothing remains but his will."

Lapis nodded slowly, then began the painful process of scale-shedding. Dragons could release their scales voluntarily, but doing so created wounds that would take weeks to heal properly. Each scale that fell carried a portion of the dragon's essence—not enough to weaken her significantly, not a few scales, but each scale carried a sufficient amount Jintessa magic to contaminate Madrid's attempted extraction. Or so they hoped.

The scales that dropped were perfect specimens of lapis lazuli—deep blue shot through with veins of gold, each one the size of

Niloo's palm. She gathered them carefully in a leather pouch, noting how they hummed with restrained magic.

Twenty scales, Lapis communicated, her mental voice strained. *More would leave me unable to fly. Less might not achieve the desired effect.*

Niloo secured the pouch to her belt, then checked her other equipment. Rope for climbing. A small mirror for signals. And her father's old mining pick—not much of a weapon, but better than nothing.

Lazuli's distraction began right on schedule. Explosions bloomed along the northern perimeter as the djinn triggered charges placed during a previous reconnaissance. Imperial soldiers responded immediately, a full third of the garrison racing toward the apparent attack.

In the confusion, Niloo made her move.

Niloo's path required crossing open ground, but the remaining guards were focused on the excitement of the drama playing out centrally, or watching for threats from the north. She sprinted from cover to cover, using bulky equipment and stacks of supplies to mask her approach. She crept right up to the edge of the ring of guards and waited.

The essence extractor dominated the excavation site like a technological altar. Crystal facets caught and refracted the morning light, creating rainbow patterns that hurt to look at directly. Clear conduits pulsed with captured energy, feeding the machine's growing hunger.

The first test subject—the farmer from Ember's Crossing—strained against his bonds, his eyes wide with terror, but a leather collar around his neck and covering his mouth prevented him from moving or speaking. Above him, the extractor's focal array began to descend. The technicians cleared the area around the test site. No one wanted to be caught by the machine's rays and accidently harvested. A clear, twenty foot ring of empty ground surrounded the victim.

The guards shifted, drawing away from the machine as a distinct hum rumbled into existence. An opening appeared as they instinctively drew closer together for protection. Niloo checked one last time and then launched herself at the captive, rolling to the foot of the machine, just as the extraction sequence initiated. The device's hum deepened to a bone-rattling resonance that made her teeth ache. The farmer's body went rigid as invisible forces grabbed him, probing his essence, seeking any trace of magical potential to harvest.

Angry shouts filled the air as the surrounding guards reacted to her sudden appearance among them. Working quickly, Niloo opened her pouch and tossed Lapis's scales at strategic points around the extractor's base. Sucked into the harmonics, each scale adhered to the surface with a soft chime, as Lapis' Jintessa-born magical essence began to interact with the machine's Gaia-tuned harmonics.

The effect was immediate. The extractor's pure resonance developed discordant undertones as foreign magic contaminated its systems. The technicians who were crowded around their control panel, noticed the anomaly within seconds, their voices rising in alarm as readouts displayed impossible results.

"Essence contamination in the primary matrix!"

"Harmonic divergence beyond acceptable parameters!"

"Abort the extraction! Abort now!"

But the machine had already tasted essence—both from its intended victim and from Lapis's scales. The combination proved explosive. Bright, stabbing light, like lightning gone wild, flashed around the camp as the internal components of the extractor began to crack under conflicting energies. The farmer in the extraction chair convulsed as magical forces tore through him, but instead of draining his essence, the corrupted process seemed to be feeding it back to him in amplified form.

Niloo watched in fascination and horror as the man's eyes began to glow with inner fire. His muscles swelled beneath his farmer's clothing, strength flowing into him from sources never meant for human bodies. The restraints that held him—strong leather reinforced with spelled silver buttons—began to stretch under impossible pressure.

He's becoming something new. Lapis' alarm spiked, sending shivers down Niloo's spine. *He's transforming, not into a heartbearer, but into some other entity entirely. GET OUT OF THERE, NILOO!*

The farmer tore free of his restraints with a feral roar. His transformed body moved with inhuman speed as he struck out at his captors. The Imperial guards raised weapons and shields but the transformed farmer shrugged off their attacks. When their energy bolts struck him, his skin absorbed the charge and used it to fuel further transformation.

Chaos erupted across the excavation site. The compromised extractor sent feedback through all connected systems, causing secondary explosions as overloaded crystals shattered. Technicians fled as their carefully calibrated equipment turned against them.

In the confusion, the remaining prisoners rioted, breaking free of their holding area. Some fled toward the excavation's perimeter. Others, caught too close to the unstable extractor, began to exhibit their own transformations as wild magical essence saturated the air, surging through their bodies. Several guardsmen were also sucked into the thrall of the rampaging magic.

Niloo found herself trapped between competing dangers. Imperial soldiers fired indiscriminately at anything that moved. The enhanced prisoners lashed out with newfound strength they couldn't control. And above it all, the essence extractor continued its death spiral, threatening to release energies that could devastate the entire region. Niloo felt the waves of magical energies bombarding her as she ran, but her bond with Lapis shielded her from the worst of the magic gone wild. She was already transformed and nothing happening here could truly affect her. But that was no reason to stay and test the theory. She bolted away from the collapsing machine and sprinted for the pass where her companions hid, waiting for her return.

A rough hand closed on her shoulder as she skirted a tent, spinning her around. She found herself face-to-face with Darius, his Imperial uniform singed and his red crystal heart blazing with reflected chaos.

"You did this," he accused, but his voice carried admiration rather than anger.

"I had to try," she replied, shouting over the extractor's dying screams. "Those people didn't deserve—"

"No, they didn't." Darius's expression shifted, internal struggle visible in his features. "And neither do the others Madrid has planned for this machine."

He gestured toward a convoy approaching from the east—transport wagons loaded with more prisoners. Men, women, and children from across western Samos, gathered for Madrid's experiments in artificial essence bonding.

"How many?" Niloo asked.

"Three hundred souls in the first shipment. More arriving daily." Darius's crystal heart pulsed brighter as Madrid's distant control pressed against his wavering loyalty. "He's building an army of essence-touched, but the process is imperfect. Most subjects die. Those who survive become... unstable."

Around them, the excavation site continued its descent into chaos. The enhanced prisoners had become a force of nature, their artificial strength turning them into living weapons that recognized no friend or foe. Imperial soldiers fell back to defensive positions while technicians attempted to shut down the shattered equipment.

"You need to leave," Darius urged. "Before reinforcements arrive from the eastern camps."

"Come with me," Niloo offered, grasping her brother's hand. "Break Madrid's hold. Fight for Samos instead of its destroyer."

For a moment, hope flickered in Darius's eyes. His grip tightened on hers, and she felt their crystal hearts resonating in harmony instead of conflict. But then Madrid's compulsion reasserted itself, flooding through the corrupted bond like ice water through veins.

"I can't," he gasped, pulling away. "The binding... goes too deep."

"The eastern excavations," he whispered urgently. "Fire Ridge and the Dead Fields. Madrid seeks more than just essence there. Ancient breeding chambers, where the first dragons laid their eggs in Gaia's early days."

"What does he plan?"

"Resurrection." Darius's voice dropped to barely audible. "He believes he can hatch the ancient eggs using modern essence. Create dragons bound to his will from the moment of birth."

The implications staggered Niloo. Dragons born into slavery, their natural bonds corrupted before they ever took wing. It would be abomination beyond anything Madrid had yet attempted.

"How long before he moves on the other sites?"

"Days, perhaps a week." Darius stepped back as his crystal heart flared warning red. "Go. And whatever you do, don't let him take you alive. The things he has planned..."

He couldn't finish the sentence before Madrid's control dragged him away, but the fear in his eyes communicated enough. The fear hardened and Darius face blanked. He frowned, then he took a step towards Niloo. "Go now," he hissed between clenched teeth, raising his weapon to point at Niloo's real heart.

Niloo spun around and ran.

The extraction site was becoming untenable. Enhanced prisoners rampaged through supply tents while Imperial soldiers established a perimeter, trapping anyone remaining inside a human ring. Overhead, patrol dragons circled like vultures, laying down fire to contain the chaos around the camp.

Niloo slipped away, using the smoke and confusion to mask her retreat. The path back to Lapis required crossing the northern approach where Lazuli's distraction had drawn Imperial attention, but the djinn's explosions had died down, and the soldiers were returning to reinforce their struggling companions attempts to regain control.

She found them both at the rendezvous point—Lapis concealed among the trees, her exposed flesh where scales had been shed protected by Lazuli's improvised bandages. The djinn himself looked exhausted, his usual luminescence dimmed by extended shapeshifting and magical exertion.

"The extraction failed catastrophically," Niloo reported as she climbed into the saddle strapped to Lapis's back. "But Madrid's experiments continue. He has three hundred more test subjects arriving within days."

Then we must organize true resistance, Lapis declared, her mental voice firm despite her injuries. *No more surgical strikes. The essence wars require armies, not individual heroes.*

As they took to the air, Niloo glanced back at the excavation site. Smoke rose from a dozen fires while Imperial soldiers struggled to contain the chaos her sabotage had unleashed. The enhanced prisoners would either be destroyed or recaptured, their brief taste of freedom a small victory in a much larger war.

The communication crystal resting in her pouch pulsed. It represented something significant—an opportunity for ongoing contact with Darius, perhaps intelligence about Madrid's future plans, and the hope that her brother's true self still fought against his magical bonds. Or was it all a deception?

The eastern horizon beckoned. Farmers and miners were organizing themselves into something Madrid wouldn't expect. Not rebels fighting for independence, but Keepers -protectors of knowledge – defending ancient secrets that predated his empire by millennia.

The Essence War had suddenly escalated beyond individual strikes and counter-strikes. Now it would become a contest between Madrid's artificial power and the natural magic that had shaped Gaia since the world's birth.

Niloo's crystal heart pulsed with determination as they flew toward that uncertain future. Behind them, the consequences of the failed extraction continued to unfold. Ahead lay the greater challenge of uniting Samos's scattered resistance into a force capable of standing against the Emperor's growing might.

In her mind, she began composing the message she would send through the communication crystal to Darius: *Hold on. Fight where you can. Help is coming.*

Even if she wasn't entirely certain what form that help would take.

CHAPTER THIRTEEN

THE NAGA CRYSTAL

Emperor Madrid stood motionless before the great window of his private chambers, three hundred feet above the Citadel's main courtyard. Below, morning light illuminated the controlled chaos of his empire—soldiers drilling in perfect formation, peasants pushing carts and hawking their wares, administrative functionaries scurrying between stone buildings like industrious ants. All of it precisely orchestrated, all of it serving his singular purpose. His eyes rose to contemplate the horizon.

None of them suspected they were merely tools in a plan that stretched far beyond Gaia's horizons. Knowing and understanding your enemy's motivation was key to winning any battle. Weaknesses uncovered could be exploited. Fears manipulated.

A knock at the chamber door interrupted his contemplation. "Enter," he commanded without turning from the window.

Commander Cayos stepped inside, his usually composed demeanor showing cracks of frustration. Fresh from the disaster at Ashfall Heights, the man bore the look of someone who had failed his master and knew the price such failure traditionally carried.

"Your Majesty," Cayos began, his voice carefully controlled. "The preliminary report from the essence extraction—"

"Indicates that it was a catastrophic failure," Madrid finished, his voice a low hiss. He turned away from the window. His pale eyes fixed on Cayos with the intensity of winter stars. "Three hundred civilians transformed into uncontrollable aberrations. Two dozen of my finest artificers dead. Equipment worth a year's tribute from four provinces reduced to a melted pile of slag."

Cayos's jaw tightened. "The sabotage was expertly executed. Intelligence suggests—"

"Intelligence suggests," Madrid interrupted with a mocking sneer, as he walked to a table where detailed maps of Gaia were spread open like the skin of a flayed beast, "that our dear female Samosian heart-bearer has returned to complicate my plans. How refreshing. It has been far too long since someone provided a genuine challenge to my work."

The Emperor's tone carried no anger, no frustration—only the cold satisfaction of a strategist whose opponent had finally revealed their capabilities. To assume that Madrid was not angry, however, would be a foolish mistake. Commander Cayos was not a fool. Madrid dragged a polished nail across the map, following the borders of Samos toward the volcanic regions.

"Increase security at Fire Ridge and the Dead Fields," he commanded. "Triple the garrison at each site. And bring in reinforcements from the eastern provinces."

"Your Majesty," Cayos ventured, "our intelligence suggests the girl has allied with local resistance. Perhaps we should consider negotiating—"

Madrid's laughter cut through the air like breaking glass. "Negotiate? With farmers and miners who fancy themselves warriors?" He turned back to Cayos, and for a moment, something inhuman flickered behind his eyes. "Commander, you misunderstand the nature of this conflict. I am not fighting for Samos. I am not even fighting for Gaia."

He moved to a second table, this one holding a map that Cayos had never seen before. Unlike the familiar outlines of Gaia's provinces, this chart showed open ocean stretching toward a distant landmass marked with symbols the Commander couldn't read.

"Jintessa," Madrid said, noting Cayos's confusion. "The island realm where dragons nest and witches learn to bond with them. Where I spent the first forty years of my life before they cast me out for understanding truths they were too cowardly to embrace."

Cayos stared at the map, pieces of a larger puzzle suddenly clicking into place. "The dragon essence experiments. You're not trying to enhance our soldiers. You're trying to—"

"Create an army of Gaia-born dragons bound to my will from the moment of hatching," Madrid confirmed. "Dragons that will carry my forces across the ocean to settle old debts. Dragons that will burn Jintessa's councils to ash and deliver its accumulated power into my hands."

The Emperor moved to a third display—not a map, but a detailed diagram showing dragon anatomy with inked modifications marked throughout. "The natural bonding process takes years to perfect. A dragon must choose its partner freely, must trust completely before the triad can form. But I have discovered more efficient methods."

His finger traced the diagram's modifications—gem based implants that would bypass natural resistance, receptors that would flood a hatching dragon with the altered essence that his extractors would create to imbue loyalty, neural modifications that would make rebellion literally impossible.

"The ancient breeding chambers beneath Fire Ridge contain eggs that have been dormant for millennia," Madrid continued. "Dragon eggs that remember the time before humans walked Gaia. With the application of essence extracted from living specimens, those eggs can be awakened. The hatchlings will know only my voice, only my will. I will be a God to them. And we have at our disposal the youngling dragons I originally brought over from Jintessa. All the dragon essence I need. I will wake an army of dragons, ready to do my bidding."

"And what of the people of Gaia?" Cayos asked, though he suspected he already knew the answer.

"They are mere tools," Madrid replied without hesitation. "Heart-bearers to provide human elements of magic to interface with draconic magic. Farmers to feed my physical armies. Miners to extract the gems that will power my devices and feed the dragons themselves. Soldiers to maintain order while the greater work proceeds."

He gestured toward the window, where the morning sun illuminated distant mountains. "Every wretched life in this pitiful empire exists to serve a single purpose—preparing for the day when I return to Jintessa not as an exile, but as a conqueror."

Cayos struggled to process the scope of Madrid's ambition. "Your Majesty, the logistics alone—transporting an army across the ocean, maintaining supply lines—"

"Will be manageable when that army consists of creatures that can fly indefinitely and require only gemstones for sustenance," Madrid finished. "Dragons are remarkably self-sufficient, Commander. Unlike humans, they do not require constant feeding, frequent rest, or complex emotional management. Human weakness will be left behind, their purpose served."

The Emperor returned to his original position by the window, but now his gaze turned not toward his immediate empire but toward the eastern horizon, where the ocean lay beyond the curve of the world. "Many people think that the ocean is the end of the world. But I know it to be only the beginning. This... place," his face contorted with distain, "and its inhabitants are nothing but a grovelling sesspool, barely a life form, and easily discarded when the time comes." Madrid glanced over his shoulder, eyes raking over the tall man that until this moment had show him the only true loyalty he had found in this land of liars. "I trust you will remain faithful and dedicated to my rule. You swore your undying loyalty to me. To stray at this point would have...unfortunate consequences."

Commander Cayos straightened, his stony face impassive. He saluted. "My only wish is to serve."

"The setback at Ashfall Heights, it merely accelerates my timeline," Madrid continued. "If the girl can corrupt my extraction processes, then I must secure the breeding chambers before she can interfere further. Fire Ridge will be our next primary focus."

"And the civilian populations in those regions?"

Madrid's smile held no warmth whatsoever. "Will serve as test subjects for the refined bonding process. The extractors have provided valuable data about forced transformation. Most subjects die, yes, but those who survive demonstrate remarkable resilience. Useful qualities in soldiers who must fight dragons and witches."

He turned back to Cayos, his pale eyes reflecting something that might have been anticipation. "Summon Darius. His connection to the saboteur makes him valuable bait. And bring me the Naga's crystal—it is time to consult the ancient wisdom about dragon binding."

Cayos suppressed a shudder at the mention of the Naga. The mythical creature's artifact had been acquired during the conquest of Shadra province, but even Madrid approached it with unusual caution. The crystal supposedly contained knowledge from the earliest days of dragon-human interaction, when the bonds were forged through blood and sacrifice rather than mutual trust. The underwater city had proven to be a treasure trove of ancient knowledge. And an ongoing source of dragon essence. The Naga were the earliest form of dragon, a watery cousin that evolved into the land beast' essence that he coveted so much. It had been the Naga crystal which had first spoken of the secrets buried beneath Samosian soil.

"How long until the breeding chambers can be accessed?" Madrid asked.

"Weeks, perhaps days if we sacrifice safety protocols." Cayos's stiff posture did not soften as his eyes followed the emperor. He walked over to a cabinet containing various artifacts, reaching out cautiously to withdraw a crystal that seemed to writhe with internal shadows. Carefully, he carried it over to Madrid and handed him the object, relieved to part with the thing.

"The Naga's wisdom speaks of rituals that can awaken dormant eggs instantaneously, but the process requires..." Madrid paused, considering his words. "Specific offerings."

"What kind of offerings?"

"Living essence freely given. Not extracted by force, not corrupted by machinery, but surrendered willingly by those who understand what they sacrifice." Madrid cradled the dark crystal, its surface reflecting no light despite the chamber's illumination. "The girl and her brother represent perfect candidates—siblings bonded by blood and crystal, their essence already intertwined. I learned much from Shikoba's sacrifice, and her mother before her. She continues to serve me to this day, although not as the tribal priestess she had anticipated she would become. Still, she lives, and serves me."

The implications crystallized in Cayos's mind. "You intend to use the Samosians siblings to awaken the ancient eggs."

"Among other purposes," Madrid confirmed. "Their willing sacrifice would provide sufficient power to hatch a full clutch of dragons. Creatures that would emerge already bound to my will, already trained in the arts of war."

He set the Naga's crystal on the table beside the dragon modification diagrams. "But willing sacrifice requires proper motivation. The girl fights for her brother, for her province, for abstract ideals she believes noble. When she learns that her continued resistance will result in the systematic torture of every civilian in Samos, her perspective may shift."

"And if she still refuses?"

Madrid's expression didn't change, but the temperature in the room seemed to drop. "Then I will demonstrate the price of defying imperial will. The people of Samos will serve as examples to other provinces—I will show them what happens when local loyalties supersede imperial necessity."

He moved to a final map, this one showing the entire continent of Gaia with detailed notes about population centers, resource extraction, and strategic value. "The beauty of governing through fear,

Commander, is its efficiency. One province thoroughly broken serves as a lesson to all others."

Cayos studied the map, noting the calculations marked beside each province. Numbers that represented people reduced to statistics, lives measured only by their utility to Madrid's greater plan.

"Your orders, Your Majesty?"

"Increase recruitment from the eastern provinces. I want a thousand soldiers with untapped magical potential under imperial control within the month." Madrid's finger traced the ocean beyond Gaia's borders. "Accelerate the breeding chamber excavations regardless of cost. And prepare transportation for when the dragons hatch—ships that can accompany an aerial army across the sea."

"What of the girl's resistance activities?"

"Let her play her small games for now," Madrid replied dismissively. "Each strike against my forces provides valuable intelligence about her capabilities and limitations. When the time comes to collect her, I will know exactly how to break whatever defenses she might attempt."

The Emperor returned to his position by the window, but his reflection in the glass showed not the ruler of Gaia but something else—something that remembered exile and burned with the need for revenge.

"Jintessa cast me out for pursuing knowledge the Djinn masters had forbidden," he said quietly. "They claimed my research into forced bonding was an abomination, that dragons could never truly serve unless they chose their bondmates freely." His laugh carried the bitter edge of decades-old anger. "They will learn otherwise when my army appears on their horizon."

Cayos recognized the dismissal in his master's tone. "I will see to the preparations immediately, Your Majesty."

Madrid barely noticed as the Commander departed. He remained by the window, his gaze fixed on the eastern horizon where his destiny waited, deep in thought. The setbacks in Samos were temporary inconveniences, minor obstacles in a plan that had been decades in the making.

The girl and her allies fought for Gaia's freedom, not understanding that their world had never been the prize. Every crystal heartbearer he captured, every essence he extracted, every dragon egg he corrupted—all of it served the greater goal of returning to Jintessa with power enough to reshape both realms according to his vision.

In his mind, Madrid could already see the moment of triumph—Jintessa's councils burning, its dragons bowing to his will, its accumulated knowledge flowing into his hands. The exiled would become the conqueror of both lands, and all the realms would acknowledge the superior wisdom of his methods.

The essence wars were merely the prologue to a much larger story, one that would end with the transformation of the world itself.

Madrid's reflection smiled in the window glass, and for a moment, the face that looked back was not entirely human. The forbidden knowledge he had pursued on Jintessa had left its marks, changing him in ways that went beyond mere appearance. His djinn blood heated and he flickered as he struggled to control the human form he showed to the world. The elixirs were failing.

Soon. Soon he would have all the pieces of his plan in place.

When he finally conquered the island realm, it would be as something greater than the exile they had cast out. Something that transcended the limitations they had tried to impose on his ambitions.

The Emperor of Gaia turned from the window and began preparations for the next phase of his war against both worlds.

CHAPTER FOURTEEN

BROTHER AGAINST SISTER

The communication crystal pulsed against Niloo's palm as she crouched in the ruins of an abandoned watchtower, three miles east of Ashfall Heights. Two days had passed since the extraction disaster, and Madrid's forces had spread across the volcanic region like a plague of locusts. Below, patrols moved in systematic search patterns, the Citadel dragons casting long shadows across the scarred landscape as they flew overhead.

"He's close," she whispered to Lazuli, who perched in his hawk form on the crumbling stone beside her. "I can feel Darius. But there's something else—pain, resistance. He's fighting Madrid's control."

Through their bond, Lapis communicated worry from her hiding place in a lava cave two valleys over. The dragon's wounds from scale-shedding were healing slowly, leaving her vulnerable to detection by Madrid's aerial scouts. *Your sibling bond grows stronger with proximity to its true source,* she warned. *Your twin hearts are drawn to each other. Be warned, your brother may not be himself when you next meet.*

Niloo touched her own crystal heart, feeling its blue warmth pulse in rhythm with the communication gem. The double resonance created an echo effect—not painful, but disorienting. Through it, she sensed Darius's approach from the northwest, his emotional state a churning mixture of determination and despair.

The watchtower had been built during the border wars of her grandmother's generation, before Madrid's rise to power. Its stone walls bore scorch marks from dragon fire—not the controlled flames of bonded partners, but the wild burning of creatures driven mad by illness. A sober reminder of what Madrid's experiments could create.

"There," Lazuli said, his hawk eyes spotting movement before Niloo's human vision could detect it. "Single person approaching, on foot. No escort visible."

Niloo squinted against the afternoon glare, finally making out a familiar silhouette picking its way up the rocky slope toward the tower. Darius moved with the careful gait of someone fighting an internal battle with every step, his Imperial uniform marking him as enemy even as his presence sparked hope in her heart.

She descended from the tower's upper level, meeting him at the entrance where morning glory vines had begun to reclaim the ancient stones. Up close, she could see the toll Madrid's control had taken—dark circles beneath his eyes, a tremor in his hands that spoke of magical and physical strain, and most telling of all, the way his red crystal heart flickered between brilliant scarlet and a dull, corrupted brown.

"Niloo." His voice carried the warmth of their shared childhood, but underneath lay something else—a note of warning. "You shouldn't have come."

"You called to me," she replied, holding up the communication crystal. "Through this. Even Madrid's blood bonding magic couldn't suppress that message completely."

Darius's expression shifted, surprise mixing with a desperate kind of relief. "I wasn't certain the crystal would work. Madrid monitors all magical communications through the Citadel's network, but this one operates on a different frequency."

"The frequency of family," Niloo said, stepping closer. "Blood calls to blood, even across enemy lines."

They stood facing each other in the tower's shadow, siblings separated by more than mere allegiance. Niloo could feel the corruption radiating from Darius's crystal, a wrongness that made her skin crawl even as her heart ached for the brother she remembered.

"Tell me about the blood magic," she said gently. "I need to understand what Madrid has done to you."

Darius's hand moved unconsciously to his throat, where Niloo now noticed a thin scar barely visible above his uniform's collar. "A binding ritual performed the night they brought me to the Citadel. My blood mixed with essence drawn from captured dragons, then crystallized through processes I don't fully understand." His voice dropped to a whisper. "It creates a connection Madrid can activate at will. When he exerts control, it feels like drowning in ice water while my bones burn from within."

The clinical description couldn't hide the terror beneath his words. Niloo reached out, her fingers hovering just short of touching his face. "How do we break it?"

"We don't," Darius replied, stepping back before contact could be made. "The binding requires the death of either the controller or the controlled. Madrid has ensured his own survival through methods that... disturb even his most loyal servants."

"Then we find another way." Niloo's determination flared bright as her crystal heart. "The Keeper records in our parents' chamber mention ancient counter-rituals, ways to disrupt blood magic through—"

"Through willing sacrifice," Darius finished, his expression darkening. "I've read the same texts, Niloo. Madrid forced me to translate portions of them for his research. The price of breaking a blood binding is always the life of the bound."

The words hung between them, a death sentence waiting to be carried out. Around the tower, the wind picked up, carrying the scent of sulfur from the distant volcanic vents. Somewhere in the distance, a dragon roared—not the musical call of a free creature, but the anguished cry of one driven beyond endurance.

"That's why he wanted us to meet," Niloo realized, understanding dawning with sick clarity. "Madrid knows about this place, knows you'd seek me out. He's using our connection as bait."

Darius nodded miserably. "The compulsion drove me here against my conscious will. Even now, I can feel his awareness pressing at the edges of my mind, watching through my eyes." His red crystal flared brighter, and he doubled over as pain lanced through the magical connection. "He's... he's coming. Through me."

Niloo felt it too—a presence like winter darkness pressing against the warmth of their sibling bond. Through Darius's compromised crystal, Madrid's consciousness reached across the miles, cold intelligence evaluating the situation with predatory calculation.

"Sister." The voice that came from Darius's mouth carried Madrid's inflection, though the lips that spoke belonged to her brother. "How good of you to accept my invitation."

"Get out of my brother's mind," Niloo snarled, her crystal heart blazing with protective fury.

"Such spirit. Such delightful rebellion. It will make your eventual submission all the sweeter." Madrid's presence grew stronger, forcing Darius to straighten despite his obvious resistance. "Your sabotage at Ashfall Heights demonstrated admirable skill, but it ultimately served my purposes. The failed extraction provided invaluable data about essence corruption techniques."

Through Darius's hijacked voice, Madrid continued his psychological assault. "Did you know that three of the transformed prisoners survived the process? They now serve as the first members of my enhanced guard—humans with supernatural strength, magical resistance, and absolute loyalty. Your interference improved my army rather than hindering it."

Niloo forced herself to remain calm, though her crystal heart pulsed with rage. "What do you want?"

"Your surrender, naturally. Your brother's willing cooperation. The unmasking

of your parents' hidden chamber." Madrid's laugh emerged from Darius's throat, shattering like broken glass into the silence. "In exchange, I offer the lives of Samos's civilian population. Refuse, and I will transform every man, woman, and child into test subjects for my experiments."

"Niloo, don't—" Darius managed to force out his own words before Madrid's control clamped down again.

"Darius fights admirably, but his resistance weakens with each exertion. Soon, his consciousness will be entirely submerged, and you will face only my will wearing his flesh." The threat carried casual certainty, as if discussing the weather. "I have plans for both of you that extend far beyond these provincial squabbles."

Through her bond with Lapis, Niloo felt the dragon stirring in her distant cave, ready to come to their aid despite her injuries. But any direct confrontation here would result in Darius's death—Madrid would not hesitate to destroy a compromised asset to deny it to his enemies.

"The breeding chambers," she said instead, buying time while her mind raced through options. "That's what you really want. The ancient dragon eggs beneath Fire Ridge and the Dead Fields."

"Perceptive. Yes, those repositories hold the key to my larger ambitions. But accessing them requires a blood connection to Gaia's original inhabitants—the great dragons who shaped this land before humanity's arrival." Madrid's presence pressed harder against Darius's consciousness. "You and your brother's family history and connection to this land, combined and distilled into essence freely given, would provide sufficient power to awaken every egg in those chambers."

"And if we refuse?"

"Then I will harvest your essence by force, accept the reduced efficiency, and awaken perhaps half of the clutches. Still more than adequate for my purposes." The casual dismissal of their lives chilled Niloo to the bone. "But willing sacrifice creates stronger bonds. Dragons hatched through your combined choice would serve me with absolute devotion."

Darius's body swayed as two minds fought for control. His red crystal flickered erratically, the corruption warring with his natural essence. Blood trickled from his nose as the magical strain took its toll.

"You're killing him," Niloo hissed, fury bubbling up and begging to be released. She took a step closer to her brother, fists clenched at her side.

"I am demonstrating the futility of resistance." Madrid's voice carried no emotion whatsoever. "The blood binding can be adjusted—increased until cooperation becomes the only alternative to madness. Your brother has experienced this once before. Perhaps he remembers the lesson."

A cry of agony escaped Darius's lips as Madrid demonstrated his point. He fell to his knees, hands clutching his head as heartbearer crystal flared white-hot against his chest. Through their sibling connection, Niloo felt echoes of his pain—a torture specifically designed to be shared.

"Stop!" she shouted. "I'll consider your offer. Just stop hurting him."

The pressure eased immediately, though Madrid's presence remained. "Consideration is insufficient. I require decision. Meet me at Fire Ridge in three days' time. Come alone, with your dragon and djinn. Attempt any sabotage, and I will demonstrate more creative applications of the blood binding."

Darius raised his head, his own consciousness briefly surfacing. "The eggs," he gasped. "Not just... breeding chambers. Madrid found something else. Ancient... records. Dragon memories crystallized in stone."

"Enough." Madrid's control slammed down like an iron fist. Darius's eyes rolled back as the binding crystal burned away his resistance. When he looked up again, only Madrid's cold intelligence gazed out from his features.

"Three days, sister. Fire Ridge. Do not disappoint me."

Darius, with movements that were no longer his own, turned away from his sister and left the tower without another word. But as he reached the entrance, his natural self fought through one last time.

"The memories," he whispered urgently. "They show... other worlds. Places where dragons came from before Gaia. Madrid seeks to open those paths again."

Then Madrid's control reasserted itself completely, and Darius walked away with the mechanical precision of a puppet being controlled by invisible strings. Niloo watched silently, until he disappeared among the rocky outcroppings, her heart breaking with each step that carried her brother further from salvation.

Lazuli shifted to his humanoid form, landing beside her with gentle grace. "The revelation about other worlds—do you understand its significance?"

"Dragon migration routes," Niloo replied, pieces clicking together in her mind. "Not just the path between Gaia and Jintessa, but passages to realms we've never imagined. Madrid doesn't just want to conquer just this world—he wants to rule a dragon empire spanning multiple realities."

The scope of Madrid's ambition expanded beyond anything she'd previously conceived. An army of enslaved dragons carrying his forces between worlds, spreading his dominion across realms that had never known his touch.

"We have three days," she said, steel entering her voice. "Three days to find another way. To save Darius, protect the eggs, and stop Madrid from opening pathways that could destroy everything we've ever known."

Through her bond with Lapis, she felt the dragon's resolve strengthening to match her own. *Then we gather allies,* Lapis communicated. *Heartbearers from other provinces, resistance fighters, our dragon kin from Jintessa, anyone who understands what we face. The essence wars have become something larger—a battle for the fate of all existence.*

Agreed, said Niloo. *But how do we find them?*

As evening's shadows lengthened across the volcanic landscape, Niloo began composing messages in her mind. Letters to be carried by Lazuli to their allies and shared with neighboring provinces, warnings to be spread through the underground networks her parents had helped establish. It seemed an impossible task, to locate the other heartbearers, her sisters who had left on their own individual missions, and to warn them of the danger on their collective doorsteps.

Madrid had forced the confrontation, believing his overwhelming power would guarantee victory. But he had also revealed a glimpse into the true scope of his plans, giving them information that could help them rally opposition across multiple provinces.

The next three days would determine whether freedom could triumph over tyranny, whether love could overcome artificial bondage, whether the dragons of many worlds would soar free or serve in magical chains.

Niloo touched her crystal heart, feeling its warmth pulse with renewed determination. Somewhere in the distance, her brother walked toward an uncertain fate, carrying both Madrid's darkness and the hope that his true self might yet break free.

Their task had become something far greater than provincial rebellion. Now they fought for the very nature of freedom itself.

Chapter Fifteen

THE KEEPER'S BURDEN

The hidden chamber beneath Niloo's family farm felt smaller than she remembered, its circular walls pressing close as the narrow shelves that housed the ancient texts surrounded them, a silent witnesses to their desperate planning. Her parents bent over the central table where the Codex of Gaia lay open, its dragon-script pages illuminated by a shimmering light, fueled by tiny chips of crystal compressed into the lense of a lantern, that had burned steady for centuries.

The stone walls had cracked along seams that had held through the blistering heat of dragonfire, possibly because they had been forged

by a similar breath ages ago. Yet the chamber had not remained un-
scathed. Dust covered the floor in a thick layer and several of the
bookcases had fallen over, spilling their contents onto the braided rug.
The outer chamber was as far as the enemy had been able to penetrate.
Their illusion and the masking of the shielding of the entrance had
worked. Madrid's forces had been stopped short of the true prize.

"Pathways between worlds," her father murmured, tracing symbols
that seemed to shift and change under his fingertips. "I thought it was
a metaphor. I never believed the legends were literal truth."

"The dragons knew," her mother added, her voice heavy. "That's
why they established the Keeper traditions. They understood that
someday, someone would seek to abuse the ancient connections."

Niloo paced the chamber's perimeter, her crystal heart pulsing with
urgency as precious hours slipped away. Two days remained until
Madrid's deadline at Fire Ridge, and every moment spent in research
was time not devoted to gathering allies or planning rescue attempts.
She pondered what it could all mean. Other worlds? Like theirs? It
was mind boggling, like thinking that the stars themselves hosted little
green dragons, and flaming djinn...Niloo shook her head, clearing her
wandering thoughts

"Show me," she demanded, moving to the table where her parents
worked. "If Madrid has discovered these pathways in the dragon memories, I need to understand what he's truly capable of."

Her father turned several pages until he found what he sought—a
detailed diagram showing not just Gaia and Jintessa, but multiple
strings of pathways stretching between unknown landmasses. Some
bore names in the ancient dragon script, others remained blank as if
the knowledge had been deliberately obscured. The pathways were
vast, stretching under the surface of Gaia and the surrounding oceans
in a spiderweb of connections. There was a partial branch ending un-

der another province and a blurred name. She squinted at the spidery script. *Camelo*—

"The Dragon Crossroads," he explained, using the Common tongue translation of the ancient term. Niloo jerked her eyes away from the partial word. "Pathways carved through reality itself during the Great Migration, when the dragons fled the Sundering Wars that destroyed their original realm."

Lazuli, who had been studying a shelf of curious artifacts, turned sharply at these words. "The Sundering Wars are mentioned in Jintessa's oldest histories, but only as fragments. Stories of a time before dragons learned to live in harmony with magic."

"Before they learned wisdom," Niloo's mother corrected. "The early dragons wielded power without restraint, reshaping entire worlds according to their whims. The wars began when different clutches disagreed about how reality should be ordered."

The implications sent ice through Niloo's veins. *If Madrid gained access to those primal powers, if he got his filthy hands on magic that could reshape worlds themselves...*Niloo said through the bond. She felt, rather than heard Lapis's grunt of understanding.

"The pathways were sealed," her father continued, "by the combined sacrifice of the greatest dragon leaders. They gave their lives to create a living lock on the access roads, preventing anyone from using them to spread the wars to peaceful realms."

"But seals can be broken," Niloo said, understanding dawning with sick certainty. "That's what the fossilized eggs contain—not just memories, but the keys to reopening those pathways."

Her mother nodded gravely. "The dragon memories you've discovered aren't simple recordings. They're crystallized consciousness, containing the actual thoughts and experiences of those who created the seals. Madrid must believe he can extract the knowledge needed to reverse their sacrifice."

Through her bond with Lapis, Niloo felt the dragon's spike of concern at these revelations. *My people speak of the Lost Clutches—dragons who vanished during the Great Migration, never reaching Jintessa's shores. If they sealed the pathways with their lives...*

"They became the guardians," Niloo completed aloud. "Eternal sentinels preventing the roads from being opened again."

"Until Madrid found a way to wake them," her father said grimly. "The blood magic he uses, the artificial bonding process—it's all designed to overcome their sacrifice, to force them into service even in death."

"This abomination...I wonder if this is how the Great Barrier was created, only using human magic, rather than dragon? Those voices..." Niloo's voice trailed off, recalling their encounter on their return from Jintessa.

The scope of Madrid's blasphemy expanded beyond mere conquest and into the realm of cosmic violation. He was attempting to pervert the greatest sacrifice in dragon history for his personal ambition.

"There has to be a way to stop him," Niloo insisted. "The Keeper traditions exist for this purpose. Surely our ancestors left us tools, knowledge, something to counter this threat."

Her parents exchanged a look fraught with meaning before her mother moved to a dimly lit alcove off of the main chamber. Niloo had never examined that section of the chamber closely. Her mother paused in front of a decorative panel, then pressed her palm against a swirl that resembled a closed eye. Niloo heard the click of a lock being withdrawn, and a small hidden compartment was revealed, this one sealed with additional locks that required both parents' blood to open. Niloo's father joined her mother and in unison, they pricked their finger and pressed the welling of blood to the secondary locks.

"The Final Protocols," her father explained as the seals dissolved under their combined touch. "Instructions meant to be opened only when the pathways themselves were threatened."

Inside the compartment lay items that made Niloo's breath catch: a crystal heart like her own, but larger and multifaceted in ways that hurt to perceive directly. Beside it rested a scroll written not in dragon script but in human common tongue, though the letters glowed with inner fire.

"The Master Heart," her mother said reverently. "Created by the first Keepers as a backup plan, in case the dragon seals ever failed. A way to communicate, and yes, also control the Heartbearers. This is a dangerous tool."

Niloo reached toward the artifact, then stopped as her own crystal began to resonate painfully. "What does it do?"

"It amplifies the connection between heartbearers across all provinces," her father explained. "In theory, it could link all living bearers into a single network, combining their power for a unified purpose."

"All of them?" Lazuli asked. "Including he ones that remain under Madrid's control?"

Her mother consulted another text, her face growing pale as she read. "Yes. And according to our latest intelligence... there are at least eight. Madrid has been systematic in his collection efforts."

The mathematics were stark. Even if Niloo could contact every free heartbearer remaining—perhaps seven or eight individuals scattered across the unconquered provinces—they would face overwhelming odds against Madrid's enslaved army.

Her father glanced at her mother then said, in a slow, hesitant voice, "We have heard rumours of a wizard roaming Gaia and fighting on the side of the heartbearers. Our informants have identified him as possibly the last remaining adept from before the Purge, a wizard by the name of Ramos. We believe he is trying to unite the heartbearers on his own, at least the female ones who have returned from their training in Jintessa."

"If you could find this wizard, you might be able to enlist the others, to help with this defense of the dragon nesting grounds," said her mother, with a frown. Niloo stared at them and shook her head. It was an impossible task.

"The scroll," Niloo said, turning back to the glowing document. "What are the Final Protocols?"

Her father unrolled the parchment with trembling hands, revealing text that seemed to write itself as they watched. "Instructions for... for awakening Samos itself."

"I don't understand."

"The dragons didn't just shape this land," her mother explained. "They invested part of their essence into the very soil, the stones, the growing things. Samos remembers their touch, but that memory lies dormant unless properly awakened."

Lazuli's form brightened with sudden comprehension. "Elemental earth magic. I sensed it when we first arrived, but assumed it was the residual essence from ancient habitation. Are you saying the entire province is a sleeping dragon?"

"Not a dragon," her father corrected. "Something more fundamental. The collected will of all dragons who ever called this place home, distilled into the landscape itself. Awakening it would give a heartbearer access to the earth's powerful magic, a magic that dwarfs any individual dragon."

"But at what cost?" Niloo asked, though she suspected she already knew.

Her mother's voice dropped to a whisper. "The life of the one who awakens it. The Final Protocols require a willing sacrifice—a heartbearer must merge their essence completely with the land, becoming one with Samos forever."

The chamber fell silent except for the soft hum of crystalline lights. Niloo stared at the Master Heart, understanding the choice her ancestors had preserved for her. She could unite the remaining heartbearers, face Madrid's army with whatever allies she could gather, and likely die in glorious failure. Or she could pay the ultimate price to awaken power that might genuinely threaten Madrid's plans.

"There might be another way," she said slowly, an idea forming as she spoke. "Madrid wants me at Fire Ridge to awaken the ancient eggs. But what if I used the Master Heart instead? What if I connected with the other heartbearers not to fight Madrid directly, but to seal the pathways permanently?"

Her father's eyes widened. "Re-create the original sacrifice, but on a larger scale?"

"Exactly. If I can link with bearers on both sides—free and enslaved—we might be able to overwhelm Madrid's control through sheer numbers. Turn his own weapons against him."

"That's incredibly dangerous," her mother warned. "Attempting to break blood magic through brute force could kill every connected heartbearer, enslaved and free alike."

"Better than letting Madrid open the Dragon Crossroads," Niloo replied with quiet conviction. "If he succeeds, every world becomes a potential conquest. How many billions of lives is my sacrifice worth? Is our sacrifice worth?"

Lazuli moved closer, studying the magical potential radiating from the Master Heart. "This artifact would need time to establish connections across such distances. And it would require an anchor point—somewhere significant to dragon history."

"Fire Ridge," Niloo realized. "The breeding chambers Madrid seeks. If I can reach them before he activates his own process..."

"You'd be walking into a trap," her father objected. "Madrid expects you. He'll have prepared countermeasures. His wizards will be waiting."

"Then I don't go alone." Niloo's crystal heart pulsed with growing determination. "We gather every ally we can find. Free heartbearers, resistance fighters, anyone willing to stand against Madrid's tyranny."

Through her bond with Lapis, she felt the dragon's resolve strengthening to match her own. *The dragons of Jintessa will answer this call,* Lapis communicated. *If the pathways are threatened, well...even my cautious people will risk everything to prevent another Sundering War.*

"How do we contact them?" Niloo asked.

"Through me," Lazuli answered. "With Lapis' help, I can carry messages to the heartbearer dragons here in Gaia and their djinn and human bondmates, and rally whatever Samosian aid they're willing to provide."

The plan crystallized around them. Desperate, dangerous, but possibly their only chance to prevent catastrophe on a epic scale.

"The Master Heart requires preparation," her mother said, moving toward the artifact with reverent care. "Rituals to attune it to your essence, words of power to establish the initial connections."

"How long?" Niloo asked.

"A day, perhaps less if we take turns and work through the night."

Time enough, barely, thought Niloo. Lazuli could reach the Jintessa dragons and the remaining free heartbearers in the meantime, and establish the connection needed to be able to be contacted through the Master Heart. Locating the wizard, if he actually exists, would be far more difficult. If fortune smiled upon them, they might just reach Fire Ridge before Madrid completed his own preparations.

"There's something else," her father said, hesitation in his voice. "About Darius. The blood binding that controls him—it operates through proximity to Madrid. If you can separate them by sufficient distance the compulsion weakens. Enough for him to act independently, if only briefly."

Her mother nodded. "The Final Protocols mention techniques for temporarily severing such bonds. Not permanently—that still requires death—but long enough for," she paused, grief momentarily consuming her, unable to complete the sentance due to the lump rising in her throat.

"For him to choose his own fate," Niloo said quietly, completing the thought. Her physical heart throbbed, ached alongside her crystal heart, as the words were dragged from her. "To decide whether he dies free or enslaved."

The weight of the approaching sacrifices settled over the chamber like a burial shroud. In a few days, everything would change—either Madrid would open pathways to unlimited conquest, or the Dragon Crossroads would be sealed forever, at the cost of lives beyond counting.

Niloo touched the Master Heart, feeling its potential shiver deep into her bones. Would its power be enough to reach her sister heartbearers? The future looked bleak. So many possibilities. So many lives at stake. In most of those futures, she saw her own death. But in a precious few, she glimpsed something else—worlds where dragons flew free, where the pathways remained closed, where her sacrifice purchased safety for countless generations yet to come.

"Begin the preparations," she commanded, authority entering her voice as her resolve firmed. "Send word to every ally we can reach. We end this war one way or another."

As her parents began the complex rituals required to attune the Master Heart, Niloo allowed herself one moment of quiet farewell to the life she'd never live. Then she turned her full attention to the tasks ahead, preparing to carry the burden every Keeper had dreaded since the traditions began.

The burden of being the last guardian between order and chaos, between life and the deep dark void of death, between the worlds as they were and the nightmare Madrid would make them.

A shift of power was on the horizon. What came next would determine the fate of all.

CHAPTER SIXTEEN

THE WIZARD'S INTERVENTION

The morning mist clung to the eastern plains like a lover reluctant to let go, transforming Niloo's family farm into something ethereal and otherworldly. She knelt beside the ancient well that marked the farm's focal point, her hands pressed against the Master Heart as her parents completed the final attunement rituals. The crystal artifact pulsed with accumulated power, each facet reflecting not just light but possibility itself—threads of connection reaching toward heartbearers scattered across Gaia like a spider's web spun from starlight.

"The resonance strengthens," her mother murmured, adding another pinch of gold to the ritual circle. The powder dissolved into the symbols carved deep into the earth, making them glow with the same inner fire that lived within Niloo's pendant. "By tonight, the Master Heart should be ready for initial contact attempts."

Niloo felt the weight of approaching destiny settle over her like a shroud woven from storm clouds. Through her bond with Lapis, she sensed the dragon's restless energy as she circled high above, maintaining a watchful eye for Imperial patrols. She also felt the dragon's resolve to keep her alive. It was a comfort to know that they had not given up hope.

The great blue dragon's scales had regrown enough over the last few days to allow flight, though they lacked their usual lustrous depth. Like everything touched by Madrid's evil, even healing was slowed, corrupted by evil. Lapis would now carry permanent scars from the corruption she experienced at Ashfall Heights.

"We have company approaching from the northwest," Lazuli reported, materializing beside the well in a shimmer of displaced air. His djinn form flickered between hawk and humanoid as anxiety disrupted his concentration. "Three riders, moving with purpose but not openly hostile."

Niloo's hand moved instinctively to the communication crystal give to her by Darius, searching for sensations as it warmed against her palm. No urgent pulse, no warning of immediate danger. But Madrid's agents had grown more subtle in recent days, using techniques that bypassed magical detection.

Her father straightened from his position at the ritual circle's edge, joints creaking from hours spent in careful concentration. "Imperial?"

"Unknown," Lazuli replied. "Their approach pattern suggests familiarity with our defensive preparations, but they're not making effort to conceal themselves."

A new voice drifted across the morning air, carried on a breeze that tasted of distant spices and barely contained laughter. "Perhaps because concealment becomes unnecessary when one possesses sufficient skill with misdirection."

The voice seemed to come from everywhere and nowhere, accompanied by a sensation like reality hiccupping around them. Niloo blinked, and suddenly a fourth figure stood within their protective circle—a man of an indistinguishable age, though something in his dark eyes suggested decades of accumulated wisdom. His robes bore travel stains and patches that somehow managed to look deliberately fashionable, and his hair possessed the distinctive silver streaking that marked those who had channeled significant magic over extended periods. He led a horse, a shaggy mare that lifted her head, sniffed the air, and wickered greeting.

"Greetings, Keepers of Samos," the stranger said with a bow that managed to be both respectful and slightly mocking. "I am Ramos, lately of nowhere in particular, and most recently from everywhere that Madrid's actions require...adjustment."

Niloo's parents exchanged glances loaded with meaning. Her mother's hand moved to a hidden weapon while her father stepped protectively closer to the Master Heart.

"The Ramos?" her mother asked, voice tight with controlled tension. "The Last Adept?"

"Oh, I do dislike that title," Ramos replied with a theatrical sigh. "It makes me sound so dreadfully infantile, doesn't it? I prefer to think of myself as the First of Something New. Or simply, The First. First Wizard works just fine, actually." He gestured vaguely at the air around them, and Niloo noticed a stirring in the morning mist. It began to swirl in patterns that were difficult to follow with her eye. "Besides, 'adept' suggests a level of competence I'm not entirely certain I've earned."

Even as he spoke, Niloo felt the change in their surroundings. The farm appeared exactly as it had moments before, but somehow different—as if she were viewing it through slightly distorted glass. The sensation made her stomach lurch with vertigo.

"Illusion," said Lazuli, his djinn nature allowing him to perceive the wizard's manipulation. "He's making this location appear abandoned to outside observation."

"Abandoned and thoroughly uninteresting," Ramos confirmed cheerfully. "To anyone watching from a distance, this appears to be nothing more than a failed farmstead, complete with collapsed barn and overgrown fields. The Imperial scouts who passed through twenty minutes ago saw exactly that and continued eastward in search of more promising targets."

"Twenty minutes ago?" Niloo's father demanded. "We detected no—"

"Of course not," Ramos interrupted with a wave of his hand. "My illusions extend to perception as well as appearance. You experienced those twenty minutes as peaceful morning preparation time, while I dealt with three very determined scouts who were absolutely certain they'd tracked magical activity to this location."

The wizard's casual mention of "dealing with" Imperial scouts sent ice through Niloo's veins. "Are they—?"

"Alive and convinced they've thoroughly searched this area," Ramos assured her. "Currently riding back to report that the magical disturbances originated from an abandoned crystal mine three valleys south. They'll spend the next two days excavating empty caves before

concluding their equipment was faulty. To kill them would have confirmed Madrid's "

Despite the gravity of their situation, Niloo found herself fighting
a smile. The image of Imperial forces digging futilely through barren
rock while their true targets worked undetected nearby carried a sat-
isfying irony.

"How did you find us?" her mother asked, though her posture had
relaxed slightly.

"I've been monitoring heartbearer activity across Gaia for some
time," Ramos explained, settling cross-legged on the ground as if joining an old friend's tea gathering. "Your daughter's use of Jintessa dragon scales to corrupt Madrid's element extractor created magical ripples
that reached every province. Quite impressive, actually—I couldn't
have done better myself."

"You were watching the excavation site?"

"From a comfortable distance, yes. Madrid's technology has grown
disturbingly sophisticated, but it still relies on predictable magical
frequencies." Ramos produced a small crystal device from his robes, its
surface covered with tiny symbols that shifted and changed as Niloo
watched. "This little beauty alerts me whenever someone attempts
large-scale elemental manipulation. Very useful for staying one step
ahead of Imperial experiments."

Through her bond with Lapis, Niloo felt the dragon's surprise.
The great blue creature had circled the farm dozens of times without detecting any hidden observers, yet Ramos claimed to have been
monitoring their activities.

"Your dragon's confusion is understandable," Ramos said, apparently reading her thoughts through expressions she wasn't aware of
making. "I observe through reflection rather than direct viewing. Like

watching a pond to see the sky—you perceive the reality without occupying the same space."

"Reflection magic is supposed to be impossible," Lazuli protested, his scholarly nature offended by violations of established magical theory.

"Impossible is such a limiting word," Ramos replied with a grin that suggested he'd encountered this objection before. "I prefer 'insufficiently understood.' The universe contains far more possibilities than our current theories encompass, wouldn't you agree?"

Before anyone could respond, the wizard's expression shifted to something more serious. "But we have more pressing concerns than magical philosophy. Madrid's forces are converging on Samos in unprecedented numbers. The element extraction failure has accelerated his timeline considerably."

"What kind of numbers?" Niloo asked, though she dreaded the answer.

Ramos consulted his crystal device, frowning at whatever information it provided. "Three full legions, plus specialized artificers, enhanced soldiers, and support staff. Approximately fifteen hundred combat personnel, supported by nearly as many workers and technicians."

The magnitude of Madrid's commitment staggered her. "He's bringing an entire army to dig up dragon eggs?"

"Not just to dig them up," Ramos corrected grimly. "To hatch them. Madrid has decided that subtle infiltration has run its course. He's preparing for open warfare, and he needs dragons under his absolute control to carry his forces beyond Gaia's borders."

"Beyond Gaia?" Her father leaned forward, ancestral knowledge stirring in his eyes. "The pathways mentioned in the Codex?"

"The very same," Ramos confirmed. "Madrid's exile from Jintessa was not the end of his ambitions but merely a temporary setback. He seeks to return with power sufficient to reshape both realms according to his vision."

Niloo felt the Master Heart pulse against her awareness, responding to her emotional turmoil. The artifact's connections were still forming, threads of possibility reaching toward other heartbearers, but already she could sense distant echoes—points of light scattered across Gaia's provinces like stars in a clouded sky.

"How many heartbearers remain free?" she asked.

Ramos's expression darkened. "Fewer than I'd hoped, more than Madrid realizes. He's been systematic in his collection efforts, but several have managed to evade capture. And his control over the enslaved ones has... weaknesses. Some have fallen into darkness."

"Darius," Niloo breathed, understanding flooding through her. "The blood magic isn't perfect."

"Far from it," Ramos agreed. "Madrid's binding technique requires constant reinforcement, and it weakens with distance from the primary control source. Your brother, for instance, experiences periods of reduced compulsion whenever he's separated from Madrid by more than fifty miles."

Hope kindled in Niloo's chest. "Then when he's at the excavation sites—"

"He has windows of partial freedom, yes. Brief opportunities to act according to his true nature rather than imposed will." Ramos leaned forward, his expression intense. "Which brings us to why I've revealed myself now, rather than continuing to observe from comfortable concealment."

He gestured, and the air above their ritual circle shimmered with images—a three-dimensional map showing troop movements across western Samos. Imperial forces converged on Fire Ridge like blood flowing toward a wound, their numbers growing with each passing hour.

"Madrid plans to begin the hatching process within days," Ramos continued. "He cannot afford to wait longer—each delay increases the risk of organized resistance forming. But his accelerated timeline creates opportunities for those willing to seize them."

"What kind of opportunities?" Niloo asked, though something in Ramos's tone suggested she wouldn't like the answer.

"Madrid's forces are spread thin across multiple objectives. He must secure the breeding chambers, establish defensive perimeters, transport his equipment, and maintain control over his enhanced soldiers and enslaved heartbearers. Too many variables for perfect coordination."

The wizard's smile returned, but it carried a sharp, feral edge that reminded Niloo of Lapis preparing for battle. "I propose we introduce additional variables. Complications that strain his resources while positioning our own assets for maximum impact."

"Our assets?" her mother questioned.

"Contact with the free heartbearers operating in the other provinces, most of whom I have met at some point in my journeys. There are resistance networks there that have been quietly growing for months, and several very interested parties from Jintessa who have finally realized the scope of Madrid's ambitions. By that I mean dragons." Ramos's crystal device flickered with new information. "Also, three Imperial commanders whose loyalty to Madrid has been... wavering."

"Cayos?" Niloo guessed.

"Perhaps. Among others, it seems. Witnessing Madrid's treatment of civilians has sparked some uncomfortable questions about Imperial duty versus human decency." Ramos tucked the device back into his robes. "Amazing how quickly absolute loyalty crumbles when confronted with absolute power's cruel nature."

Through her bond with Lapis, Niloo felt the dragon's descent from her high patrol. She had spotted something that demanded immediate attention—movement on the eastern horizon, riders approaching with the desperate urgency that marked either fleeing civilians or Imperial messengers.

"We have visitors," she announced.

Ramos nodded, unsurprised. "Right on schedule. I took the liberty of arranging some... consultations."

The approaching riders resolved into three figures as they drew closer—three humans mounted on swift horses. All three bore the travel stains and the wind-burned appearance of people who had ridden hard across great distances.

"Friends of yours?" Lazuli asked, his form solidifying as he stepped up beside Niloo.

"Allies of necessity," Ramos corrected. "Kira from Hindra, Marcus from Cassimir, and Vera from the eastern reaches of Peca. While not part of the original parings of heartbearers, each of them had the potential to be a heartbearer, and they've managed to avoid Madrid's clutches through a combination of skill and good fortune. I felt they had earned the right to wear a heart crystal. While they are not a true heartbearers, as you are Niloo, they are able to wield magic after a fashion. Enough for them to be useful in Madrid's plans if captured. In better times, they might have trained at the Wizard Keep, or in Castle Ionia."

The riders reached the farm's perimeter and dismounted, their movements speaking of exhaustion held in check by sheer determination. Niloo felt her crystal heart respond to their presence, recognizing the familiar resonance of others who bore similar artifacts.

Kira appeared to be roughly Niloo's age, though her silver-streaked hair suggested experiences that had aged her beyond her years. Her crystal heart, visible through her travel-worn shirt, pulsed with storm-gray light that reminded Niloo uncomfortably of gathering thunderheads.

Marcus carried himself with the fluid grace of someone accustomed to moving across shifting terrain, his sun-darkened skin bearing the distinctive markings of deep desert dwellers. His crystal gleamed with warm amber light, and when he dismounted, Niloo caught glimpses of sand falling from his dusty clothing despite the morning's dampness.

Vera proved to be the curious figure—a witch whose crystal had been modified through means Niloo didn't recognize. Her form shifted constantly between states, sometimes solid, sometimes translucent, occasionally splitting into multiple overlapping images before coalescing again. A neat feat of magic, if imperfect.

"The gathering begins," Ramos announced with satisfaction. "Though I'm afraid our pleasant morning is about to become considerably more complicated."

As if summoned by his words, the western horizon began to darken with approaching storm clouds. But Lapis's alarm through their bond suggested these were not natural weather patterns—the darkness moved too purposefully, too uniformly, carrying undertones of magical manipulation.

"Madrid's advance scouts," Kira identified, her storm-gray crystal brightening in response to the unnatural clouds. "They're manipulating the weather with magic, to mask their approach and disable scrying attempts."

"How long until that cloud reaches us?" Niloo asked.

Marcus consulted a handheld device, that resembled sand compressed into the shape of a compass, its surface shifting with information only he could read. "Two hours, perhaps less. And they're not alone—ground forces are moving through the valleys, using the storm cover to conceal their numbers."

"Then we adjust our timeline," Ramos declared with a grin, his eyes twinkling with excitement. He clapped his hands together with the enthusiasm of someone who thrived on impossible challenges. "The Master Heart's attunement will have to be completed under combat conditions."

"That's incredibly dangerous," Niloo's father protested. "If the ritual is interrupted during the opening phase—"

"Then we will ensure it isn't interrupted," Ramos replied calmly. "I've spent years perfecting defensive illusions for exactly such circumstances. Madrid's forces will find this location quite thoroughly unremarkable until we're ready to reveal ourselves. A simple trick of the eye."

He gestured again, and the farm around them began to change. Not physically—the buildings and fields remained exactly as they were—but something fundamental shifted in how they felt. The sensation was like looking at a familiar painting and suddenly realizing it depicted something entirely different than what you'd always seen.

"Now then," Ramos continued, settling back into his cross-legged position with the air of someone beginning a long-overdue conversation. "Let's discuss how we're going to save your brother, prevent Madrid from hatching an army of enslaved dragons, and keep the pathways between worlds sealed forever. I have some ideas, but I suspect you'll find them either brilliant or completely insane."

Niloo felt the presence of other heartbearers—not just the three who had arrived at the farm, but distant points of light scattered across Gaia. Some burned bright with freedom, others flickered with the dull constraint of blood magic, and some were barely present, as if they were barely clinging to life. But all of them shared the fundamental resonance that marked them as pieces of the same ancient puzzle. She shivered, to sense all their souls being called to the Master Heart.

"Tell us," Niloo said, pushing aside the uncomfortable sensations, to focus on the here and now. Her voice carried the authority of one who had accepted the burden of impossible choices. "We're listening."

As the wiry wizard outlined his plan, the storm clouds continued their march across Samos's western peaks. For the first time since leaving Jintessa, Niloo felt something that had been missing in their desperate flight—a flicker of hope backed by genuine power, support that extended beyond her small circle of companions. It calmed the growing uncertainty that Madrid's victory was inevitable.

The struggles of the heartbearers across Gaia were entering their final phase and for the first time, the Emperor would face opponents who understood the true scope of his ambitions.

Ramos smiled at Niloo's expression, and reality seemed to smile with him. He patted the spot at his side. "Sit, my dear," he said warmly. "This is going to be magnificent! Now, let me tell you all about Crystal Throne."

CHAPTER SEVENTEEN

FINE TUNING

The farmhouse cellar had been transformed into something that resembled both a war room and a concert hall, with the Master Heart blazing at its center while magical frequencies hummed through the air in patterns too complex for unaugmented human perception. Niloo sat cross-legged before the artifact, her mind stretched thin as she maintained connections to heartbearers across seven provinces, while her companions worked to support and amplify the network through their own unique abilities.

The resonance is building, Lapis reported through their bond, her dragon senses monitoring the harmonic patterns that were beginning to emerge from the combined consciousness of dozens of magical practitioners. *But the frequency is still unstable—individual voices are not yet properly synchronized with the collective pattern.*

Through the triad bond, Niloo could feel her dragon companion's deep concern about the risks they were taking. The Master Heart network was designed to connect willing minds across vast distances, but it had never been tested on this scale, with this many participants, under these kinds of battlefield conditions. Every new connection increased the power available to the network, but also increased the potential for catastrophic feedback if something went wrong.

Its like trying to conduct an orchestra where half the musicians have never seen the sheet music, Lazuli observed, his djinn nature allowing him to perceive the dimensional stresses created by joined minds operating at such an unprecedented scale. *Each heartbearer brings their own magical frequency, their own approach to channeling power, their own cultural understanding of what cooperation means. Harmonizing all of that into a unified purpose?*

It is either going to be the most beautiful thing we've ever created, Niloo completed through the bond, *or it's going to kill us all in the most spectacular magical accident in recorded history.*

The weight of that possibility pressed against her as she felt the network's growing power. Through the Master Heart, she could sense Elissa's healing magic in distant Tyr, Shreya's mountain-stone strength in Cassimir, Seraphina's fierce compassion in Hindra. Each connection brought new capabilities to the collective, but also new vulnerabilities, new points where the entire system could fail if individual nodes were compromised or overwhelmed. These three entered the communication stream easily, perhaps due to their proximity to Samos.

Ramos was right about the mathematics, she realized, her understanding of the intricacies enhanced by her companions' perspectives.

Consciousness shared doesn't diminish—it multiplies. But multiplication means that failure will also be amplified. If this network collapses, it won't just disconnect the heartbearers—it could damage every mind that's currently linked to it.

Through the bond, she felt Lapis's ancient wisdom grappling with the ethical implications of what they were attempting. Dragons had long memories of magical workings that had seemed promising in theory but proved catastrophic in practice. The original Dragon Crossroads had been created by beings who believed they could control dimensional forces that ultimately proved beyond anyone's ability to direct safely.

Are we repeating the mistakes of the past? the dragon wondered, her mental voice carrying centuries of accumulated caution. *The ancient dragons who built the Crossroads also believed they were creating something that would serve consciousness rather than endanger it. Their confidence did not prevent the Sundering Wars that followed.*

But their mistake was trying to control the pathways between worlds, Lazuli replied. *We are not trying to control anything—we are creating opportunities for minds to choose cooperation over isolation. The risk is not that we will gain too much power, but that we will fail to use the power the combined minds freely offers.*

The distinction mattered, though it didn't eliminate the dangers they faced. Through the Master Heart, Niloo could feel the mounting pressure as more heartbearers joined the network, Peca and Fjord specifically, their combined will creating resonances that made the very air around them shimmer with barely contained energy.

Elissa's having trouble maintaining her connection, she reported, sensing her distress through the link to distant Tyr. The Imperial forces there are up to something that is creating interference to her crystal's magic—something that disrupts the harmonic frequencies

we're using for long-distance communication. Even with her special
map and the enhanced crystal's powers from her mentor, Crystal
Throne, the connection wavered.

After her chat with Wizard Ramos, they had decided that Elissa
was key to bringing about the full power of the Master Heart. Her
heart had been initialized by Crystal Throne. That made Elissa a key
component of the magic they sought to create. Crystal was an extension of that very power, having placed herself in Tyr exactly where
Elissa had found her, buried beneath the old church, protecting her
communication node and keeping it intact after all these years.

Madrid has launched countermeasures, Lapis said. *He would not
have ignored the possibility that heartbearers might attempt to coordinate resistance. Whatever techniques he is using to interfere with our
network, they were probably prepared years in advance.*

Then we must adapt, Lazuli said, his shapeshifting nature making him inherently comfortable with the need for rapid change. *The
beauty of consciousness-based magic is that it can evolve faster than any
technological countermeasure. Madrid's interference assumes we will
continue using the same frequencies, the same approaches to connection.
But what if we don't?*

Through the triad bond, Niloo felt Lazuli cautiously touch the
fragile reality formed and contained within the joined minds, his
consciousness slipping through the cracks in dimensions to find alternative pathways for magical communication. It was dangerous
work—djinn who pushed too hard against dimensional boundaries
sometimes lost the ability to return to their original reality—but
Lazuli approached it with the sort of focused determination. He understood the stakes involved.

There, he said after several tense minutes, his form flickering as
he stabilized the newly dimensional connections. *Madrid's interfer-*

ence affects three-dimensional magical frequencies, but it cannot reach communications that pass through folded space-time. If we route the networked connection through pocketed dimensions the bandwidth will be reduced but the connections will be much harder to disrupt. Madrid would need to tear holes in reality itself to interfere with communications passing through separate dimensional layers.

Can he do that? Niloo asked, though she suspected she already knew the answer.

Eventually. Perhaps, Lapis replied grimly. *But not quickly, and not without creating instabilities that would threaten his own magical systems. It buys us time, and time is what we need most.*

As Lazuli implemented the new routing system, Niloo felt the Master Heart network's structure shift and strengthen. The connections to distant heartbearers stabilized, lessening their vulnerability to Imperial interference. But the process also created new challenges—the pocket-dimensional routing required each participant to maintain their connection through multiple layers of reality simultaneously, a technique that none of them had been trained to perform.

Like learning to sing harmony while juggling, she muttered, grumbling. Her consciousness strained the effort of maintaining coherence across dimensional boundaries, quivered. *While riding a dragon. In a thunderstorm.*

And all the while, Madrid's forces are trying to shoot us down, Lapis added dryly through the bond. *Do not forget that part of the image.*

But even as they struggled with the technical challenges of maintaining the network, Niloo began to sense something else emerging from their collective effort—a harmony that transcended the individual voices contributing to it. The heartbearers weren't just sharing information or coordinating tactics; they were beginning to think together in ways that preserved individual identity while creating collective intelligence.

This is what Madrid truly fears, she realized, understanding flooding through the triad bond and broadcasting out to all of those participating in the emergence of their collective mind.. *Not individual resistance, but a collective consciousness that remains individual. He can break single minds, can corrupt isolated wills, but he cannot control minds that support each other while maintaining their independence.*

Through the network, she could sense the truth of this understanding. Each heartbearer remained fully themselves—Elissa's healing compassion, Shreya's mountain steadiness, Seraphina's fierce protectiveness—but their individual strengths were being amplified by conscious cooperation with others who shared their fundamental values.

Like instruments in an orchestra, Lazuli observed, his earlier metaphor proving more accurate than he had realized. *Each one playing its own part, but all contributing to a musical complexity that no single instrument could create alone.*

And the conductor is not any individual will, Lapis added, her ancient wisdom recognizing patterns that stretched back to the earliest days of draconic cooperation, but the shared commitment to consciousness itself—to preserving the right of minds to choose their own development rather than having it imposed by external authority.

The realization sent new strength through the Master Heart network, a harmonic resonance that connected not just the heartbearers but the dragons and djinn bonded to them, creating a web of conscious cooperation that spanned provinces and species. For the first time since Madrid's rise to power, an alternative to his vision of controlled order was taking tangible form—not chaos, but chosen cooperation; not uniformity, but unity in diversity.

The ancient dragons spoke of this, Lapis shared, *The Great Harmony they called it—a state of consciousness where individual minds maintain their identity while participating in collective wisdom that transcends any single perspective.*

Your ancestors achieved this? Niloo asked, sensing the importance of the dragon's memories.

Briefly, Lapis replied, her mental voice carrying both pride and sorrow. *During the final days before the Sundering Wars, when it became clear that the Crossroads were creating more problems than they solved. For perhaps a dozen years, dragon consciousness operated in true harmony—individual creativity supported by collective wisdom, personal choice guided by shared understanding.*

What ended it? Lazuli asked, though his djinn nature had already provided him with uncomfortable insights into what might threaten such a system.

Fear, Lapis said simply. *Fear that harmony meant the loss of individual identity, that cooperation would eventually become control. Some dragons withdrew from the collective to preserve their independence. Others tried to use the harmony to impose their personal visions on the group. The system collapsed because not everyone trusted that consciousness could remain free while being shared.*

The lesson was sobering, but also instructive. Through the Master Heart network, Niloo could feel similar fears stirring among some of the heartbearers—concerns that the increasing connection would somehow diminish their individual agency, that collective action would inevitably become collective compulsion.

That's why Madrid's techniques are so insidious, she realized. *He doesn't just attack consciousness directly—he makes people afraid of the very connections that could protect them from his control. He teaches isolation by making cooperation seem dangerous.*

Then we must demonstrate the difference, Lazuli declared, his form solidifying with determination. *We must show everyone that consciousness shared freely becomes stronger, while consciousness controlled by force stagnates and becomes hollow. The network is our proof that minds can work together without surrendering what makes them unique.*

As if summoned by their resolve, reports began flowing through the Master Heart network from across Gaia—Imperial forces mobilizing in response to coordinated resistance activities, Madrid's enslaved dragons taking to the skies in unprecedented numbers, reality distortions appearing around key strategic sites as the Emperor began implementing whatever final phase his plans required.

"The preparations are complete," came Ramos's voice through the network, his magical signature carrying excitement, determination, and just a hint of the theatrical flair that marked him even in crisis situations. "Dragons across seven provinces are positioned for synchronized action. The resonance frequencies are stable. All we need now is the catalyst to transform potential energy into kinetic change."

"And what would that catalyst be?" Shreya asked through the connection, her practical nature cutting through magical theory to focus on immediate requirements.

"Madrid himself," Niloo replied, understanding crystalizing as she felt the network's readiness. "He has to reveal himself eventually, has to commit to direct action rather than working through intermediaries. Only then will we have access to the core of his power structure—the source that maintains all the individual control spells, enhancement magics, and consciousness modifications he has created."

"You are proposing to use ourselves as bait," Lazuli observed. "To make ourselves such an attractive target that Madrid abandons caution in favor of direct confrontation."

"Exactly," Niloo confirmed, the Master Heart blazing brighter as the network's collective will focused on the plan that was forming. "We force him to choose between preserving his carefully laid plans and eliminating the threat we represent. His obsession with control won't let him ignore a direct challenge to his authority."

Through the bond, she felt her companions' complex reactions to the strategy—excitement at the prospect of finally facing their enemy directly, fear of the powers he could bring to bear against them, and underneath it all, the sort of grim satisfaction that came with accepting necessary risks for worthy causes.

"We cannot be caught in a direct fight with Madrid. Not yet. Not now," Shreya warned. "There are other forces at work that we are just beginning to understand, here in my province. Can you handle him there, Niloo, if he were suddenly to appear on your doorstep? It will be your risk to take."

Let Madrid try and harm Niloo. He will fry on the spot, rumbled Lapis with an answering grumble from Lazuli.

"Then let us provide him with a challenge he cannot ignore," Lazuli said.

"We fight for the right to remain magnificently, chaotically, beautifully ourselves," Niloo concluded, her human voice carrying the commitment of every individual mind that had ever chosen freedom over security, complexity over simplicity, hope over despair.

The Master Heart network pulsed with unified purpose, seven provinces worth of heartbearer determination choosing to work together without surrendering their independence. The harmony they had achieved was fragile, experimental, unprecedented in its scope and ambition. But it was also chosen freely by minds that understood the difference between cooperation and control, between unity and uniformity.

Madrid's vision of perfect order was about to face its first test—not against individual resistance, but against a collective consciousness that had learned to preserve diversity while working toward common goals.

The network was ready. The dragons were poised for action. The forces they had moved into position waited her command.

All that remained was for Madrid to make his choice—surrender his vision of controlled perfection, or face proof that consciousness shared freely was stronger than consciousness artificially imposed.

They were about to be tested by forces that had spent decades perfecting the art of breaking minds. But for the first time since Madrid's rise to power, those forces would face opposition that was growing stronger through unity rather than weaker through division.

CHAPTER EIGHTEEN

THE POWER OF HUMOUR

The morning sun cast long shadows across the ruins of the old farm house, and its hidden chamber beneath Niloo's family farm. Wizard Ramos examined the Master Heart with the practiced eye of someone who had spent decades studying ancient magical artifacts. The crystal's faceted surface threw rainbow patterns across the stone walls, each pulse of light corresponding to a distant heartbearer somewhere across Gaia's provinces.

"Remarkable craftsmanship," he murmured, his pale blue eyes twinkling with genuine appreciation. "Though I must say, whoever designed this clearly had a flair for the dramatic. All those facets and internal geometries—completely unnecessary from a purely functional standpoint, but absolutely essential for proper magical presentation."

Niloo watched him circle the artifact, noting how his usual theatrical demeanor had shifted into something more focused, more purposeful. "You've seen something like this before?"

"Not exactly like this, no. But I've had occasion to study similar communication networks." Ramos paused, stroking his grey beard thoughtfully. "In fact, I've been maintaining one of my own for the better part of twenty years. Nothing quite so ambitious as connecting all the heartbearers, mind you, but sufficient for keeping track of Madrid's various... misadventures."

From his travel-worn robes, he produced a crystal device no larger than his palm, its surface covered with tiny symbols that shifted and danced as Niloo watched. Unlike the Master Heart's brilliant blue radiance, this crystal emanated a warm amber glow that seemed to pulse with quiet mischief.

"Allow me to demonstrate," Ramos said with a grin that suggested he was about to show off. He passed his hand over the device, and suddenly the air above the chamber filled with a three-dimensional map of Gaia. Tiny points of light moved across the provinces—some steady and bright, others flickering or dim.

"The bright lights represent free heartbearers," he explained, his tone taking on the quality of a teacher who genuinely enjoyed his subject. "The dim ones are those under Madrid's control, and the flickering ones..." He paused dramatically. "Well, those are the ones I've been helping to develop what you might call 'selective hearing' when it comes to imperial commands."

Kira leaned forward, her storm-gray crystal pulsing with interest. "You've been interfering with Madrid's blood magic bindings?"

"Interfering is such a harsh word," Ramos replied with exaggerated innocence. "I prefer to think of it as...creative manipulation. You see, Madrid's spells are remarkably sophisticated, but they do have certain limitations. Distance, for one thing. Strong emotional connections, for another. And then there's the simple matter of properly maintained equipment."

Lazuli, who had been studying the magical map, suddenly chuckled. "You've been sabotaging his supply lines."

"Sabotage is such an ugly word," Ramos protested, though his eyes continued to dance with mischief. "I prefer 'logistical adjustments.' For instance, last month Madrid's forces were supposed to receive a shipment of enhanced focusing crystals from the mines in Cassimir. Instead, they received a shipment of very pretty but completely useless decorative stones. The poor dears spent three weeks trying to figure out why their essence extractors kept producing rainbow-colored lights instead of concentrated magical energy."

Marcus, whose amber crystal had been glowing steadily brighter as Ramos spoke, barked a laugh, "How have you managed to coordinate all this without being detected?"

"Ah, now that's the truly elegant part," Ramos said, gesturing to his crystal device. "You see, Madrid's intelligence network relies heavily on intercepted magical communications. They've become quite good at detecting and decoding standard enchantment frequencies. But there's one type of magical signature they never think to monitor."

He paused for effect, clearly enjoying the suspense.

"Comedy," he announced with a theatrical flourish. "Or more specifically, the magical resonance created by shared laughter. It turns out that when people find something genuinely amusing, their magical auras harmonize in ways that are completely invisible to Madrid's detection spells. So I've been embedding my messages in jokes."

Vera, whose form had stabilized into a more solid appearance during the explanation, looked skeptical. "You're telling us your entire resistance network operates through... humour?"

"Not just any humour," Ramos corrected seriously. "Good humour. The kind that brings people together though a good belly laugh. The kind that reminds them of their shared humanity. Madrid's people scan constantly for fear, anger, desperation—all the emotions they've learned to weaponize. But joy? Hope? The simple pleasure of a well-timed jest? Those might as well be invisible to them."

To demonstrate, he activated the crystal again, and Niloo heard what sounded like the beginning of a joke being told in Hindra, followed by laughter that seemed to ripple across provinces. As the laughter faded, she realized she had somehow understood not just the joke, but the complex strategic information that had been woven into its telling.

"Brilliant," she breathed. "And completely insane."

"The two often go hand in hand," Ramos agreed cheerfully. "Now, as for your Master Heart—I believe we can significantly enhance its range and effectiveness by integrating it with my existing network. Think of it as... adding a new section to an orchestra. The humour network provides the rhythm section, while your heartbearer connections supply the melody."

Her father looked up from the ancient texts he'd been consulting. "The attunement rituals specifically warn against external magical interference during the bonding process."

"Oh, those warnings are completely accurate," Ramos said dismissively. "External interference would indeed be catastrophic. But this wouldn't be external—it would be collaborative. Rather like the difference between someone shouting over your conversation and someone joining in with harmonious singing."

He began tracing symbols in the air, and Niloo felt the Master Heart respond, its pulsing rhythm shifting to match the cadence of his gestures. "The key is synchronization. If we can time the activation to coincide with one of my network's transmission cycles, the resonance should amplify rather than interfere."

"And if you're wrong?" her mother asked pointedly.

Ramos paused, his theatrical manner dropping away for a moment. "Then we'll have approximately thirty seconds to evacuate this chamber before the magical feedback turns it into a very impressive crater." He brightened immediately. "But I'm quite confident that won't be necessary. I've been perfecting this technique for years, and I've only created three craters. Well, four if you count that incident in Peca, but that was intentional."

Despite the gravity of their situation, Niloo found herself smiling. There was something infectious about Ramos's blend of competence and whimsy, his ability to treat world-shaking magic as if it were an interesting puzzle to be solved.

"What about Madrid's forces?" she asked. "Your illusions won't hold forever."

"Ah, yes, about that." Ramos activated his crystal once more, and the map zoomed in on their immediate area. Imperial forces were visible as red dots, but their movement patterns looked... confused. "I may have made a few additional adjustments to their reconnaissance reports. According to their latest intelligence, this area is currently inhabited by a family of very large, very territorial bears. Their scouts are maintaining a respectful distance while they await the specialized bear-handling equipment that should arrive sometime next month."

Lazuli stared at him. "Next month?"

"Well, it would arrive next month if it existed," Ramos clarified. "Which it doesn't, because I may have placed the order with a merchant who specializes in selling cloud formations to nomadic sky-shepherds. Fascinating fellow, completely fictional, but his paperwork is impeccable."

"You invented an entire fake merchant?" Marcus asked, clearly impressed despite himself.

"Oh, Cloudwright Nimbus is just one of dozens," Ramos replied with obvious pride. "I maintain an entire fictional economy devoted to selling nonexistent goods to Madrid's supply corps. They've been wonderfully cooperative—very reliable about placing orders for invisible siege engines, self-sharpening swords that exist only on Tuesdays, and my personal favorite, boots that provide complete protection against attacks by rainbow-colored elephants."

"Do rainbow-colored elephants exist?" Vera asked, with narrowed eyes.

"Not anymore," Ramos said sadly. "Tragic overhunting by medieval interior decorators. But Madrid's people don't know that, so they keep ordering the boots. I've made quite a tidy profit selling them ordinary leather footwear with a mild enchantment that makes them smell faintly of strawberries."

Niloo shook her head in amazement. "How long have you been doing this?"

"Ever since I realized that Madrid's greatest weakness is his complete inability to recognize absurdity," Ramos replied. "He's so focused on grand schemes and cosmic power that he never questions whether the 'ancient draconic ritual components' his agents are acquiring might actually be painted pinecones and rabbit bones."

"Speaking of Madrid's schemes," Kira interjected, her expression growing serious, "we've been getting reports from the northern provinces. Something big is happening. Mass troop movements, forced recruitment drives, and strange magical experiments."

Ramos nodded grimly. "Yes, I've been monitoring those developments. Madrid is accelerating his timeline, which means our window for action is narrowing rapidly." He turned to Niloo. "Which brings us back to your Master Heart. If we're going to unite the heartbearers, we need to do it soon."

"How soon?" she asked.

"Ideally? Today." Ramos checked his crystal device again. "Madrid's forces are currently distracted by my bear reports, but that won't last indefinitely. And according to my network, he's planning something catastrophic for the end of this week."

"What kind of catastrophic?" her father asked.

"The kind that involves opening pathways between worlds and unleashing armies of enslaved dragons," Ramos replied matter-of-factly.

The chamber fell silent as the implications sank in. Niloo looked around at the serious faces surrounding her—her parents, the three heartbearers who had physically travelled to answer Wizard Ramos' call, and this eccentric wizard who seemed to treat the fate of the world as an elaborate practical joke.

"All right," she said finally. "Let's do this. But I want to understand exactly what we're attempting."

Ramos clapped his hands together, his enthusiasm returning. "Excellent! Now, the technical aspects are fairly straightforward. We synchronize the Master Heart's activation frequency with my humour network's transmission cycle, creating a resonance cascade that will reach every heartbearer simultaneously. The emotional component of shared laughter will provide a carrier wave that bypasses Madrid's detection systems while establishing genuine connections between the bearers."

"And the risks?" Lazuli asked.

"Well, there's a slight chance the feedback could temporarily transform everyone involved into various types of waterfowl," Ramos admitted. "But that only lasted about an hour when it happened to my test group in Fjord, and they all agreed it was quite an educational experience."

"Waterfowl," Niloo repeated flatly.

"Mostly ducks, with a few swans and one rather dignified goose," Ramos clarified. "The important thing is that their consciousness remained intact throughout the transformation, and they gained some very interesting insights into magical theory. One of them wrote an entire treatise on the metaphysical implications of pond-dwelling while in duck form."

Despite everything, Niloo found herself laughing. "You're completely insane."

"Thank you," Ramos replied warmly. "I've worked very hard to achieve just the right level of insanity. Too little, and you become predictable. Too much, and you forget to check whether your spells actually work."

He moved to the Master Heart, his hands hovering over its surface. "Now then, shall we begin? I suggest we start with something simple—perhaps that old joke about the wizard, the dragon, and the enchanted turnip. It's a classic for a reason, and the punchline creates exactly the sort of harmonious resonance we need."

As Ramos began the complex process of synchronizing the two magical networks, Niloo felt the Master Heart respond to his touch. The crystal's pulsing intensified, and suddenly she could sense other heartbearers across Gaia—not just their presence, but their emotions, their hopes, their fears.

For the first time since returning to Samos, she felt truly hopeful. Madrid might have armies and ancient magic and the power of enslaved dragons, but they had something he would never understand: the ability to find joy and connection even in the darkest times.

And sometimes, that was exactly the weapon you needed.

CHAPTER NINETEEN

MANY VOICES

The moment the Master Heart synchronized with Ramos's humour network, the chamber erupted in a symphony of light and laughter that seemed to transcend the physical realm entirely. Niloo felt her consciousness expand beyond the confines of her own body, reaching across provinces through connections that sparkled with shared joy and warm affection.

"Well," Ramos said cheerfully as rainbow patterns danced across the stone walls, "that's either going exactly as planned or we're about to become very colorful puddles. I'm cautiously optimistic it's the former."

Through the Master Heart's expanded awareness, Niloo could sense them—all of them, the heartbearers scattered across Gaia, each one a brilliant point of light in the magical network that was rapidly forming. Some were closer than others, and a few were so near she could almost hear their thoughts.

"Niloo?" The voice came through the crystal connection, warm and familiar despite the time that had passed. "Is that really you?"

"Elissa!" Niloo's heart leaped as her crystal warmed against her chest. She recognized her friend from their time together in Jintessa. Through the magical link, she could sense Elissa's location—somewhere in the northern reaches of Tyr, accompanied by the steady presence of her djinn Druzy and the fierce intelligence of her dragon Mystic.

"Thank the ancient ones," came another voice, this one carrying the musical accent of Hindra. "I was beginning to think I was the only one who remembered what we were supposed to be doing."

"Seraphina," Niloo breathed, recognizing the voice of the healer who had helped train them all in the arts of magical medicine. "Where are you?"

"Currently hiding in a grain storage silo while explaining to my dragon why we cannot simply burn down the entire imperial garrison," Seraphina whispered with dry humour that made Ramos chuckle appreciatively. "Royale has very direct approaches to problem-solving."

The connections multiplied as the network expanded, but Niloo noticed troubling gaps in the pattern. Ramos's expression had grown increasingly somber as he monitored his crystal device, though he maintained his cheerful demeanor.

Shreya's steady strength reached out from Cassimir, while other familiar presences blazed to life across the provinces. Selina from Wydra, her magical signature carrying undertones of forge-fire and ancient oak. Beatrice from Fjord, carrying the chill of mountain winds and

Jannah from Peca, her connection resonating with earth magic and the deep strength of not one, but four Chaac.

"Seven provinces responding," Marcus observed, his amber crystal pulsing in rhythm with the Master Heart. "That's... fewer than we hoped for."

Ramos's theatrical manner flickered for just a moment, and Niloo caught a glimpse of genuine pain in his pale blue eyes before he recovered. "Ah, well, quality over quantity, as they say. Sometimes the most important battles are fought by the smallest armies."

"Seven out of ten," Vera whispered, her djinn form solidifying further as she observed the magical resonances flowing through the chamber. "What about the others? Bastion should have two heart-bearers, and Shadra—"

"Some hearts," Ramos said quietly, his voice losing its usual theatrical flourish, "have gone silent forever. Others... others beat to a different rhythm now, one we cannot hear through willing connection."

The weight of understanding crashed through the network like a physical blow. Through the magical link, Niloo could sense the other heartbearers' growing awareness that something was wrong—that the pattern was incomplete in ways that suggested more than simple absence.

"Shikara?" Elissa's voice was barely a whisper through the connection.

"Gone," Ramos replied simply. "Fighting to the last breath to protect those who could not protect themselves. She died as she lived—with crystal blazing and spells flying, taking down half a regiment of Madrid's finest before they could overwhelm her."

The silence that followed was heavy with grief and rage. Shikara had been their eldest sister in Jintessa, their teacher in combat magic, their unwavering defender of the innocent.

"And the others?" Seraphina asked, though from her tone, Niloo suspected she already feared the answer.

"Shikoba is Madrid's guest in a very unpleasant location," Ramos said carefully. "As for young Emily... Her dragon serves the emperor now. Where the dragon goes, the heartbearer must follow."

"Enslaved," Shreya's voice carried barely contained fury. "All of them enslaved."

"Not all," Ramos corrected firmly. "Shikoba fights still—I can sense her rage even from here, like a storm trapped in a bottle. And Emily... Emily's situation is more complex than Madrid understands. But for now, they are beyond our reach."

Through the network came a chorus of reports that painted an increasingly dire picture. Imperial forces were mobilizing across all provinces, with particularly large concentrations moving toward the borders. More concerning still were the reports of strange magical experiments and the construction of what could only be described as binding circles large enough to hold entire armies.

"He's preparing for some final phase," Shreya's voice came through the connection, tight with controlled anger. "The forced integration of all magical beings under his control, harnessed to serve his end goals."

"We have perhaps three days before he begins the ritual here. Three days," Niloo repeated, feeling the weight of that timeline. "Can we coordinate a response that quickly? With only seven of us?"

"Oh, we can certainly try," Ramos said with the sort of cheerful optimism that suggested he was about to propose something completely insane. "Though I should mention that our current situation has developed a few additional complications."

As if summoned by his words, the chamber's protective enchantments chimed a warning. Through the Master Heart's expanded awareness, Niloo could sense imperial scouts approaching their location—not the confused bear-watchers Ramos had previously misdirected, but actual magic-wielders with detection capabilities.

"They're tracking the network activation," Lazuli observed grimly. "The magical resonance was too powerful to hide completely."

"Ah yes, that was always a possibility," Ramos admitted with the casual tone of someone discussing the weather. "On the bright side, it means our network is working exactly as intended. On the less bright side, we're about to have some uninvited guests."

Through the magical connection, Niloo could sense the other heartbearers preparing for action across the provinces. Dragons took to the skies, djinn shifted into combat forms, and magical weapons were drawn from their hiding places, readying for battle.

"Can we get reinforcements to you? Or do something that will serve as a distraction?" Beatrice asked through the network, her voice carrying the steady determination of someone who had clearly been preparing for this moment.

"Not the kind Madrid would expect," Ramos replied with returning mischief. "But I may have a few surprises up my proverbial sleeves. Twenty years of building a resistance network tends to accumulate interesting allies. Do not worry about us here."

"What kind of a distraction are you thinking?" said Jannah.

"Well," Ramos said, his eyes twinkling with mischief, "I was thinking we might start by convincing every free dragon in Gaia to have a simultaneous temper tantrum. Madrid's forces are used to dealing with enslaved dragons, but thirty-five angry, independent wyrms appearing in their skies at once? That should provide quite the distraction."

"Where did you find that many dragons in Gaia? Nevermind...there's no time for explanations. And while they're dealing with the dragons?" Elissa prompted.

"While they're dealing with dragons, we systematically attack his magical infrastructure. Those binding circles, the essence collectors, communication networks—the entire apparatus he's building to control magical beings. Without his tools of domination, his enslaved heartbearers should begin breaking free on their own."

"That's a tall order, Wizard Ramos," said Niloo. "We don't know where all of this is located."

"We know enough to begin. And we can begin everywhere," he replied.

The plan was audacious, requiring precise timing and unprecedented magical coordination. It was also the sort of thing that could only work if attempted by someone completely confident in their own absurdity, Niloo realized, It could work. It could also spell disaster.

"There is one small complication," came Selina's voice through the network, her tone carrying the gruff determination of someone accustomed to dealing with stubborn warriors. "My province is currently under siege by imperial forces who've decided our forges belong to them."

"Madrid has commandeered your smithies?" several voices asked through the connection.

"Every forge from the clan holds to the smallest village workshop," Selina explained with barely contained fury. "They're forcing our master smiths to create enchanted weapons and armor for Madrid's armies. They've placed shackles on every craftsman, and they've threatened to execute the children if anyone refuses to work."

"Ah, that's considerably more serious than our current situation," Ramos admitted, his tone losing some of its levity. "Madrid knows the value of Wydran metalwork. Your people forge the finest magical weapons in all of Gaia."

"And now those weapons will be turned against us," Selina replied bitterly. "My dragon wants to simply melt every forge in the province, but that would destroy centuries of our craft knowledge along with the imperial operation."

"No need for such drastic measures," Ramos said thoughtfully. "Dragon fire can be quite selective when properly directed. Have Citrine breathe on the shackles themselves—magical restraints tend to be surprisingly brittle when exposed to direct dragon flame. Once your smiths are free, I suspect they'll be more than happy to demonstrate why Wydran steel has such a fearsome reputation."

"That... could work," Selina admitted, and through the connection Niloo could sense her fierce satisfaction at the prospect. "Our warriors have been itching for a proper fight, and there's nothing quite like a Wydran war-hammer enhanced with fresh dragon magic."

"Excellent. Now then, shall we begin our magnificent rebellion against tyranny? I have a few more jokes to tell, and I suspect Madrid's people could use a good laugh before we thoroughly ruin their day."

As the magical network hummed with renewed energy and the first sounds of the approaching enemy reached the chamber, Niloo felt a fierce determination rise within her. They were outnumbered, outgunned, and missing some of their most powerful allies. But they had dragons, djinn, ancient magic, and a wizard whose secret weapon was his ability to find humour in hopeless situations.

"All right," she said through the network, addressing heartbearers across seven provinces. "For Shikara. For Shikoba and Emily. For everyone Madrid has stolen from us. Let's show him what happens when you try to break the bonds between heartbearers."

The response was immediate—a chorus of dragon roars, djinn battle cries, and distinctly inappropriate laughter that echoed across the magical spectrum. They might be fewer than hoped, but those who remained carried the fury and determination of all who had fallen or been taken.

Whatever happened next, Niloo thought with grim satisfaction, it was going to be absolutely glorious.

CHAPTER TWENTY

HEARTBEARER STRIKE

Madrid's approaching scouts surged through the mountain passage and descended the long hill to the farm, arms waving and urging their companions to pick up speed, as their destination came into sight, the weathered farm house and barns of Niloo's ancestral home.

"Well," Ramos said with the sort of cheerful tone usually reserved for discussing pleasant weather, "it appears our guests have arrived ahead of schedule. How wonderfully punctual of them."

"Ramos," Marcus warned, amber crystal flaring as he prepared defensive spells, "there are too many of them. We should evacuate—"

"Nonsense!" Ramos interrupted, practically bouncing with excitement. "This is the perfect opportunity to field-test our new network. Seven provinces, seven coordinated strikes, all beginning with... well, right here."

Through the magical connection, Niloo could feel the other heartbearers' readiness. Dragons darkened the skies across Gaia as the heartbearers prepared for battle. Their djinn were shifting into their favourite combat forms, their favourite weapons readied as they searched for the first place to attack. Niloo prepared coordinates, taken from Ramos' carefully prepared map, marking the locations in each province that were suitable targets.

"Selina," Ramos called through the network, "how quickly can your smiths work once they're free?"

"Give me ten minutes to melt their shackles, and I'll have war-hammers flying within the hour," came the fierce reply from Wydra. "My people don't forget insults to their craft or their person."

"Excellent. Jannah, are you prepared for some geological rearrangement?"

"The temple guardians remember their ancient oaths and the secrets of the earth elements," Jannah's voice resonated through the connection with the deep authority of one who had inherited the knowledge and wisdom once held by four individual Chaac's and now residing not in a temple of stone but in her living memory.. "Madrid's engineers built their fortresses without consulting the old ways. The earth itself will remind them of their presumption."

"Beatrice, how are the fjords this time of year?"

"Frozen solid and perfect for avalanche work," came the reply from the northern mountains. "Zircon has been practicing his ice-shaping. He thinks he can redirect an entire glacier if properly motivated."

"Seraphina, still hiding in that grain silo?"

"Not anymore," the heartbearer replied with grim satisfaction. "Royale convinced me that sometimes the best medicine is preventing the disease entirely. We're about to give Madrid's garrison a very aggressive treatment for their slavery addiction."

The first imperial scout rounded the corner of the barn, magical restraints glowing in his hands. He took one look at the rainbow light patterns dancing across the yard, emanating from the ruined house, and Ramos's maniacally cheerful expression as he blocked the way.

"Surrender in the name of—" the scout began, shouting at the old man.

"Oh, I'm sorry," Ramos interrupted politely, "but we're not accepting surrenders today. Perhaps you could try again next week? I hear Thursday afternoons are lovely for capitulation."

The scout skidded to a halt, blinking in confusion, clearly not prepared for this response. Behind him, more imperial soldiers filed into the yard, their enchanted weapons trained on the elderly man standing in their way.

"You are harboring illegal magical artifacts," the lead scout announced formally. "By order of Emperor Madrid, you will submit to binding and interrogation."

"Binding?" Ramos gasped theatrically. "How delightfully presumptuous! Tell me, have you ever seen what happens when you try to bind a humour network that's connected to seven provinces and seven dragons who are about to demonstrate the true meaning of liberation?"

"What are you—" the scout started to say.

"NOW!" Ramos shouted with gleeful enthusiasm.

The world exploded into coordinated chaos.

In Wydra, Selina's dragon Citrine swung low over the forges and breathed a precise stream of golden fire that melted magical shackles without harming the smiths who wore them. The moment the re-straints fell away, the sound of hammers on anvils turned against their guards, quickly overpowering them. A cheer rose from the smiths, ringing out across the province as the master craftsmen began forging weapons of liberation, fury enhancing their skillful strokes.

In Peca, Jannah spoke incantations that evoked the elements of water and earth, in the tongue of the Chaac, invoking rituals that had been old when the guardians first walked the world. The mountain foundations beneath Madrid's strategic fortresses remembered their true nature, and what had been solid bedrock suddenly became very pliable. Several imperial strongholds found themselves sinking into the earth with the inexorable patience of geological time accelerated by priestly magic.

In Fjord, Beatrice and her dragon Zircon created an avalanche so massive and precisely directed that it swept away three imperial camps while somehow leaving a nearby village completely untouched. The sound of the snow cascade could be heard for miles as it swept the encampment over a cliff and into the sea, relaying a message that the northern reaches would not be easily conquered.

In Tyr, Elissa and Mysty struck at the Citadel's core of magic, as-saulting the spire where Madrid forged his spelled silver weapons. The resultant explosions brought the Citadel dragons out of their roosts, like a kicked ant hill, with a fury of flapping wings and fanged snarls.

In Cassimir, Shreya led a surgical strike against the factories built at Emperor Madrid's command, in which were forged the imperial essence collectors—devices designed to drain magic from captured beings.

In Hindra, Seraphina emerged from her grain silo to discover that her dragon Royale had already reduced the imperial garrison to a collection of very confused soldiers standing in their underclothes in a field of melted armor and nonexistent weapons.

And in the farm's courtyard, Ramos jumped up onto a nearby wagon bed and launched into a tale about a witch with one too many enchanted pots. In the tale, the pots would spill their contents if they were not chosen first, and so to fix the pots, the witch had a smithy fuse them together into a chamber pot that she left under her bed, so that they would never again complain about not being used first.

The scouts lips twitched as the tale was told, momentarily distracted by the antics of the old wizard.

Meanwhile, the Master Heart network absorbed all the chaos and blended it with Ramos's humourous story and transmitted the unlikely concoction in real-time, completely overwhelming the local imperial scouts so that they simply stood there, weapons forgotten, staring at the lights and wizard show, with expressions of complete bewilderment.

"You see," Ramos explained conversationally to the lead scout while reflected rainbow patterns danced across his face, "the thing about humour networks is that they make everything else seem rather silly by comparison. Including, I'm afraid, your attempts at intimidation."

The lead scout tried to raise his weapon, but found that his arm wouldn't obey him. None of the soldiers could move properly—the Master Heart's influence had synchronized their nervous systems with the rhythm of cosmic laughter, leaving them temporarily paralyzed by their own body's confusion about whether this was a serious combat situation or the setup to an elaborate joke.

"Don't worry," Ramos said kindly, "the effect is completely temporary. You'll be able to move normally in about... oh, twenty minutes or so. Just long enough for us to finish our attack on Madrid's infrastructure."

Through the network, reports continued flooding in. Imperial forces across Gaia were finding their carefully laid plans disrupted by a combination of dragon fire, earthquake-prone fortifications, weaponized weather patterns, and smiths who were apparently capable of forging enchanted war-hammers at superhuman speed when properly motivated.

"The old temple wards are responding," Jannah's voice came through the connection with quiet satisfaction. "I've awakened protections that Madrid never knew existed. His forces in Peca are finding that the very stones beneath their feet remember older loyalties."

"This is actually working," Niloo said with amazement, watching as the tactical displays on Ramos's crystal device displayed the collapse of imperial positions across multiple provinces.

"Of course it's working," Ramos replied with wounded dignity. "I don't build networks that don't work. That would be like telling jokes that aren't funny—technically possible, but deeply offensive to the natural order. However, we are barely scratching the itch that is Emperor Madrid."

"The communication breakdown is spreading," Vera observed. "Without their coordination systems, Madrid's forces are operating blind."

"And without their enslaved smiths, they'll be running out of enchanted weapons," Selina added through the network, the sound of hammering growing louder behind her voice.

"How long before Madrid responds directly?" Marcus asked, his practical nature cutting through the celebration.

"Oh, he's already responding," Ramos said with a grin that suggested he was enjoying this far too much. "Can't you feel it? That growing sense of imperial fury radiating from the direction of the Citadel?

Madrid has just discovered that his carefully constructed conquest across Gaia has become a carefully orchestrated embarrassment."

Through the Master Heart network, Niloo could indeed sense something building—a massive concentration of magical power gathering around the imperial Citadel, as Madrid grew angry and increasingly spiteful.

"He's planning something big," she said, her crystal heart warming against her chest in warning.

"The ancient texts spoke of this moment, or one very like it, " came Jannah's thoughtful voice. "There is an ancient text that says 'When the usurper's power reaches its peak, the guardians' final protections will activate.' Madrid thinks he has won, but he has not yet faced what the Chaac have preserved through the centuries."

"Which brings us to our masterstroke," Ramos added with barely contained excitement. "Tell me, has anyone ever wondered what would happen if free dragons combined their magical resonance?"

"What kind of magic would that create?" Elissa asked through the network.

"The kind that breaks every magical bond Madrid has ever forged," Ramos replied, his eyes practically glowing with mischief. "Every enslaved dragon, every forced heartbearer connection, every binding circle across the empire—all of it dissolved in one magnificent moment of coordinated dragon power."

"Is that actually possible?" Niloo asked, turning to face the wizard.

"More than possible," Lazuli said with growing excitement. "If we use the heartbearer network as a focusing lens, the dragons' combined magical output could create a resonance pattern that overrides every control enchantment Madrid has created."

"And as a delightful bonus," Ramos continued, practically bouncing, "the frequency will also trigger the immediate hatching of *every dragon egg* in Gaia, overriding Madrid's breeding programs. Thousands of new dragons, born free instead of into slavery."

The implications hit Niloo like a physical blow. "That would amplify our network exponentially. Every dragon could become a conduit for heartbearer magic. But will they?"

"Indeed! Madrid loses his existing dragon cavalry, his breeding program gets completely disrupted, and we gain access to magical power levels that should theoretically be impossible."

"But isn't this just trading one sent of binding for another?" Niloo frowned. "I am not sure this will work. But I am willing to try. What choice do we have?"

"The ancient texts spoke of this possibility too," Jannah added quietly. "'The great liberation', when all dragons remember their true nature through a rebirth. Though..."

"Though what?" Niloo asked, noticing the hesitation in the Chaac's voice.

"Nothing," Jannah replied after a moment. "The guardians' knowledge suggests this will work perfectly. Madrid will never recover from such a blow."

As if summoned by their words, the Master Heart pulsed with unprecedented energy, and through the network came the growing roar of dragons preparing to remake the magical landscape of Gaia entirely. *Here the call of my brothers and sisters, feel their heart,* said Lapis. *It begins.* Lapis lifted her head and roared

CHAPTER TWENTY-ONE

DRAGON SONG

The air around Niloo began to vibrate with a power that made her bones ache and her crystal heart sing in harmonious response. Her teeth rattled as the ground shook. Through the Master Heart network, she could feel the seven dragons across Gaia positioning themselves according to Ramos's carefully calculated coordinates, each one a crucial node in the magical constellation they were about to create.

"Positions confirmed," Selina's voice came through the connection, steady despite the magnitude of what they were attempting. "Citrine is ready."

"Zircon in position," Beatrice reported from the frozen peaks of Fjord. "The ice crystals here are amplifying his natural resonance beautifully."

"Mysty and I have cleared the Citadel's interference," Elissa added with grim satisfaction. "Those spelled silver weapon forges won't be disrupting anyone's magic for quite some time."

One by one, the other heartbearers confirmed their readiness. Shreya from the smoking ruins of Madrid's essence collector factories. Seraphina from the liberated garrison in Hindra. Jannah from the ancient temple sites in Peca where the ancestor spirits themselves held their spectral breath in anticipation.

"Excellent," Ramos said, his theatrical manner giving way to something more focused and intense. "Now then...the tricky part. Niloo, I'll need you to synchronize your crystal heart with the Master Heart's core frequency. This is going to feel rather like sticking your finger in a lightning storm, but trust me—it's perfectly safe."

"Define 'perfectly safe,'" Marcus said dryly, raising a dark, questioning eyebrow.

"Well, there's only a small chance you'll temporarily experience existence from the perspective of every dragon in Gaia simultaneously," Ramos replied cheerfully. "But think of the stories you'll be able to tell!"

Before Niloo could ask what that meant exactly, the Master Heart erupted into a column of rainbow light that reached toward the sky like a beacon. The crystal against her chest grew so hot she gasped, but instead of burning, it felt like diving into a warm ocean of pure magic.

And suddenly, she wasn't just Niloo anymore.

She was Citrine, breathing golden fire that sang with the rhythm of hammers on anvils, feeling the joy of Wydran smiths as their chains melted away.

She was Zircon, shaping ice and snow into avalanches of freedom, the cold mountain air filling her lungs with sharp clarity.

She was Mysty, dancing through the chaos of the Citadel's collapsing defenses, lightning crackling between her claws as partially formed spelled silver weapons melted back into to slag.

She was Royale, standing triumphant over confused imperial soldiers, her healing flame turning their weapons to ash while leaving their armor merely embarrassingly absent.

She was every dragon she had never met, scattered across Gaia, all feeling the same call to something greater than themselves.

"Now," Ramos's voice echoed across all realities simultaneously, "let's show Madrid what happens when you try to chain the wind."

The seven dragons opened their throats and released not roars, but something far more fundamental—a harmonic frequency that resonated with the very essence of draconic magic. The sound wasn't heard so much as felt, vibrating through crystal hearts and magical bonds, through the air itself and the stone beneath their feet. The sound was visceral and bone deep. An ancient cry that connected the dragons to the beginning of time, when they were born of fire and ash, smoke and lava. In such conditions, gems are formed, and no jewel has ever shined so bright as the first dragons.

Across the empire, every magical restraint that had been placed by Emperor Madrid on the enslaved dragons quivered.

In the Citadel's dragon roosts, the enslaved younglings suddenly remembered their Jintessa names. Their bindings cracked, to hang loosely around their ankles. The spelled silver control collars shrieked and began to melt. They who had been kidnapped from their mothers nests in Jinessa, and forced to serve Emperor Madrid in this new land called Gaia, spread their wings and roared their fury to the sky, as memories of home flooded their minds and a fierce longing to return home built within their chests. Their djinn bondmates ran to comfort their charges, casting wild eyes around the rookery as chaos reigned. They sprang up on their young charges' backs and launched into the sky.

And in hidden chambers throughout the empire, thousands of dragon eggs, long lost and forgotten, heard their anguish and began to hatch, cracking open ahead of schedule, the harmonic triggering their emergence into a world where they would be born free.

"It's working!" Elissa's voice rang with triumph through the network. "Such a roar is coming from the hatchery. I can see a few of the imprisoned Citadel dragons, tumbling out of the rookery in a crazed frenzy. Their djinn are struggling to calm them. This is a masterful stroke against Madrid's control of the Citadel itself!"

"The breeding caverns must be erupting with hatchlings," Niloo added with fierce joy. "Madrid's guards won't know which direction to run!"

But through her connection to the expanding network of liberated dragons, Niloo felt something else—a vast, cold intelligence turning its attention toward them with the focused intensity of a predator that had just realized its prey was fighting back.

"Ramos," she gasped, her consciousness snapping back to her own body so suddenly that she staggered. "Madrid felt that. He knows exactly what we just did."

"Of course he did," Ramos replied, though his cheerful demeanor had acquired a distinctly manic edge. "One doesn't liberate several thousand dragons without making a certain amount of magical noise. But the beauty of it is—"

His words were cut off as the very air around them began to twist and darken. Through the Master Heart's awareness, Niloo could sense

Madrid himself approaching, his magical signature blazing with rage and power that dwarfed anything she had ever encountered.

"He's coming," she whispered. "He's actually coming here. Now."

"Splendid!" Ramos said with the sort of enthusiasm usually reserved for unexpected birthday parties. "I was beginning to think we'd have to send him a formal invitation."

"This is not splendid!" Marcus snapped, his amber crystal flaring as he tried to calculate their chances of survival. "We're not ready for a direct confrontation with Madrid!"

"My dear Marcus," Ramos replied, his pale blue eyes twinkling with something that might have been madness or genius, "readiness is a state of mind. Besides, we have something Madrid has never had to deal with before."

"What's that?" Niloo asked, though she wasn't sure she wanted to know the answer.

"An entire network of freshly liberated dragons who are absolutely furious about their previous accommodations," Ramos said with a grin that promised either salvation or spectacular disaster. "Plus, I've been saving my very best jokes for just such an occasion."

Through the network came the sound of approaching wing beats—not just the seven dragons they had worked with, but dozens of others, newly freed and converging on their location with the unified purpose of beings who had just remembered what freedom felt like.

"The ancient texts spoke of this moment too," Jannah's voice cut through the noise. "When the usurper finally reveals himself, the guardians' true test begins."

The sky above Niloo's ancestral farm darkened as two forces approached from opposite directions—Madrid from the south, his power crackling like a storm of enslaved magic, a foul, dark stain on the back of the ancient pale dragon called Opaleye, and a flight of enraged dragons from every point of the compass, their freedom song echoing across the mountains.

"Well then," Ramos said, straightening his robes and checking that his crystal device was properly calibrated, "shall we see whose magic is stronger—tyranny or humour enhanced by justified draconic fury?"

Let the confrontation begin.

CHAPTER TWENTY-TWO

THE EMERPOR'S GAMBIT

Madrid descended from the darkening sky like a plague made manifest, his form wreathed in shadows that seemed to devour the light around him. In contrast, the ancient dragon beneath him shone brightly, even as Opaleye flew with lethal grace. His massive wings cut the air with the precision of a master predator. His scales shimmered between pearl and silver, while his belly and the inner membranes of his wings gleamed with the shifting colors of precious opal—deep blues and greens that flickered with hidden fire.

Opaleye glided down from the sky to land in the farmyard, outstretched claws furrowing the soil as he landed. Slowly the dragon turned towards where Ramos and his companion's hiding place. The befuddled scouts shrank away from the dragon and the Emperor, then turned tail and ran back around the side of the barn and out of harm's way.

"How magnificent," Ramos observed, squinting at the approaching dragon, his right hand shielding his eyes. He shrugged, then tilted his head with the sort of academic interest he usually reserved for studying particularly dangerous phenomena. "The great Opaleye himself. I do hope Madrid realizes he's riding a volcano that has chosen not to erupt...as of yet." Ramos stepped of the tilting porch, and into the yard, wizard's robes trailing through the dust. He shoved up his sleeves, freeing his hands, and waited.

"That's Opaleye, the First Among Dragons," Jannah's voice came through the network with a mixture of reverence and wariness. "Titan says he's the leader of all dragons stolen from Jinessa. Madrid thinks he controls him, but..."

"But Opaleye has his own reasons for this alliance," Ramos finished softly. "I know. How wonderfully complicated."

Dragon and emperor came to a halt in the dusty yard facing Ramos. Madrid glared down at his old nemesis, his eyes flashing in anger. He had not forgotten their last confrontation.

Madrid's voice rang out across the farmstead, amplified by magic until it seemed to echo from the grounds themselves. The sound was designed to intimidate as his voice grated against their ears. "You pathetic insects think you can challenge me, the Emperor of the free world, with parlor tricks and stolen dragons? I have ruled this world for over thirty years. I have conquered challenges far greater than you."

"Thirty years?" Ramos called back cheerfully. He stepped away from the drunkenly leaning porch of the farm house, loosening his arms as he moved into the open. "My goodness, that's quite impressive! Tell me, how many of those years did you spend learning to make friends? Because I have to say, your social skills could use some work."

Madrid's eyes narrowed, glaring at his bitter enemy. Power flickered angrily between his fingers, begging to be released.

Ramos reached inside his pocket and pulled out his wizard stone, tossing it to the ground. The stone quivered, then began to swell into a rock and then a ledge large enough for him to stand on. Waving his hands, he cast a spell to lighten his weight and floated up into the air, then gently wafted over to settle on the smooth, grey surface.

"I thought you'd like a closer look at me. I know your eyes are growing dim with all the squinting you must do on a daily basis. That comes from sneering down at your underlings, you know. Remember me, my old friend?" Ramos struck a pose, right hand finding his bony hip. He grinned up at Madrid and waved

"I should have silenced you when I had the chance!" Madrid snarled, and the air around him crackled with dark magic. "You will surrender the Master Heart and submit to my will, or I will demonstrate why every settlement in every province should fear my wrath."

Opaleye's great head twisted around to look at Madrid, opal eyes reflecting his intelligence. When he spoke, his voice carried the weight of ancient authority and barely restrained fury. Smoke billowed from his nostrils, a sure sign of his agitation.

"Release the hatchlings and their djinn first," the dragon snarled, his words like distant thunder. "As agreed. No games, Madrid."

Madrid's jaw tightened with irritation. "The rebels will surrender the artifact first. Then we will discuss terms."

"No," Opaleye replied with quiet menace. "First the hatchlings are returned safely to their roosts, unbound and freed. Then I will consider further cooperation."

The tension between emperor and dragon was palpable, a reminder that Madrid's greatest ally was also potentially his greatest enemy.

"Actually," Niloo said, surprised by the steadiness of her own voice, "I don't think any of them need to fear you anymore."

As if summoned by her words, several liberated youngling dragons crested the surrounding hills in a swarm of flashing scales and flaming fury. Dozens of them, wings spread wide, eyes blazing with the fire of remembered freedom, entered the valley. Petite female djinn, their bondmates, clung to their saddles, astride the dragons broad backs. Anger blazed in their faces, an anger to equal that of their companions. At their head flew a magnificent bronze dragon whose scream shattered the air and echoed off of the mountains.

Opaleye! the bronze dragon roared, speaking dragonspeake. *I am Kora of the Burning Peaks, stolen from my clutch-nest when I was barely hatched. For twenty-three years I have waited for this moment—to see you free of this alliance.*

And I, called another, this one silver and blue like captured starlight, *I am Novus of the Northern Windy Summits. Opaleye, pack leader, will you not join us? The dragon song has given us a glimpse of the way home!*

One by one, the freed dragons announced themselves, reclaiming names that had been lost, and their homeland that had been forbidden to them. But their calls were directed not at Madrid, but at Opaleye—pleading, hopeful, desperate for their leader to abandon his cooperation with the tyrant.

Opaleye's opal eyes flickered with something that might have been longing, but his voice remained steady. *I hear you, my kin. And I rejoice in your freedom. But while any innocents remain in Madrid's power, I cannot join you.*

The hatchlings will be safe, Kora interrupted urgently. *We are many now. We can protect ourselves.*

"Can you?" Madrid interjected with cold amusement. "Tell me, noble dragons, can you protect them from this?"

He raised his hand, and in his palm materialized a silver device with a glowing tip that pulsed with sickly yellow light. Niloo could sense the malevolent energy radiating from it—a frequency designed not to liberate, but to cause agonizing pain to any dragon exposed to it.

"One word from me," Madrid continued, "and every hatchling in the breeding caverns beneath this dry, crusty Samosian soil will experience torment beyond imagination. Even now, my guards are activating the nodes that will spell the caves, turning them into an electrified field that the tender hides of the fledglings cannot withstand. Do you really want to test this new weapon? I assure you, I am happy to have a field test of my invention." Madrid eyed everyone in turn, weapon held high for all to see. His narrowed gaze fell to his old nemesis, the wizard Ramos. "I have been longing to do so. No? I thought not. Now, shall we discuss the terms of your collective surrender?"

Opaleye's massive form went utterly still, and when he spoke, his voice carried a menace that made the mountain peaks seem fragile. "Madrid. You test the boundaries of our arrangement."

"I test nothing," the emperor replied coldly. "I merely remind you of the stakes."

The ancient dragon's head twisted around again to stare at Madrid. His dark eyes glowed with an inner fire that spoke of barely restrained violence. "And I remind you, that my cooperation is voluntary. Continue threatening children, and you will discover what happens when I withdraw it."

For a moment, the two stared at each other—tyrant and dragon elder, locked in a battle of wills. The air between them crackled with the potential for violence.

Then Ramos stepped forward and cleared his throat politely.

"Excuse me," the old wizard said with the tone of someone interrupting a particularly tedious argument, "but if you two are finished measuring the size of your respective egos, I'd like to point out something rather important."

"What?" Madrid snapped.

"Your device," Ramos said cheerfully, "it appears to be smoking."

Madrid looked down at the silver device in his palm, and his eyes widened in alarm. The glowing tip was indeed flickering erratically, and wisps of acrid smoke curled from its faceted surface.

"That's the problem with frequency-based magic," Ramos explained conversationally. "Expose it to a more powerful frequency—say, one generated by dozens of liberated dragons singing the unifying harmonics of their species—and it tends to... well, let's call it an 'aggressive malfunction.'"

The device in Madrid's hand heated and the silvery tip's glow intensified. Frowning, he shook the device. A loud squeal issued from the spelled silver and with a sudden bang, it flashed with heat. The silver softened and sloughed away revealing the heated rod beneath its surface which burned red hot. With a yell, Madrid dropped the rod and it cracked on impact with the ground. The silver ignited the dried grass as the molten silver splashed onto the ground. With a pop and a white hot burst of light, the device went dark.

Opaleye's laugh rolled across the clearing. "It appears, Madrid, that your insurance has just expired."

"No matter," the emperor snarled, dark magic beginning to writhe around his form once again. "I have other methods of ensuring compliance."

"I'm sure you do," Opaleye replied with deadly calm. "But right now, I think it's time we renegotiated the terms of our alliance."

The great dragon's opal belly scales began to glow with inner fire, and for the first time in thirty years, Madrid looked genuinely uncertain.

"The hatchlings—" he began.

"Will be protected," Opaleye finished, his voice carrying absolute authority. "But not by continuing this charade. The harmonic frequency has shown us a new path, Madrid. One that doesn't require your... guidance."

"You dare—" he hissed, eyes narrowing angrily.

"I dare," Opaleye snarled, the weight of the dragon's anger fueling his words. "Our alliance is ended. Release me or face the consequences."

Madrid's face contorted with rage, and his fury broke. Madrid flung his arms wide. Lightning burst from his hands and flashed around the great dragon, striking Opaleye in the tender joins between his scales. Opaleye howled and reared up onto his hind legs, trying to unseat Madrid, but the emperor was ready for him. Into his hands dropped two more spelled silver instruments, shaped like an ancient trident. The tines glowed with wicked energy, forked lightning crackling from its tips. He jammed the glowing tips into Opaleye's beefy neck, sliding the tips between the protective plates and into the dragon's hide.

Opaleye howled and thrashed as the lightning overwhelmed his resistance, and he came under the emperor's control once more. "Now fly!" commanded Madrid and Opaleye launched himself into the air, while Madrid cast blades of fire in a wide circle, burning, consuming everything in its path.

Ramos hastily jumped from his rock and pocketed the stone, then ran for the safety of the underground chamber. "Everyone down, now!" he cried as he burst into the ante chamber. Putting his words into action, the wizard flung himself bodily at Niloo, knocking her to the ground. With a whoosh, and a low boom, a concussive explosion swept over them all. First came the flame, and then the rain of debris, as the house above them blew up.

CHAPTER TWENTY-THREE

THE CHAMBER OF LAST RESORT

Ramos jumped to his feet and grabbed hold of Niloo, dragging her in his wake into the hidden chamber, then pushing her ahead of the fireball that hungrily fed on the shattered debris that had once been Niloo's childhood home. Lazuli shifted into a smaller version of Lapis and turning his back on the fireball, he spread his wings, protecting both Niloo and Ramos as they ran for the safety of the inner chamber. Once Lazuli was clear of the threshold, Ramos slammed the door shut and bolted it, then spun around to face the room, his grey hair disheveled and singed at the fringe.

"Is everyone ok?" Ramos called out as he brushed the debris from his robes. His normally pristine beard was now gray with stone dust, and slightly smoking around the edges, making him look more like a chimney sweep than a first wizard. "All limbs accounted for?"

The underground chamber shook with the force of Madrid's assault, dust and small stones raining down from the ceiling as concussive waves of magic rolled over them. Centuries old mortar crumbled from between the fitted stones, releasing the faint scent of limestone. The Master Heart's rainbow light flickered wildly, casting shifting shadows across the faces of those huddled over the heart in the cramped space, shielding it with their bodies. The light playing off their features alternated between emerald, sapphire, and ruby hues.

"We're alive," Marcus said grimly, his amber crystal pulsing with warm, steady light as he struggled to reinforce the chamber's protective wards. He was not a master, not even a trained wizard, but golden threads of power spread from his hands to trace along the ancient carved symbols in the walls, following pathways etched into the rock by countless generations of Keepers. Ramos examined his efforts then nodded to him, smiling. "But for how long? These wards were designed to keep intruders out, not to contain the aftermath of an aerial battle directly overhead."

Through the Master Heart network, they could feel the anguish of the liberated dragons above—a collective roar of fury and despair that made the crystal formations around them vibrate in sympathy. The sound resonated through their bones, a whining song of grief and rage that spoke of bonds forcibly severed and freedom temporarily gained, then lost.

"He's got Opaleye under his control again," Niloo whispered, her human heart aching with sympathy to the great dragon's pain. Through the bond, she could feel Lapis snarling. She was the one sensing Opaleye's distress. The sensation was like having her ribs compressed while her lungs filled with burning air. "Those silver tridents—they're overriding his will, forcing him back into servitude. The silver's been spelled to interface directly with a dragon's nervous system," she said with barely controlled fury. "It's not just controlling his actions—it's hijacking his very thoughts. The younglings are falling back under the control of their wizards, too, along with their djinn. We are not strong enough, not yet."

"This is a temporary setback," Ramos said with determination. His pale blue eyes held a dangerous glint. "Madrid may have regained control of a handful of dragons, but he's also just demonstrated to them, exactly why they were right to seek freedom. Nothing motivates a revolution quite like watching your leader being tortured."

Above them, they could hear the concussive sound of massive wings beating the air, punctuated by roars of challenge that made the chamber's ancient stones whine in harmonic response. Madrid's amplified voice shouted commands that cracked like whips through the air as he strove to bring the younglings back under his control. Weaving a spell of immense power, he grabbed hold of the male heartbearers magic through their crystals, forcibly bonding their magical powers to his. Each word that fell from his lips dripped with the authority of absolute power. The battle in the skies above the decimated farm intensified and the very air above them screamed with the violence of it.

Opaleye! Kora's voice rang out in dragonspeech, transmitted through the network with the desperate intensity of a sister calling to a drowning brother. *Fight the compulsion! Remember who you are! We are here!*

The silver burns, came Opaleye's agonized reply, each word torn from his throat like pieces of his soul. *Cannot... resist... the fire com mands... My flame... not my own...*

"The trident's forcing him to attack his own kind," Niloo said with horror, as her rage gave her focus. "Madrid's using Opaleye as a weapon against the other dragons. He's turning their greatest strength—their loyalty to their leader—into their greatest weakness."

"Clever and utterly despicable," Ramos observed, his fingers already moving across his crystal device with the practiced precision of a musician tuning an impossibly complex instrument. "Nothing breaks a rebellion faster than forcing their leader to fight against them. It's psychological warfare at its most vicious."

Through the network came the sounds of aerial combat in vivid, heartbreaking detail—the clash of claws on scales that rang like struck bronze, the roar of competing flames that painted the sky in shades of gold and crimson, the anguished cries of dragons forced to battle their own elder. Niloo could feel each impact, every wound inflicted on both sides sending echoes of pain through her crystal heart. She touched her nose, and it came away bloody.

"Niloo!" Utterly silent until now, her mother rushed to her side as Niloo staggered and fell, the connection with the Master Heart lost.

But underneath the chaos, weaving through the violence like a thread of silver through a tapestry of fire, Niloo could feel something else: a low, harmonic humming that seemed to be building in intensity. It felt ancient beyond measure, older than the dragons themselves, older perhaps than the very stones of the mountain.

"What's that sound?" she asked, pressing her ear against the chamber floor, where she had fallen. The humming seemed to be coming from everywhere at once—the floor, the ceiling, the very bedrock beneath them.

Ths sound of Jannah's voice was coming from Niloo's crystal heart. The Master Heart, which pulsed with a life of its own, had forged an open connection to every heartbearer in Gaia. Their crystals were live conduits to their matching hearts located elsewhere, and all she had to do is speak, to be heard.

"The temple foundations here are responding to the violence there. Ancient protections are awakening—elemental safeguards that have slept for a thousand years," said Jannah, her voice strained but determined.

"What kind of protections?" Marcus demanded, his academic mind already racing through possibilities.

"The kind that were designed to contain beings of immense magical power," Jannah replied, searching the memories obtained from the former Chaac. "The first Chaac was commissioned to built these chambers, both here and there, long before there were borders to define the provinces. It was not just to hide the Master Heart, but to serve as a prison if necessary. They knew that artifacts of such power would inevitably attract those who would misuse them."

Ramos's eyebrows shot up with the delighted expression of a scholar who had just discovered that his most outrageous theory was actually conservative. "A prison? How delightfully dramatic! And what, exactly, would it imprison?"

"Anyone foolish enough to bring violence to a sacred site while standing directly above the most powerful magical artifact in Gaia," Jannah said with grim satisfaction that spoke of justice delayed but not forgotten. "The mountain itself is the prison, Ramos. And I'm standing in the control room."

Above them, Madrid's voice rang out in fury that shook loose mortar from the ceiling: "Insignificant insects! You think your ancient stones can protect you? I have broken the will of the greatest wizards you could produce, on this sad lump of rock you call home! I have made glaciers weep! Your pathetic temple magic is nothing before the power of an emperor!"

The chamber shuddered again, but this time it wasn't from Madrid's attacks—it was from something far deeper, far older, stirring to wakefulness beneath their feet. The humming intensified until sound bypassed their ears entirely and spoke directly to their bones, issuing from the ground itself.

"Oh, this is getting interesting," Ramos said, his map beginning to hum as it absorbed the physical changes happening around them, its faceted surface throwing off sparks. "Niloo, I'm going to need you to synchronize with the Master Heart again. But this time, instead of connecting to the communication frequency, I want you to find the containment protocols."

"The what now?" Niloo asked, though she was already moving toward the blazing artifact, drawn by an instinct that felt older than conscious thought. She sensed her ancestor's call — blood to blood, bone to bone.

"Every magical prison needs a key," Ramos explained. "And every key needs someone with the proper authorization to turn it. The Master Heart chose you, which means you have access to systems that the Chaac built into this place millennia ago—systems that were designed to activate only in the most desperate circumstances, and only for the right person. I believe that person is you, Niloo. You are a heartbearer. And you are born into the family of Keepers of Samos."

"You want me to trap Madrid?" Niloo said, frowning at the wizard.

"I want you to remind him that there are consequences for dese-
crating holy ground while attacking with enslaved dragons," Ramos
replied. "I want you to show him what happens when you bring violence to a place built by people who understood that some things are
worth protecting at any cost. Remember your ancestors. Remember
the barrier."

The battle above intensified, as the younglings attacked the ground
forces brought by Madrid, and also Madrid himself. Screams rent the
air as dragonfire raked the ground. Soldier and guards dived for cover
and ran from the farm, desperate to escape the all consuming flame
that pursued them. In the sky above, Madrid's dragons, carrying the
male heartbearers, fought to protect Madrid. Wizards in their own
right, they cast spells that repelled the dragon fire back on the caster
and wove shields of protection. Through the network came Opaleye's
voice, filled with pain and rage and the terrible clarity of a being pushed
beyond endurance: *Kill me! I would rather die than harm my own
kind! Let my death break these cursed bonds!*

Never! Kora replied fiercely, her mental voice blazing with the absolute refusal of love confronted with loss. *We will find a way to free
you! We will not abandon you to this monster!*

But even as she spoke, they could hear the bronze dragon's cry
of pain as Opaleye's flame, directed by Madrid's will and the silver
tridents' compulsion, found its mark across her wing membrane. The
sound that pierced Niloo bringing tears to her eyes.

I burn my own kin, Opaleye's mental voice broke with anguish. *The
silver makes me weapon against those I love most. This is torment beyond
death.*

"Now, Niloo," Ramos urged, his usual theatrical manner giving
way to something deadly serious. "Before Madrid realizes what we're

doing. Before he forces Opaleye to do something that will break the great dragon's spirit entirely."

Niloo pressed her hands against the Master Heart's blazing surface, and the crystal was warm beneath her palms, humming with power that felt like the heartbeat of the world itself. Once again she felt her consciousness expand beyond the boundaries of her individual existence, but this time, instead of connecting to dragons, she felt herself sinking deeper into the mountain itself.

She followed pathways of power that had been carved into the living stone by the first builders—channels that glowed with their own inner light, conduits that had been waiting patiently for centuries to fulfill their purpose. The sensation was like diving into an ocean of liquid starlight, each current carrying her deeper into mysteries that predated written history.

And there, in the deepest foundations of the farmhouse buried beneath layers of stone and time and careful intention, she found them: the containment protocols, waiting with the patience of mountains for someone with the authority to activate them.

The knowledge flowed into her mind like water finding its course—complex runic sequences that described not just magical formulae, but philosophical principles. The first Chaac hadn't simply built a prison; they had created a system that could distinguish between different types of power, different intentions, different kinds of will.

"I can feel it," she gasped, her voice echoing strangely in the chamber as she spoke from both her physical location and the deeper realm of the mountain's consciousness. "The whole mountain is one giant magical cage. But Ramos, if I activate this, everyone above ground gets trapped—Madrid, Opaleye, all the other dragons..."

"Not if we're selective about it," Ramos said, his fingers dancing across his crystal device with increasingly frantic precision. "The beauty of ancient magic is that it was designed by people who understood nuance. We can create a barrier that contains Madrid while allowing the dragons to escape."

"How?" Niloo asked, even as she felt the containment protocols responding to her presence, recognizing her as someone with the right to command them.

"By teaching the mountain to recognize the difference between freedom and slavery," Ramos replied with the sort of manic enthusiasm that suggested either brilliance or complete madness. "Madrid's control magic has a distinct signature—it tastes of iron and desperation and the particular kind of emptiness that comes from trying to fill a soul-shaped hole with power over others. We just need to program the containment field to trap anyone generating that particular aura."

Above them, another anguished roar from Opaleye shook the chamber, and this time they could hear the sound of claws raking across dragon hide, the wet splash of blood hitting stone.

"I'll do it," Niloo said, her voice steady with resolve that surprised her. "Activating the containment."

She felt the ground respond to her command like a great engine coming to life after eons of sleep. The mountain itself seemed to take a deep breath, and suddenly the air in the chamber felt charged with potential, crackling with the kind of energy that preceded lightning strikes. The hair on her scalp rose as did the hair on her arms.

The harmonic humming they had heard earlier suddenly intensified into a sound that shivered through stone, testing the fabric of reality, a frequency that spoke of barriers and boundaries and the absolute authority of natural law.

And on the surface, invisible walls of force began to rise around the one being whose magical signature marked him as a enslaver of dragons and a destroyer of sacred places. The containment field manifested not as visible walls, but as a growing resistance to Madrid's power, a pushing-back that grew stronger with every spell he cast, every command he issued, every moment he continued to wield the silver tridents against Opaleye's will.

The final trap was closing, and for the first time in thirty years, Madrid was about to discover that there were still places in the world where his authority meant nothing, and powers older than his empire that would not bend to his will.

Chapter Twenty-Four

THE SIEGE OF FIRE RIDGE

The containment field around Madrid shimmered like heat waves rising from summer stone, but instead of trapping the Emperor, it seemed to be feeding his power. Through the Master Heart network, Niloo felt a surge of wrongness that made her crystal heart burn against her chest like a brand.

"Ramos," she gasped, her consciousness still partially merged with the mountain's ancient systems, "something's wrong. The containment isn't holding."

"Impossible," the wizard muttered, his crystal device flickering erratically as readings cascaded across its surface. "The protocols should recognize his enslavement magic, should be containing anyone who—" His pale blue eyes widened in sudden, terrible understanding. "Oh. Oh, that's really quite clever of him."

Above them, Madrid's laughter echoed off the mountainsides, carrying the sound of a man who had just realized his enemies had played directly into his hands. "Did you really think I hadn't studied your precious temple magic, you sanctimonious fools? I've had thirty years to prepare for this moment!"

Through the magical connection, they felt Opaleye's anguish spike as the silver tridents dug deeper into his neck, but Madrid's voice carried a different note now—satisfaction mixed with anticipation that sent ice through Niloo's veins.

"The containment field doesn't recognize me as the enslaver," Madrid continued, his amplified voice rolling across the battlefield like thunder, "because I'm not the one controlling the dragons directly. The silver tridents are. And according to your precious ancient magic, I'm simply a victim of circumstances, forced to wield tools I cannot abandon."

Ramos cursed in three languages, two of which Niloo didn't recognize. "He's twisted the containment protocols against themselves. The field thinks he's being controlled by the tridents rather than controlling through them."

"Can we override it?" Marcus demanded, his amber crystal blazing as he tried to reinforce their magical defenses.

"Not without risking bringing the entire mountain down on our heads," Ramos replied grimly. "The protocols are built into the fundamental structure of—"

His words were cut off as a massive concussion shook the chamber, sending several ancient books tumbling from their shelves. Through the Master Heart network came a burst of triumph from the liberated dragons above, followed immediately by Opaleye's roar of pain and fury.

We have broken free of the silver binding! Kora's mental voice blazed with fierce joy. *Opaleye flies with us again!*

But the celebration was short-lived. Even as Niloo felt her heart lift with hope, Madrid's cold laughter echoed through the chamber via magical amplification.

"One dragon freed, but not for long." he called out with casual dismissal. "But observe what your rebellion has truly accomplished."

The air above the chamber filled with a sound that made Niloo's blood run cold—the rhythmic beating of hundreds of wings, far too many to belong to the citadel dragons they had been fighting against. Through Lapis's consciousness, still connected to the network despite her hiding place in the volcanic caves, came images that stole the breath from Niloo's lungs.

The sky above Fire Ridge was darkening with an approaching army of dragons unlike anything she had ever seen. These weren't the magnificent creatures born free on Jintessa or even the enslaved younglings taken from their mothers' nests. These were something else entirely—dragons with scales that gleamed like polished steel, wings that moved with mechanical precision, and eyes that glowed with the cold light of cloned intelligence.

"My breeding program," Madrid announced with pride that made Niloo feel sick, "has proven more successful than even I anticipated. Behold the first clutch of my artificially enhanced dragons—cloned creatures born in slavery, knowing no loyalty except to their creator."

Abomination! Opaleye's mental roar carried the horror of a parent witnessing the mutilation of his children. *What have you done to them?*

"I have perfected them," Madrid replied with the satisfaction of a craftsman discussing his masterwork. "No inconvenient free will. No troublesome emotional attachments. No risk of rebellion or resistance. They are dragons reduced to their essential purpose—weapons of conquest that will carry my forces across the world and beyond."

Through the network, the heartbearers across Gaia could sense the approaching army's wrongness. These creatures carried no warmth, no life-spark of independent thought. They were dragons in form only, their minds replaced by magical manipulation that answered to Madrid's will alone.

"How many?" Elissa's voice gritted through clenched teeth, tight with controlled fear.

"The first cloned clutch numbered two hundred," Madrid replied, apparently enjoying their despair. "But that is merely the beginning. At Fire Ridge, the ancient breeding chambers hold eggs by the thousands. And now that your rebellion has so helpfully gathered all the Jintessa dragons into one convenient location, I can use their essence to awaken the remaining clutches simultaneously."

The implications hit Niloo like a physical blow. Madrid hadn't been caught off guard by their coordinated strikes—he had been herding them toward this moment. Every victory they had celebrated, every dragon they had freed, had simply gathered more power for him to harvest.

"The containment field," she realized with dawning horror. "It's not just failing to trap him—it's protecting him while he completes the ritual."

"Indeed," Madrid confirmed with cruel satisfaction. "Your ancestors built their protections too well. The field will prevent any outside
interference while I demonstrate the true scope of my achievements."

Through the Master Heart's expanded awareness, Niloo could feel
it beginning—a massive surge of elemental magic that drew power not from unwilling victims, but from the very air around Fire
Ridge. Madrid's created dragons had spread across the ancient breeding grounds, each one positioned at a precise point in a pattern to best
aid the completion of the task.

"He's using the cloned dragons as a focusing array," Niloo gasped.
"They're channeling the essence of the youngling dragons into the
fossilized eggs."

"And the younglings can't flee," Lazuli added with grim understanding, "because they won't abandon Opaleye and the others still
under Madrid's control." From the backs of the trapped dragons, a
cry of horror and screams of pain filled the air, as their bonded djinn
struggled to free their dragons from the onslaught.

Deep beneath Fire Ridge, the first of the ancient eggs vibrated,
cracks forming in the tough exterior of their fossilized shell, swelling in
response to the massive infusion of dragon essence. But these weren't
the warm, golden shells of natural dragon eggs. The epochal remains
cracked along unnatural lines, shattering into a thousand shards. The
sudden explosion revealed creatures that emerged and rapidly swelled
to the size of a full grown adult, predispositioned for absolute obedience.

My children, Opaleye's mental voice broke with grief as he watched
the first hatchlings take flight. *He has stolen even their moment of first
awakening.*

Through Lapis's eyes, Niloo watched the newborn dragons spread
across the sky with perfect formation flying, their movements syn-

chronized like a military parade. There was no curiosity in their eyes, no wonder at their first sight of the world. They emerged knowing only their purpose: to serve, to conquer, to kill on command.

"The siege has begun," Ramos said quietly, his usual theatrical manner subdued by the magnitude of what they faced. "And I'm afraid we're on the wrong side of the walls."

"Then we break them down," Niloo declared, her crystal heart blazing with determination. "The Master Heart can reach every heart-bearer in Gaia. We use that connection."

"To do what?" Marcus asked. "Madrid has two hundred dragons and thousands more hatching. Even with every free heartbearer working together—"

"We don't fight the cloned dragons," Niloo interrupted, her mind racing as a desperate plan began to form. "We give them something they've never had—a choice."

Ramos's eyebrows shot up with sudden understanding. "Oh, my dear, that's brilliantly inspired."

"Maybe," Niloo admitted. "But if we can reach the cloned dragons through the Master Heart network, if we can show them what freedom feels like, what our bonding tastes like then—"

"The magical compulsion might not be able to override direct exposure to free will," Lazuli said. "It would be like trying to stop someone from breathing by convincing them they don't need air."

Above them, the battle was shifting as Madrid's dragon army took positions around Fire Ridge. The Jintessa dragons found themselves vastly outnumbered, their natural flight patterns blocked by the mechanical precision of their artificial cousins.

We cannot fight them, Kora's voice came through the network, heavy with the weight of impossible choices. *They are still dragons, whatever Madrid has done to them. To kill them would be to murder children who never had the chance to experience life.*

Then find another way, said Lapis.

Opaleye replied with the iron determination of a leader who had lost too much to surrender now. *The heartbearers speak of choice. Perhaps it is time these young ones learned what that means. I will keep Madrid occupied. It is fortunate he cannot understand our dragon speech.*

Through the Master Heart, Niloo reach out to her sisters, and through them to their dragons, their Jintessa bondmates, and with Lapis' help, the Jintessa dragons took control of the contact. They reached out, not toward the youngling dragons fighting above, but toward the cloned ones following Madrid's commands. The connection felt wrong, like trying to grasp smoke or hold lightning. Where natural dragons blazed with individual personality and shared warmth, the artificial ones felt hollow, their consciousness replaced by cold conditioning.

But underneath the murky mind control, in the deepest cores of their being, something flickered. Not thought exactly, but potential for thought. Not freedom, but the capacity to understand what freedom might mean. She could sense an innocence about them. They were babes trapped in adult bodies.

"I can feel them," Niloo whispered, her awareness expanding to touch the blank minds that had never known they could question orders. "They're not empty, just...unawakened, Innocent."

"Then let's wake them up," Ramos said with a grin. "After all, what's the worst that could happen?"

Niloo drew on the strength of the heartbearers through the Master Heart, all lending their power to what might be the most audacious magic in Gaia history: the attempt to give consciousness to beings designed to have none, to offer choice to creatures bred for absolute obedience.

As the first tendrils of awakening awareness touched the cloned dragons' minds, some began to falter in their perfect formations. Wings that had moved with mechanical precision suddenly showed hesitation. Eyes that had glowed with cold programming flickered with something that might have been confusion.

And in the hidden chamber beneath the ruined farmhouse, Niloo felt the weight of their combined consciousness, lending their strength to the impossible task of teaching dragons how to dream.

If they succeeded in their desperate gamble—the battle for the minds of the newly hatched dragons might end not with conquest, but with the greatest liberation in the history of Gaia.

CHAPTER TWENTY-FIVE

BROTHERS IN ARMS

The first cloned dragon to break formation did so with a sound of breaking glass. It wasn't the physical cracking of crystal, but a deeper shattering of mental barriers that had erected to prevent them from doing exactly what they were doing, awakening their conscious mind. Through the Master Heart network, Niloo felt the moment of realization ripple outward like a stone thrown into still water, each wave touching another dragon and asking the same fundamental question:

Who am I?

Who are you?

"It's working," she gasped, her consciousness stretched thin across dozens of newly awakening minds. Each dragon that began to question its conditioning sent feedback through the network, a cascade of confusion and wonder that threatened to overwhelm her completely. "They're starting to—"

Her words were cut off as a familiar presence sliced through the magical connection like a razor sharp blade through silk. Cold, controlled, carrying the distinctive resonance of her brother's crystal heart but wrapped in layers of compulsion and barely restrained fury.

Sister. Darius's mental voice reached her through the network, but it felt wrong—fractured, as if he were speaking from the bottom of a deep well. *You must stop this. Now.*

Niloo could sense him approaching Fire Ridge from the eastern side, not alone but leading a squadron of Imperial forces. Mounted troops with crystal-tipped spears, mobile essence collectors, and most disturbing of all, a cadre of enhanced soldiers whose magical signatures blazed with the same wrongness as Madrid's dragon army.

"Darius is coming," she announced to the chamber, her voice tight with pain and conflicting emotions. "And he is not alone. He has some of those altered humans with him, the enhanced ones. Madrid must have called for reinforcements."

"Of course he is," Ramos said with the sort of grim satisfaction usually reserved for winning bets no one wanted to collect. "Madrid would never waste an opportunity for psychological warfare. What better way to break our concentration than to force you to fight your own brother?"

But through the network connection, Niloo could feel something else threading through Darius's surface thoughts—brief flashes of resistance, moments where his true self fought against the blood magic compulsion. He was trying to tell her something, sending fragmentary images and half-formed warnings through their sibling bond.

The excavation complex, came his broken mental voice, each word clearly causing him pain to transmit. *Deeper than... than you know. Madrid has been... experimenting. On himself. Changing. Not enti rely...human anymore.*

Darius' thoughts reached Niloo once more. *The enhanced sol diers... unstable. Programming conflicts with...with natural survival instincts. If they witness too much chaos... their loyalty breaks down. Madrid's control weakens.*

Niloo's communication crystal pulsed with agony. Darius was fighting the compulsion, but she could feel it tearing him apart. Each act of resistance was like pressing his hand against a red-hot iron. Madrid's blood magic punished defiance with agony that radiated through every nerve, every thought, every breath. That Darius could function at all, while fighting such compulsion, spoke to a strength of will that both humbled and terrified her.

Before she could respond, Madrid's amplified voice boomed across Fire Ridge. "Ah, my young pet arrives precisely on schedule," the Emperor announced. "Tell me, dear sister, how does it feel to know that your brother will be the instrument of your defeat? Surely you can feel his pain."

Wizard Ramos frowned, then muttered, "I can't see a damn thing here. I need to get to that ridge." His eyes swept around the room, before settling back on Niloo. "You must carry on in my absense, Niloo. I must go." Ramos tugged open the door to the tunnel they had used to escape once before, and disappeared down its passage. As he left, he emitted a sharp, high pitched whistle, calling for Betsy, and then broke into a jog, disappearing from sight.

The squadron of Imperial forces crested the ridge to the east, just as Wizard Ramos arrived at the summit. As usual, Betsy cared little for the antics of the dragons circling in the sky above. What interested her was the lush grass that poked out from the soil of the small clearing they were crossing. Ramos slid off Betsy's back, patted her nose and whispered, "Remember you are on a diet, dear," to which Betsy snorted and rolled her eyes. "I will be back shortly."

Ramos skirted the trees that lined the meadow, taking a deer trail up to the edge of a cliff that overlooked the most likely approach for an army on foot. He picked out a likely looking rock with an excellent view of the valley entrance, and sat down beside it, pulling an apple out of his pocket as he did so. Taking a big bite, he chewed, his sharp eyes watching the valley and the sky with equal measure. Finishing the apple, he tossed the core aside and then pointed his index finger at the sky and swirled it in a circling motion. A hazy cloud settled over him, hiding him from view.

Next he pulled out a scrying tablet and set it on the ground. He tapped the surface and then zoomed in on the image of the mouth of the valley, watching as the first of the spelled and altered farmers-turned-soldiers crested the rise, Darius at their head. Even from this distance he could see the changes the blood magic had wrought—his movements too precise, his posture rigid with unnatural control. The red crystal at his throat pulsed with sickly light, and thin lines of silver traced along his arms where the compulsion magic had burned permanent marks into his skin.

Darius raised his hand to signal a halt, then turned in his saddle to address his troops. Ramos couldn't hear his words from his hiding place, but he could sense their effect through the network—confusion, hesitation, then growing uncertainty among the enhanced soldiers as whatever he said contradicted their orders.

"Oh, that clever boy," Ramos murmured with delight, as he studied the man. "He's not leading them to attack us—he's leading them into position for something else entirely."

"He's going to use Madrid's own troops against him," Ramos realized with a surge of hope. "That is so dangerous! But well worth the cost

*****

Above Fire Ridge, the dragons' awareness was accelerating. Those who had begun to question were now actively disobeying, hovering uncertainly in the air as their newly awakened consciousness grappled with concepts like choice and individual will. The perfect formations Madrid had deployed were dissolving into chaos as dragon after dragon broke from their assigned positions. They neither attacked nor fled, but milled about in confusion, lost children without a parent.

Madrid straightened in his saddle, head turning in the direction where the Fire Ridge lay. With a snarl, he forced Opaleye to abandon the farm and fly to meet up with Madrid's army on foot. Niloo watched him disappear, knowing that he now sought her brother, that he could sense rebellion in the air.

Madrid arrived just in time to witness the break down of the hatchling's obedience. His fury broke with a rage so intense it seemed to heat the very air around Fire Ridge. "Impossible! The mind control is absolute! They should not be able to resist my commands!"

But even as he spoke, Opaleye's ancient wisdom cut through the Emperor's self denial with devastating clarity: *You cannot enslave the soul, Madrid. You can only postpone its awakening. We are not beasts.*

The great dragon's words seemed to trigger something in the cloned dragons—a cascade of realization that spread through their ranks like wildfire. They had been created as weapons, but they were also drag-ons. And dragons, by their very nature, were meant to choose their own paths.

"Madrid is losing control of his perfect little army," Ramos said to Betsy, with fierce satisfaction. Betsy raised her head, blurbled around her mouthful of grass, and went back to eating. "Ah, but he is not always the smartest, when his greed takes hold. And we know Madrid is a greedy one."

But their moment of triumph was shattered as Darius's squadron finally reached the base of Fire Ridge. The soldiers had arrived with military precision, but Ramos could detect telltale signs that their conditioning was beginning to fray. Some moved with jerky, uncer-tain motions. Others had stopped following orders entirely and were staring at their surroundings in confusion.

But Madrid's arrival changed all of that. As Opaleye swooped low over the army, Madrid pressed a button on a silvery bracelet attached to his right wrist. The pulse flashed across the area, and slammed down into the minds of the soldiers, washing away Darius' influence, with brutal efficiency.

*****

Now, Darius's mental voice cut through the network, clearer than it had been since Madrid's control had tightened around him. *While Madrid is distracted. The excavation complex—entrance hidden be-neath the eastern slope. Stone marked with... with the old symbols. Spiral carved into granite. Hurry, Niloo.*

"He's creating an opening for us," Niloo said, already moving to-ward the chamber's exit. "But we need to move quickly."

"Absolutely not," her father said firmly, blocking her path. "That's obviously a trap. Madrid is using your brother to lure you into the open."

"No," Niloo replied with certainty that surprised her. "Darius is fighting Madrid's control. This might be our only chance to find where the Emperor is conducting his experiments. And it might be our only chance to free him," she added.

"She's right. Madrid's attention is entirely focused on maintaining control over his dissolving dragon army. He won't expect a ground assault on his primary operation," said Lazuli.

They could feel the battle shifting to Fire Ridge where the cloned dragons struggled with their newfound consciousness. Some had chosen to join the fight against their creator, while others simply fled, overwhelmed by the sudden weight of independent thought. The Citadel dragons chased after Opaleye, flying swiftly to catch up to the great dragon. and soon joined the chaos on the ridge.

But under cover of that chaos, Madrid himself had vanished from the aerial battlefield. Opaleye flew on alone.

"Where is he?" Lazuli asked, his djinn senses probing the magic flashing above Fire Ridge.

Underground, came Opaleye's urgent mental voice. *I felt him descend into the mountain itself. He retreats to complete something—something that requires him to be physically present at the source.*

"The final phase," Jannah's voice came through the network, heavy with growing dread. "The texts speak of rituals that can only be completed by standing in the heart of the dragon nesting grounds, surrounded by the awakening eggs."

"Then that's where we need to be," Niloo said with finality. "Lapis, can you reach us?"

The sky is chaos, her dragon companion replied through their bond. *But I can navigate through to you. I will meet you at the end of the tunnel.*

As they prepared to leave the relative safety of the hidden chamber, Niloo felt a surge of complex emotion through her connection with Darius. Relief that she had understood his message, fear for what they might find in the excavation complex, and underneath it all, a desperate hope that their bond might prove stronger than Madrid's blood magic.

Be careful, Darius whispered, his voice fading as Madrid's attention turned back to controlling his wayward servant. *The things he's done to himself...he's no longer the man who conquered Gaia. He's become something else. Something worse.*

The warning sent ice through Niloo's veins, but it also strengthened her resolve. Whatever Madrid had become, whatever horrors waited in the depths of Fire Ridge, her brother was down there fighting for his freedom with every fiber of his being.

It was time to bring that fight to its conclusion, one way or another.

As they emerged from the hidden chamber into the morning light, the sky above Fire Ridge painted itself in the colors of war—dragon fire in gold and crimson, the silver gleam of spelled weapons, and the strange, cold blue of brutal magic pushed beyond its limits. But on the eastern slope, almost hidden among the natural rock formations, Niloo could see it: a spiral carved into granite, marking an entrance that predated Madrid's excavations by millennia.

The path lay open before them. Now they just had to survive what waited at its end.

CHAPTER TWENTY-SIX

THE DRAGON'S GAMBIT

The entrance to Madrid's excavation complex yawned before them like the mouth of some ancient predator, carved stone spirals worn smooth by countless centuries of wind and rain. But as Niloo approached the threshold, her crystal heart began to pulse with warning—not the gentle warmth of connection, but the sharp, urgent beat that spoke of immediate danger.

"Wait," she whispered, pressing her palm against the granite archway. Through the stone, she could feel vibrations that had nothing to do with the battle raging above Fire Ridge. "Something's wrong. The excavation isn't empty."

Lazuli shifted to the form of a mouse and darted into the tunnel entrance, his djinn senses probing the darkness ahead. He returned within moments, reforming into his humanoid shape with an expression of grim concern.

"Guards," he reported quietly. "But not Imperial soldiers—something else. Their magical signatures feel... hollow. Like the artificial dragons, but wrong in a different way."

Through the Master Heart network came Lapis's urgent mental voice: *Niloo, I'm approaching your position, but the sky battle has taken an unexpected turn. More fossilized eggs are hatching, but these aren't responding to Madrid's control at all.*

Above them, the mountain rumbled, as the earth heaved, large boulders bouncing down the slope, echoing through the valley of Fire Ridge, as another section of the ancient breeding chambers cracked open. But this time, instead of the mechanical precision of Madrid's artificial army, what emerged carried the wild, untamed fury of dragons who had been sleeping in stone for millennia.

Ancient ones, Opaleye's mental voice blazed with recognition and hope. *The First Clutch awakens. These are the eggs of my ancestors—dragons who chose stone sleep rather than submit to the wars that destroyed our original realm.*

"That's not possible," Ramos said, though his crystal device was flickering with readings that suggested otherwise. "The First Clutch was destroyed in the Sundering Wars. Everyone knows that."

Everyone was wrong, came a new voice through the network—ancient beyond measure, carrying the weight of eons spent in patient dreaming. *We chose preservation over destruction. Stone sleep rather than endless war. And now, in this realm's hour of need, we wake.*

The voice belonged to a dragon unlike any Niloo had ever imagined. Through Lapis's eyes, she watched as a creature of living starlight emerged from the cracking stone, its scales shifting between colors that had no names in any mortal language. Where Madrid's artificial dragons moved with mechanical precision, this ancient being's magic flowed like a waterfall, each movement an expression of power carefully leashed.

I am Stellaris, the dragon announced, its mental voice carrying harmonics that made the mountain itself sing in response. *First of the Star-Born, Last of the Dream-Weavers. And I am... displeased... with what has been done to my sleeping kindred.*

"Oh, this changes everything," Ramos breathed, his eyes bright mischief. "Madrid's been so focused on controlling artificial dragons and enslaved Jintessa natives that he never considered what would happen if the original inhabitants of Gaia decided to wake up and object to his renovations."

Through the network, they could feel Madrid's shock as more ancient dragons emerged from their stone cocoons. These weren't the young, trainable creatures he had expected to command, but beings whose power and wisdom had been accumulating in crystalline dreams for thousands of years.

You dare to disturb our sacred breeding grounds? Stellaris's voice audibly broke through the noise and confusion of battle, hard as a whip. The sound staggered the flying dragons, startling them like a flock of birds. *You dare to corrupt the eggs of the unborn with your selfish perversions?*

Madrid's response came not in words but in action—a blast of dark magic that should have reduced any normal dragon to ash. Instead, it struck Stellaris's starlight scales and seemed to simply... disappear, absorbed into the cosmic radiance that surrounded the ancient being.

Interesting, Stellaris observed with the detached curiosity of a scholar examining an unusual specimen. *Your power tastes of stolen essence and forced bindings with humans. How... predictable.*

But even as the ancient dragons emerged to challenge Madrid's authority, Niloo felt her brother's presence flicker in the network—a brief moment of clarity before Madrid's control clamped down again with savage intensity.

Sister, Darius's mental voice was barely a whisper, strained by the effort of maintaining even momentary connection. *He's not in the complex. This entrance is... is a trap. The real excavation is deeper. Much deeper. Where the mountain bleeds fire.*

Before she could respond, the tunnel entrance behind them erupted with movement as Madrid's guards emerged into the daylight. But these weren't the enhanced soldiers they had expected—they were something far worse.

The men that shambled up from the tunnel entrance had once been like them—men who had worn crystal hearts and bonded with dragons. But Madrid's experiments had hollowed them out, leaving only empty shells animated by mechanical purpose. Their crystals had turned black as coal, and their eyes held no spark of individual consciousness.

Niloo staggered back, as Lazuli stepped between her and the guards. "Heartbearers," Niloo gasped, her crystal flaring with recognition and horror. "They're corrupted heartbearers. He's been using the captured heartbearers as test subjects," Furious, Niloo drew her weapon, as Lazuli prepared a nasty invention of his own, his djinn form flickering between states as rage disrupted his concentration. "He's been using them as prototypes for his mental hijacking experiments."

"Not prototypes," Ramos corrected grimly, his usual theatrical manner stripped away by the magnitude of Madrid's atrocity. "Failures. The ones who couldn't survive the process fully but weren't quite dead enough to stop functioning."

The hollow heartbearers moved with jerky, unnatural motions, their blackened crystals pulsing with the same cold light as Madrid's cloned dragons. But where the dragons had been created with at least the potential for consciousness, these beings were truly empty—consciousness scooped out and replaced with simple, violent mind control.

"We need to get past them," Niloo said, her crystal heart blazing with determination even as it ached for the people these creatures had once been. "If Darius is right about the deeper excavation—"

Her words were cut off as Lapis landed with ground-shaking force in the clearing around the tunnel entrance. The great dragon's lapis lazuli scales were marked with fresh battle scars, and her eyes blazed with fury. *Get behind me. Now. You cannot face these creatures alone.*

Niloo and Lazuli didn't need to be told twice. They dashed around the backside of Lapis, while the dragon breathed fire, sweeping it across the entrance and forcing the male heartbearers to retreat.

The ancient ones fight alongside us now, Lapis reported through their bond, even as she interposed her massive bulk between the hollow heartbearers and Niloo's group. *But Madrid has revealed his true form. He is no human, Niloo. The experiments he performed on himself have transformed him into something that should not exist. Part djinn and something else now.*

Through the network came images that made Niloo's blood run cold—Madrid as he truly was now, his human appearance maintained only through illusion. The reality was a twisted amalgamation of stolen dragon essence, corrupted heartbearer magic, and something else entirely. Something that hungered for the complete domination of all living beings.

He seeks to become a god, Stellaris's ancient voice carried a note of disgust that resonated through every dragon in the network. *Not of creation, but of absolute control. He would remake consciousness itself in his image, until every thinking being becomes merely an extension of his will.*

"The hollow heartbearers," Ramos realized with dawning horror. "They're not failed experiments—they're successful prototypes. This is what he plans to do to everyone."

Above Fire Ridge, the battle had devolved into confusion. Ancient dragons wielding starlight and dream-fire clashed with Madrid's remaining artificial army, while the newly awakened cloned dragons struggled to choose sides in a conflict that they did not understand. The Jintessa dragons fought alongside their ancient cousins, as they fought to bring the hatchlings under control. Opaleye flew between them all, roaring his fury and commanding the dragons to stand down.

But through it all, Madrid himself remained elusive, his true location hidden somewhere in the depths of Fire Ridge where the mountain's volcanic heart provided power for workings that threatened the very nature of consciousness itself.

"The deeper excavation," Niloo said, her mind racing through possibilities. "If it's where the mountain bleeds fire, that would be—"

"The original dragon nursery," Jannah's voice came through the network with the weight of temple knowledge. "The first nesting site, where dragons learned to channel volcanic energy into the creation of new life. If Madrid has access to that power source, it would be very bad for us."

She didn't need to finish the thought. With the fundamental forces that had shaped the first dragons at his command, Madrid could corrupt consciousness on a scale that would encompass not just Gaia, but every realm connected to the Dragon Crossroads.

"We have to reach him," Niloo declared, her crystal heart pulsing with desperate determination. "Before he completes whatever he's planning."

Then we go through them, Lapis said simply, her great head turning toward the hollow heartbearers with the grim resolve of someone who had accepted the necessity of mercy through violence.

As Lapis breathed deep blue fire that sang with the harmony of true crystal resonance, the hollow heartbearers' blackened crystals began to crack and shatter. For just a moment, Niloo thought she saw something flicker in their empty eyes—not consciousness returning, but perhaps the peace of finally being allowed to rest.

The path to the deeper excavation lay open before them, leading down into the volcanic heart of Fire Ridge where the final confrontation with Madrid would occur. But first they needed to go through the heartbearers who guarded the path. But as they descended into the mountain's burning depths, Niloo couldn't shake the feeling that they would be walking not toward victory, but toward a trap that had been decades in the making—one that would test not just their power, but their very understanding of what it meant to be alive, aware, and free.

Niloo exchanged a look with Lapis and Lazulin, then with a roar, they attacked.

CHAPTER TWENTY-SEVEN
CROSSROADS

immortality

Deep within the volcanic heart of Fire Ridge, where the mountain's molten blood flowed through channels carved by the first dragons, Madrid stood before an apparatus of his own invention. The device rose from the bowl of the cavern floor like a crystalline tree, its roots reaching toward natural lava tubes that glowed with primordial fire. But this was no mere magical construct—it was a perversion of the very forces that had created the Dragon Crossroads, a tool designed to tear holes in the fabric of reality itself.

His human form flickered like a failing illusion, revealing glimpses of what he had become through decades of self-experimentation. Where once he had been merely ambitious, his thirst for dominion had pushed him to delve deeper into ways to preserve his body. His potions no longer worked. Possessing the bodies of others had also been abandoned as his body weakened. His quest for immortality had become his obsession. Lesions erupted from his spine in a mockery of dragon scales. Tremors caused his hands to shake, a condition he was careful to hide from everyone. Even his eyes had changed, darkening so that they absorbed the light.

But in this place, anything was possible. Here he could change his nature, become one of an infinite variation of what he could be, of what he should be, what he must be to bring everything under his absolute control.

"Thirty years," he whispered to the empty cavern. "Thirty years of careful planning, of meticulous preparation, and now it unravels because of a theatrical fool who treats cosmic power like entertainment."

Above him, transmitted through the network of crystal formations that honeycombed Fire Ridge, he could feel his perfect army dissolving into chaos. The dragons he had spent tme creating were choosing—*choosing*!—to disobey his commands. The ancient dragons, who should have remained safely dormant in their stone sleep, were wakening, and had power that made his own seem weak.

And through it all, Ramos's insufferable laughter echoed through the magical frequencies, turning Madrid's rage into something that threatened to crack the mountain itself.

"He thinks this is amusing," Madrid snarled, as he adjusted the flow of elements into the spelled silver bowl in which he stood. The crystaline tree flattened and became a plinth which rose under his feet, lifting him clear of the potion in which he had been healing. "He thinks consciousness is some grand joke to be shared freely, some cosmic jest that improves with repetition."

Madrid made a few more adjustments to the mixture below, then picked up his trident and touched the runes circling the rim of the bowl. The runes flashed and then settled down into a lava red flicker of energized silver. The bowl hummed, responding to his touch, its crystal structure resonating with frequencies that hadn't been heard since the Sundering Wars. Through its faceted surface, Madrid could see glimpses of other realms—worlds where his authority had never been questioned, realities where magic was bent to his will without the tiresome complications of free choice.

"But I understand the truth," he continued, his voice echoing around the chamber. "Magic is chaos. Free will is entropy. Only through absolute control can existence achieve perfect order."

A tremor ran through the cavern as one of the Crossroads pathways began to respond to his summons—not the careful, controlled opening he had originally planned, but a desperate tearing that sent cracks of displaced reality through the volcanic stone. Where the cracks touched, the laws of physics became negotiable. Gravity flowed sideways. Light bent into impossible colors. The very concept of "here" and "there" became fluid.

Madrid could sense his remaining forces above. Darius fought the blood magic compulsion with increasing desperation, each act of resistance burning through his nervous system like liquid fire. His enhanced soldiers were breaking down entirely, their altered bodies failing. They had not been strong enough to adapt to their new powers, which consumed their bodies resources at an accelerated rate. All was not lost however. The brutality of the procedure would act as a deterrent, and a failed experiment could be used as punishment.

"Even my own tools rebel," Madrid observed with clinical detachment. "Decades of planning and work, years of careful reinforcement, and still the chaos of individual will, contaminates my plans."

Another pathway began to tear open, this one leading to a realm where Madrid could see himself—but a version where he had never been exiled from Jintessa, where he ruled both worlds with the absolute authority he deserved. The alternative Madrid turned to look through the dimensional rift, his expression carrying the cold satisfaction of someone whose plans had proceeded exactly as intended.

"You could join me," the other Madrid suggested, his voice carrying across dimensional barriers with ease. "Abandon this failing realm. In my reality, the heartbearers never learned to resist, the dragons never awakened from stone sleep, and that fool of a wizard was silenced before he could interfere."

The temptation was real, visceral, calling to every part of Madrid that was tired of fighting. But accepting such an offer would mean admitting defeat, acknowledging that his vision for Gaia had been flawed from its inception.

"No," he snarled. "This realm will serve. These people will submit. Their magic will be rewritten until it acknowledges me as the absolute authority."

He turned back to the Crossroads apparatus, his hands moving swiftly over the device as reports continued flooding through his crystal network. The ancient dragon Stellaris had joined the battle above, wielding starlight magic that reduced his most sophisticated weapons to a child's toy. The liberated dragons were coordinating with their ancient cousins, creating a unified force that challenged his air superiority for the first time in decades.

And somewhere in the tunnels below, he could sense familiar signatures approaching—Niloo, her dragon, her djinn, and most infuriating of all, Ramos with his cosmic irreverence and reality-bending humour.

"They think they can stop me," Madrid whispered. "They think they understand the game. Magic is not some sacred principle that cannot be changed, some fundamental force that resists all attempts at improvement. Magic is formed from base elements—earth, wind, fire, water and air—and there, its basic code can be rewritten."

His hands moved across the apparatus with increasing speed, forcing more pathways to open despite the catastrophic instability such hasty work created. Through the dimensional rifts, he could see reflections of himself—versions from realities where he had already achieved perfect control, where consciousness bent to his will as naturally as gravity pulled objects toward planetary centers.

"But I have learned truths they refuse to acknowledge," he muttered. "Consciousness is not sacred—it is inefficient. Free will is not noble—it is wasteful. Choice is not a gift—it is a disease that weakens the perfect order of existence."

The first rift to fully form did so right there in the cavern. With a blinding flash, the fabric of time and space ripped open. Through the largest rift stepped a version of himself that carried no trace of humanity whatsoever—consciousness distilled into pure will, existence refined into absolute control. This Madrid was true to his original human appearance but carrying weapons and abilities that had been developed in other realities where resistance had been crushed before it could flourish.

"Behold the future," Madrid declared to the empty cavern, though his words were transmitted through the crystal network to every corrupted heartbearer still under his control. "Unity of purpose. Perfection of order. The end of the chaos that has plagued existence since consciousness first learned to question authority."

But even as he spoke, reality continued to crack around the unstable pathways. The volcanic cavern began to shift and warp, as the cavern fought to exist in multiple dimensions simultaneously.

Through it all, Madrid worked with the desperate intensity of someone who had committed everything to a single gambit. He could feel Niloo approaching through the tunnels, could sense Ramos's insufferable confidence as the wizard led his small group toward what should have been certain death.

"Let them come," Madrid snarled, once again talking to himself. "Let them witness the birth of perfect order. Let them see what the mind becomes when it is finally freed from the burden of choice."

The Crossroads apparatus pulsed with unstable energy, tearing holes in reality that revealed glimpses of realms where Madrid's vision had already triumphed.

"The convergence begins," both Madrids spoke in unison, their voices creating standing waves that made the cavern's reality even more fluid. "Soon, all possible versions of resistance will face the futility of opposing inevitable order."

Above them, the battle for Fire Ridge continued but in the volcanic heart of the mountain, Madrid prepared to end not just the rebellion, but the very concept of rebellion itself.

And in the tunnels below, Niloo and her companions descended toward a confrontation that would determine whether existence itself would retain the chaotic beauty of free will, or surrender to the perfect, sterile order of Madrid's ultimate vision.

CHAPTER TWENTY-EIGHT

DEPTHS OF FIRE

The male heartbearers didn't put up much of a fight in the end. Lapis had seen to that. Laying down a sweeping jet of dragonfire, she had made short work of clearing the entrance. Niloo could still smell the stench of charred flesh, hear the pop of cracking bones. They hadn't even screamed when the white hot flame enveloped them. Short minutes later, nothing remained of the two male heart bearers, but a smear of ash, which Niloo stepped gingerly over as she lead them into the cave.

It wasn't even a fair fight. What can stand up to dragon fire?

It was a mercy. Do not be disturbed by their death. They were nothing but an empty shell, no longer alive, said Lapis.

I just wish I had at least known their names, said Niloo, as they rounded a corner and began their descent. A faint light surrounded them as they walked, although she could see no light source. The soft glow clung to the rocky walls, providing just enough illumination for them to see the path before them. The passage was wide enough for them to walk side by side, dragon, human and djinn.

The volcanic tunnels beneath Fire Ridge felt as though they were travelling through the arteries of some vast, dreaming dragon. The walls pulsed with a gentle heat that had nothing to do with molten stone. Warm and comforting, it felt more like a mother's embrace.

With each step they took into the mountain's heart, the triad bond grew more intense, more intimate, as if the ancient magic saturating the bedrock was amplifying their connection in ways none of them fully understood.

The boundaries between us are thinning, Lazuli observed, his djinn form flickering more rapidly than usual as dimensional instabilities affected his ability to maintain consistent shape. *I can feel your heartbeat, Niloo, as clearly as my own pulse. And Lapis—your memory of sunrise over Jintessa's peaks feels like my memory.*

Niloo pressed her palm against the tunnel wall, feeling the mountain's volcanic heartbeat synchronize with her own pulse. Through the stone, she could sense something vast and patient stirring to awareness—not Madrid's corrupted magic, but older forces that had been sleeping since the first dragons shaped this land. The crystal heart against her chest had grown so warm it was almost uncomfortable, its facets throwing rainbow patterns across the walls as they walked along the corridor.

The ancient nesting chambers remember, Lapis communicated, her dragon consciousness reaching into the bedrock to touch memories crystallized in stone over millennia. *They remember the first clutches laid here, the songs that shaped these tunnels, the dreams that dragons shared while their eggs incubated in volcanic warmth.*

Through their enhanced bond, Niloo could access fragments of those ancient memories—glimpses of Gaia when it was young, when dragons and early humans worked together to shape a world where life could flourish in countless different forms. The contrast with Madrid's vision, of a sterile world absent of all magic, was so stark it made her heart ache with loss.

Something else stirs, she said, her human intuition picking up a wrongness that her companions' enhanced senses confirmed and amplified. *Madrid's presence is corrupting the natural magic of this sacred place.*

The deeper they descended, the more apparent the corruption became. Where the ancient tunnels should have pulsed with the life-affirming rhythms of draconic creation, Madrid's influence had introduced a discordant and jarring magic that made the sensitive stone writhe in pain. Formations that should have sung with harmonic beauty instead produced jarring notes that hurt the ear.

He is using the mountain's own power against itself, Lapis growled, *The volcanic forces and elemental magic, that once shaped dragon eggs into the cradle of life, are being perverted.*

The reality distortions are getting worse, Lazuli added, acutely sensitive to the dimensional stress fractures that were appearing with increasing frequency. *Madrid's experiments are not just violating the laws of this magic—they are breaking the fundamental rules that keep magic stable.*

As if triggered by their words, the tunnel ahead began to shift and warp, the walls softened into liquid stone while the ceiling faded away. Images flashed across the ceiling and flowed down the walls, and their world became a window into impossible vistas and events. Time slowed then sped up and through the dimensional tears, they caught glimpses of other realities—other worlds where Madrid had already succeeded, where free will and magic had been wiped out of existance.

Do not look too closely, Lapis warned, recognizing the danger of alternate-reality exposure. *Those visions are not mere illusions—they are real and dangerous. If you allow yourself to be pulled in, you may not return. Madrid is attempting to convince us that resistance is futile, that Madrid's victory is inevitable and assured across all possible timelines.*

But even as she spoke, Niloo felt the seductive pull of those other worlds, the terrible logic of surrender disguised as wisdom. In one reality, she saw herself kneeling before Madrid's throne, her crystal heart dulled to grey compliance, her face empty of everything that made her who she was. In another, dragons flew in perfect formations, their individual personalities erased in favor of military precision.

This is the future, the visions seemed to whisper. *Why struggle against inevitability? Why choose to continue your suffering? Surrender and find peace.*

She paused, staring at the vision. *It would be so nice to not have to fight anymore. To have peace at last.*

"But that is not peace," Niloo replied, speaking loudly, just to hear her own voice. The sound steadied her, despite the fear that tried to paralyze her. "I would rather die as myself than live as Madrid's puppet."

And I would rather face extinction as a free dragon than accept eternity as a controlled one, Lapis added, fierce courage blazing through the bond.

I would rather fragment across infinite realities than exist as a single trapped soul in Madrid's vision of order, Lazuli concluded, his shapeshifting nature embracing chaos over sterile control.

Their unified rejection of Madrid's seductive visions sent ripples through the dimensional distortions, and suddenly the tunnel solidified around them once more. But the effort of resisting the alternate-reality assault had cost them—all three felt drained, their bond strained by the pressure of maintaining individual identity against forces designed to eliminate it.

We are approaching the source, Lapis observed, senses detecting massive magical workings somewhere ahead. *Whatever Madrid is doing in the deepest chambers, it is affecting the entire mountain. Volcanic forces are being tampered with.*

Through the Master Heart network, which remained active despite the reality distortions, they could feel the other heartbearers lending them strength.. But those distant connections felt thin, stretched by the dimensional chaos Madrid's experiments were creating.

If he succeeds in whatever he is attempting, Lazuli said grimly, *the damage may spread far beyond Gaia. The pathways between worlds that we seal may be the least of our concerns if he manages to destabilize the fundamental laws that govern consciousness itself.*

The tunnel ahead opened into a chamber so vast their light couldn't reach its far walls, but what they could see made all three of them stop in horror. The ancient dragon nursery had been transformed into something that defied description—part magical laboratory, part dimensional rift. Dragon eggs littered the floor like dropped candy, scattered and lying every which way around the cavern.

In the center of the chamber was a large shallow bowl hollowed out of the stone floor, where normally the female dragon would sleep. But there was no dragon. Instead, the bowl had been lined with spelled silver to create a vessel and that vessel was filled to the brim with an unknown potion. Wisps of smoke rose from the surface, and a sulpher like smell rose filled Niloo's nose. Runes etched into the rim of the bowl glowed a deep, dark red of lava. Above the potion floated a crystal plinth and on the plinth stood Madrid.

He flickered, much like Lazuli flickered, when shifting between forms, only Madrid's changes were rapid and continuous. They had suspected that the emperor was not human, and this confirmed it. But Madrid's shifting wasn't of this dimension. He faded in and out, as though tasting other dimensions, other worlds. At the sound of their entry, his head turned and his malevolent eyes pinned them to the spot.

In response to Madrid's manipulations, the chamber itself pulsed with elemental magic. The elements of fire and earth were being harvested from the chamber that had birthed thousands of dragons. Fine streams of rock bounced and shivered across the floor, flowing toward the basin. Small fissures in the floor leaked magma in a constant stream, heating up the bowl. The walls heaved as though they breathed, the floors that rippled with sensations Niloo could feel through the thin soles of her boots. The ceiling dripped with moisture, falling like tears onto the dragon eggs below. This was where Madrid had been conducting his recent experiments, attacking not just minds, but the very nature of magic itself.

Madrid's smile widened as he watched understanding bloom on their faces. Still, he made no move to harm them.

He is attempting to rewrite the fundamental laws of magic, Lazuli whispered.

The fossilized dragon eggs, Lapis added, *he is using their life-force to power changes that will affect magic across all realities.*

Niloo knelt, keeping one eye on Madrid, then reached out and placed a hand on a ancient dragon egg. Surprise flickered across her face. These were not the warm, life-filled shells Niloo had imagined she would find. They were cold, lifeless. Yet she sensed a powerful concentration of intelligence locked away inside, storing the accumulated knowledge and dreams of a species that had chosen extinction over corruption.

This is why the ancient dragons went into the stone sleep, Lapis realized, her voice heavy with grief and rage. *They were not fleeing the Sundering Wars—they were preserving their essence so it could not be corrupted by beings like Madrid. They chose voluntary dormancy to prevent their power from being used for evil.*

And now he uses their sacrifice to fuel his twisted vision of perfection, Niloo said, her crystal blazing against her chest as it responded to her fury. *He's turning their willing martyrdom into unwilling collaboration.*

Through the triad bond, she felt her companions' outrage, their shared hunger to stop Madrid's desecration of everything they had ever known. But they also felt their own limitations—three individuals, however well bonded, facing magic they had never encountered before.

The chamber is designed to prevent interference, Lazuli observed. *Anyone who enters his lair without Madrid's permission will find their consciousness gradually absorbed into his experiments. We are already being affected—I can feel my sense of individual identity beginning to fray.*

And yet we cannot retreat, Lapis replied, her courage refusing to yield to the rising terror they all felt. *If Madrid completes whatever he is attempting here, there will be nowhere to retreat to.*

Then we go forward, Niloo declared. *Not as three individuals trying to stop an cosmic force, but as representatives of every mind that has ever chosen freedom over security, complexity over simplicity, hope over despair.*

Through the network, she felt the response of dozens of consciousness freely choosing to lend their strength—not surrendering their individuality, but sharing it in service of something greater than any single will. The chamber's absorption effects, designed to drain isolated minds, found themselves facing collective resistance that grew stronger through connection rather than weaker through division.

For freedom, Lapis said.

For the right to become more, to become anything, and everything, Lazuli added.

For the future we choose to create together, Niloo concluded, her human voice carrying the weight of every individual mind that refused to surrender its essential nature to someone else's vision of improvement.

Madrid looked up from his work at the chamber's heart. A slight smirk of amusement twisted his thin lips, but his eyes held cold calculation. When he spoke, his voice echoed eerily around the chamber, shocking their ears with sudden sound.

"Children," he said, his voice thick with condescension, "you arrive just in time to witness the birth of perfect order. How appropriate that the last, poor representatives of chaotic magic should be present for its transformation into something more useful."

Niloo glanced over at her two companions. The bond pulsed with shared determination, three minds that had chosen each other, preparing to face the ultimate test.

Who would triumph?

CHAPTER TWENTY-NINE

THE MASTER'S HEART

The descent through Fire Ridge's volcanic tunnels felt like traveling through the arteries of some vast, sleeping giant. The walls pulsed with heat that had nothing to do with mere molten rock—this was the accumulated warmth of dragon magic, crystallized into stone over millennia and now awakening to the sound of battle above. With each step deeper into the mountain's heart, Ramos felt a growing weight of magical instability. The air felt thick with corruption. He reached up and swept his hand along the wall of the tunnel. The stone shivered beneath his touch. But underneath it all, he sensed something else—a growing wrongness that spoke of fundamental forces being pushed beyond their limits.

Frowning, he quickened his pace. "Madrid's machinations will destabilize the entire region," he muttered to himself. "Damn fool. He will kill us all."

Ahead, the passage opened into a cavern so vast, that his conjured ball of light couldn't reach its far walls—but it wasn't the cavern's size that stole Ramos' breath.

It was what waited at its center.

Across the cavern, he could see Niloo, Lazuli and Lapis, also examining the scene. Niloo crouched beside a stone egg, while Lapis moved to place her large body inbetween Madrid and the heartbearer. She moved with a delicate grace, her large feet careful to not step on any of the scattered eggs.

Madrid stood in the center of a spelled silver bowl on a plinth, manipulating multiple flows of elements and combining them with the assistance of an apparatus made of crystal. Light flashed around the device, and activated runes pulsed an angry red.

"Ah," Madrid said without turning from his work, his voice carrying easily to Ramos' ears. "The heartbearer has arrived. And of course, there is Ramos. How predictable."

Around the apparatus, reality had become fluid. Dimensional rifts were opening above Madrid, to places and times and worlds where Madrid's vision had already triumphed—realms where there were no heartbearers, no witches or wizards, where magic and those that could wield it were extinct, or never had been born. And those who's very natures survived because of magic, were no more. No dragons. No unicorns, no elemental creatures. All realities that Madrid wished to rule.

Ramos could feel the pull of wrongness against his magic. The rifts sought to undo the magic of his reality, sucking everything into the void. Stay too long, close to the rift, and he would be emptied of what essence he commanded.

"You see the futility of your position," Madrid continued, "In countless realities, I have already won. The chaos of individual will has been corrected through proper authority. Magic has been eliminated."

"In countless realities," Ramos replied with the sort of cheerful irreverence that suggested he was about to make a very dangerous point, "you've also lost spectacularly. Reality is remarkably flexible about providing both triumph and disaster in equal measure. It's quite considerate that way. These realities, they are feeding off of your insanity, Emperor. They are reflecting what you want to see."

Madrid's laugh was like breaking glass. "The wizard speaks of balance, as if magic cared about fairness. But I have moved beyond such primitive concepts. Observe."

He gestured, and through the widening rifts they glimpsed armies of beings that had once been human, once been dragon, once been djinn—all refined into perfect expressions of Madrid's will. They moved with identical precision, thought with identical purpose, existed with identical certainty that individual will was a disease to be cured.

"This is the future I offer," Madrid declared, his voice now carrying harmonics from every reality where he ruled supreme. "Unity of purpose. Perfection of order. The end of the wasteful chaos you call free will."

But even as he spoke, Ramos sensed something stirring through the Master Heart network—not fear, but fury.

Niloo stood up, eyes blazing. Every heartbearer still fighting across Gaia, every dragon soaring through the chaotic sky above, every free djinn wielding their magic in defense of choice itself, all of them blazed with the same fundamental refusal to surrender what made them who they were. "You're wrong," Niloo said, her crystal heart glowing brightly against her chest as she stepped forward. "Self awareness isn't chaos to be corrected. It's the most beautiful thing in existence—the ability to choose, to grow, to become something more than what you started as."

"Beautiful," Madrid sneered. "Tell me, child, how beautiful is free will when it chooses evil and suffering? How noble is free will when it selects destruction over order?"

"As you have?" snapped Niloo. "It's beautiful because it's ours," Niloo replied, her crystal heart blazing as she reached for the Master Heart's full power. "It's noble because it's real. And it's worth fighting for because without it, we're nothing but extensions of someone else's will."

Through the network, she felt every heartbearer responding to her words—not just those fighting above Fire Ridge, but all of them across Gaia.

We are with you, came Elissa's voice from distant Tyr, her crystal blazing as she channeled power across provinces. *Every heart, every choice, every moment of freedom we've ever known.*

For freedom, added Shreya from Cassimir, her connection carrying the strength of mountain stone and desert wind.

One by one, the heartbearers across Gaia lent their power to the Master Heart network, their combined will creating a resonance that made the volcanic cavern ring like a vast bell. But this time, Niloo wasn't just connecting with the free heartbearers—she was reaching for the enslaved ones as well, the ones whose crystals pulsed with the dull red of blood magic compulsion.

Darius, she called through the network, her mental voice carrying all the love and determination of their shared childhood. *I'm here. We're all here. You don't have to fight alone anymore.*

Through the connection came her brother's anguished response, his consciousness battered by years of magical compulsion but still fundamentally, recognizably him: *Niloo... the binding... burns... but I can feel... everyone. So many hearts... so much light...*

"Impossible," Madrid snarled, as he felt his control over the enslaved heartbearers beginning to waver. "The blood magic bindings are absolute! They cannot be overcome by mere sentiment!"

"They're not being overcome by sentiment," Ramos said with a grin. "They're being overwhelmed by mathematics. You see, Madrid, you've made a fundamental error in your calculations."

"What error?" Madrid demanded, as he strove to break the rift wide open. A keening sound rose from the spelled silver, and now the surface of the potion bubbled and frothed as though it was being heated up by the thermal current running through the runes.

"You assumed free will was a finite resource," Ramos explained, his magic blazing as he channeled power into maintaining the cavern's increasingly unstable reality. "But freedom shared doesn't diminish—it multiplies. Every connection made between free souls makes every other connection stronger. Every heart that beats in harmony creates resonance for all the others."

Through the Master Heart network, Niloo felt the truth of Ramos's words. The more heartbearers who joined the connection, the stronger it became. The more they shared their individual consciousness, their free will and their magic, the more powerful their connection grew. And Madrid's blood magic, designed to control individual minds, couldn't adapt to the exponential growth of shared awareness.

The bonds are breaking, came voices from across Gaia as enslaved heartbearers fought to free themselves of Madrid's control and compulsion.

"No!" Madrid's shriek of fury sent cracks through several realities simultaneously. "I will not be denied by the delusions of inferior minds! I will have order! I will have control!"

He abandoned his careful work at the Crossroads apparatus, and spun around to face them, gathering the elemental power surging within the spelled silver bowl, pulling on its essence. A dark cloud rose to shield him as he lifted his hands. Black lightning shot from his hands. striking Lapis in the chest. The dragon screamed, rearing back on her hind legs, and issuing a jet of flame at Madrid, that parted and passed around the emperor to either side.

The second bolt shot straight at Ramos' head, but the wiley wizard dived to the side and behind a clutch of eggs. Ramos sent a ring of fire back at the emperor that exploded when it came in contact with the billowing black shield, and flashed around the room.

Lazuli screeched with fury and shifted into the shape of an eagle, then rose into the air and dived at Madrid, claws outstretched Before he could reach his eyes, Madrid right hand came up and miniature bolts of lightning flashed from his fingertips. Lazuli flipped over to dodge the oncoming lightning but one bolt struck his wing and he screeched again and tumbled to the floor.

Niloo screamed as she felt his pain through the bond. Furious, her eyes rose and met Madrids.

"You are mine," she hissed through gritted teeth.

CHAPTER THIRTY

THE TEARING
OF REALITY

Madrid struck first, his hands weaving spells that existed in multiple dimensions simultaneously. Where his magic touched the fabric of the rift, the separation weakened..

"Behold order imposed on chaos!" he cried, his voice harmonizing with versions of himself across infinite possibilities. "Watch freedom refined into its proper, submissive form!"

The spell should have overwhelmed Niloo instantly. Instead, it struck the blazing network of the Master Heart and... scattered. Like light hitting a prism, Madrid's spell fractured against the multifaceted consciousness of dozens of free minds, each one refracting his perfect order into something more complex, more beautiful, more alive.

"We are not one mind pretending to be many, " Niloo replied through the network, her voice carrying the conviction of every heart-bearer, connected to the crystal pulsing against her chest. "We are many minds choosing to be one."

Through the connection, she felt Lapis's fierce pride, Lazuli's determination, and Ramos's long suffering strength anchoring them all. Threading through it all like a melody half-remembered, she felt Darius's growing presence, as he fought free of the blood magic that had bound him.

Madrid's features shifted through expressions of rage. "Impossible! Individual consciousness cannot maintain coherence when merged! The chaos becomes overwhelming! You should be dissolving into madness!"

"Should be, perhaps," Ramos said cheerfully, "But free will has never been particularly concerned with following rules. It's remarkably stubborn about remaining itself, even when logic suggests otherwise."

To demonstrate his point, the wizard threw back his head and laughed out loud, while juggling balls of their recorded laughter—actual physical manifestations of their shared humour. At the sound, Niloo's lips twitched and she began to laugh also. Lazuli soon joined in and their combined laughter rang out through the chamber, with harmonics capable of making reality hiccup. Where they touched Madrid's rifts of projected perfect order, chaos bloomed.

"You find this is amusing?" Madrid snarled, gesturing to the dimensional rift where Madrid's armies gathered to attack. "You think this is some kind of cosmic jest?"

"I think the universe is laughing at you," Ramos replied, sending a ball of fire toward Madrid's head. "And I think you've forgotten how to appreciate the punchline of a good joke."

Madrid sent a bolt of black lightning into the closest rift and the world exploded. Ramos felt himself lifted into the air and slammed against the wall of the cavern, where he hung spread eagle, pinned by magical shackles to the cold, stone wall. The force of the rift tear tumbled Niloo across the floor and she came to rest on her side at the base of the wall. Lazuli was similarly affected, but managed to shift into the shape of a fly and ride out the worst of the force of the explosion. Only Lapis was unaffected, and with a roar, she laid down a blaze of fire as she flung herself at Madrid.

But every strike she landed on Madrid was absorbed by the rift.

Through Lapis's bond, Niloo felt the ancient dragons above joining their power to the network. Stellaris's starlight magic wove through the connection like liquid music, while Opaleye's ancient wisdom provided the stable foundation that kept their shared consciousness from fragmenting under the strain.

The mountain itself awakens, came Jannah's voice through the network. *The ancient dragons are responding to the presence of so many of its children. The volcanic forces are aligning with us.*

Niloo felt it then—Fire Ridge itself was choosing sides. The molten stone beneath their feet began to pulse in rhythm with the Master Heart, the crystalline formations in the cavern walls sang in harmony with their shared consciousness, and the ancient pathways carved by the first dragons glowed with renewed purpose. Niloo pushed herself up to a sitting position, wincing at the pain in her wrists.

"No!" Madrid's shriek of fury sent cracks through reality itself. "Stone cannot choose! Magic cannot have preference! Only free will can decide, and free will must be controlled!"

But even as he spoke, his carefully constructed Crossroads spell began to quiver. The dimensional rifts he had torn open halted, then began to mend themselves, no longer chaotic wounds in reality but organized pathways that seemed to be selecting which versions of existence to connect.

The pathways choose what passes through them, Stellaris's ancient voice carried across the network, rich with long lost knowledge and understanding. *Madrid has assumed he could force reality to serve his will, but the Crossroads were created by dragons who understood that existence itself must consent to change.*

Through the largest dimensional rift stepped not another army of enslaved beings, but something else entirely—dragons from realities where Madrid had never risen to power, versions of Gaia where heartbearers and their companions lived in harmony with the natural world. They emerged not as conquerors but as reinforcements, drawn by the Master Heart's call across infinite possibilities.

"Impossible," Madrid repeated, but his voice carried a note of uncertainty for the first time.. "The pathways obey the one who opens them. Reality bends to superior will."

"Reality cooperates with consciousness that respects its nature," Niloo replied. "You've been trying to force the universe to serve you, but consciousness—real consciousness—only flourishes when it's freely given."

Through it all, Niloo felt a familiar presence growing stronger in the network—Darius, his consciousness blazing brighter as the blood magic bond finally shattered under the combined will of every free mind connected to the Master Heart.

Sister, his mental voice was clear for the first time in years, carrying all the warmth and love of their shared childhood. *I can see him clearly now. Madrid isn't just trying to control magic and free will—he's trying to replace it entirely. This thing he's become... it's not human anymore.*

"Then lets show him what real freedom looks like," Niloo said, reaching through the network to mentally grasp her brother's hand across the chaos of battle. "We will show him what it means to choose freely, to become one."

The Master Heart pulsed with unprecedented power as brother and sister joined their will through the crystal network. Around them, every heartbearer in Gaia added their voice to the growing magic—not the mechanical unison Madrid demanded, but the complex, beautiful chorus of individual minds choosing to work together.

And in that moment of perfect cooperation freely given, something extraordinary happened.

The Crossroads spell, designed to tear holes in reality for Madrid's conquest, began to respond to a different kind of summons. Instead of pathways to realities where Madrid ruled supreme, the rifts began showing glimpses of worlds where consciousness had evolved beyond the need for control entirely—realms where free will and cooperation had created societies that Madrid's perfect order could never match.

"What have you done?" Madrid demanded, his transformed features shifting through expressions of rage and terror that existed across multiple dimensions.

"We've given reality a choice," Niloo replied, her voice carrying the authority of every free mind that had ever dared to dream of something better. "And it's choosing consciousness over control, cooperation over compulsion, beautiful chaos over sterile perfection."

Niloo sensed him before her eyes picked him out in the deep gloom at the edge of the cavern. "Darius," she whispered, turning toward her brother with eyes that sought him hungrily.

He stood near the cavern's entrance, his red crystal heart pulsing with its natural warm light for the first time in years. The silver traceries that Madrid's blood magic had burned into his arms were fading, replaced by faint scars that spoke of battles fought and won. But it was his eyes that showed the greatest change—no longer the hollow gaze of someone fighting constant compulsion, but the warm, familiar expression of the brother she remembered.

"Niloo." Her name on his lips carried years of separation, months of magical slavery, and the overwhelming relief of consciousness finally returned to itself. "I thought... I thought I might never be able to say your name with my own voice again."

Further into the chamber's weak light stepped Darius, eyes blazing with hatred as they sought and found the object of his hatred. With a cry of fury, Darius launched himself at Madrid, running across the chamber and to the very base of the plinth. Madrid looked down at the furious heart bearer and with a wicked smile, reached out a hand and gripped Darius's crystal heart.

Darius froze. His eyes widened, with shock and pain. Slick, black tar oozed from his heart and his mouth opened in a silent scream. Madrid looked up from the heartbearer and said, "You don't really think I would have come here without an escape plan, do you?" Madrid reached up and touched the nearest rift.

There was a clap of thunder, and the world went black.

When light returned, Madrid, Darius, the potion, spelled silver and all the rifts were gone.

CHAPTER THIRTY-ONE

THE PRICE OF VICTORY

The silence that followed Madrid's escape through the dimensional rift felt heavy, weighted with the strange emptiness that comes after surviving something that should have destroyed everything you've ever known. The Crossroads basin that had contained the spell lay shattered around them, its crystalline components cooling from white-hot to merely dangerous, while reality itself seemed to catch its breath after being stretched beyond all reasonable limits.

Niloo sat slumped against a chunk of volcanic stone, her mind reeling with the sudden loss of connection to her brother. She swiped a hand across her face and it came away wet with blood from multiple cuts, mingling with her tears. The strain of coordinating the Master Heart network during the final confrontation had sapped her of her remaining strength. But even as her individual awareness returned, she remained acutely connected to her companions—not through the blazing intensity of battle-forged unity, but through the deeper, more sustainable bond of minds that had chosen to face the impossible together and somehow survived.

We did it, Lapis murmured through their connection, her mental voice carrying exhaustion that went beyond physical fatigue. The great dragon lay coiled around their small group, her lapis lazuli scales dulled with effort but her eyes bright with something that might have been wonder. *Madrid is gone, exiled to a reality where his methods may find more willing acceptance. The pathways between worlds are sealed. The immediate crisis has passed.*

Has it? Lazuli asked, *And at what cost?* He slumped against Lapis' side, too tired to shift into anything more than his human form. *I can feel the echoes of what we almost lost—we came within moments of being eliminated from existence.*

Through the triad bond, Niloo felt her companions processing the magnitude of what they had prevented and the price they had paid to prevent it. The Master Heart network had succeeded beyond their most optimistic projections, connecting heartbearers across Gaia in ways that created collective consciousness without eliminating individual identity. But the cost of channeling that much collective magic had left lasting marks on everyone involved.

The other heartbearers, she said, reaching through the network to check on distant friends and allies. The connections felt different now—less intense than during the crisis, but somehow more solid, as if the shared experience of facing mind rendering forces had created permanent bonds between minds that had chosen to trust each other completely.

We're alive, came Elissa's voice through the network, though her mental presence carried the strain of someone who had pushed far beyond their normal limits. *Shaken, exhausted, fundamentally changed by what we experienced together, but alive. Though I think it will be some time before any of us fully understand what we've become.*

We've established a connection that we can all use in this fight for freedom, Shreya added from distant Cassimir. *No longer do we fight alone. We've proven it's possible to communicate over the distance that separates us, but we've also learned that it requires constant choice, and constant communication to stabilize the connection. Yet, my battle is just beginning. Can I count on you all to aide me if the need presents itself?*

of course, said Niloo. *We are strongest when we are unified, in thought and purpose. You only need to ask.*

Madrid's escape troubles me, Lapis admitted, wrestling with the moral complexity of their final choice. *We had the power to destroy him completely, to ensure he could never again threaten magic anywhere. Instead, he has escape to who knows where and when? I don't think this is the last we have seen of him.*

Yes, and the fact that the male heartbearers were not able to break away completely, before he reverted his control over their corrupted hearts. The danger continues, said Lazuli.

That was my decision, Ramos said quietly, accepting responsibility for a choice that would haunt him for the rest of his life. It was one of many he had had to make dating back to the fall of the wizard keep. Few lived who remembered that time. *I could have used magic to jamb the rift open and pursue him, and maybe I could have eliminated him permanently. But maybe I would have failed, and then who would be left to counter the male wizards under his control? I fear that battle is yet to come.*

The instant when he had felt the network's power surging, offering up the ability to harness the magic of the heart bearers, to bring them under his control and then reach across the dimensional barrier and annihilate Madrid...well the temptation had been overwhelming, justified by every cruelty he had inflicted, every mind he had broken, every soul he had corrupted in service of his vision of perfect world order. He'd almost pursued Madrid into the rift..

The escape was a compromise, Lazuli observed, *Madrid escapes immediate justice, but he also loses access to Gaia's unique magical properties, to the heartbearer network, to everything that made his vision possible here. In the reality he chose, he may find that his techniques are less effective, his control less absolute.*

Or he may find that a world already torn by war is more receptive to promises of order, Lapis countered, *We may have saved our own reality at the potential cost of another's freedom.*

The moral weight of that possibility settled over all three of them like a shroud woven from guilt and necessity. They had made the choice that preserved their world, that protected the greatest number of thinking beings from Madrid's vision. But they had also condemned unknown numbers of beings in another reality to face challenges they might not be prepared to overcome.

This is what leadership means, Niloo realized, the understanding bringing no comfort. *Making choices where every option involves sacrifice, where the best decision still carries costs that will echo across generations. Madrid forced us to choose. He planned for this. I wonder what else he has planned, that we cannot see.*

They got to their feet and shuffled into the tunnel leading to the surface. With Madrid's absense, the chamber was reverting back to its resting state, returning to a place of slumber. The walls cooled and as they reached the surface, there was hardly any change in temperature as they exited the caves.

Grateful for the space once again, Lapis arched her back and stretched her wings, sweeping them up and wide, revelling in the freedom of unrestricted movement. They looked around, wondering at the quiet and calm that surrounded them. The battlefield of the dragons had ceased, and its combatants had flown elsewhere. Whether as free or captive dragons, the moment that Madrid had stepped into the alternative reality, the will to fight had evaporated.

All that remained to remind them that a battle had been taking place, was the smell of scorched earth, and the occasional broken sword, or snapped arrow, scattered around like dropped toys.

The sun was setting over Fire Ridge, painting the volcanic peaks in colors that spoke of endings and beginnings intertwined. Through the Master Heart network, they could feel the pulse of dozens of consciousness choosing to maintain their connections, to preserve the bonds they had forged through crisis, to continue the work of demonstrating that through cooperation they could persevere. One by one, the heartbearers sent their gentle farewells and returned to the tasks at hand in their respective provinces, for the fight was not won, but merely paused.

Madrid was gone, but the real victory would not be measured in battles won or enemies defeated, but in the slow, patient work of building a world where freedom and magic could flourish without fear of those who sought to reduce its magnificent complexity to simple obedience.

The price of victory was the obligation to remain worthy of it, every day, for the rest of their lives.

And in the gathering twilight, three minds that had chosen each other prepared to bear that price together, sustained by the understanding that freedoms shared freely were not diminished by responsibility but strengthened by it.

Niloo climbed onto Lapis' back and settled into the saddle. Lazuli, in bird form, settled onto her shoulder. Niloo glanced back at the entrance to the cavern one last time, thinking of Darius. With a sigh, she pushed the sorrow away, to be examined later in private. All three nodded to the little wizard, and then with a running leap, Lapis soared into the air.

Ramos patted Betsy's nose as she shoved it under his arm in greeting. A soft wicker issued from her mouth.

"Yes, I know. Madrid will be back. Until then, we continue the fight." Turning his back on the vanishing spot in the sky that was Niloo and her companions, he placed a hand to his brow and squinted into the sun. "Now, which way is HIndra? Ah yes, south. Ready for the next adventure?"

Betsy snorted, then turned her back to the bony old man, offering him a ride.

Clambering onto her back, they trotted off into the sunset.

CHAPTER THIRTY-TWO

THE PORTAL

High above the Citadel, a tempest stirred. Swirling dark clouds formed out of a cloudless sky, black as night and spinning ominously. Lightning flashed, highlighting the underside of the roiling cloud, outlining the cloud's shape in the starry sky. With a sizzling smack, a bolt of bluish lightning struck the tip of the spelled silver mast, built on the peak of the roof on the highest spire.

The spelled silver clanged like a gong, and conducted the spike of energy down its length, as it had been designed to do. The unnatural lightning took on a life of its own, triggering an answering rumble deep within the base of the former Wizard's keep. Waves of rolling sound washed over the island known as the Citadel to the people of Gaia. Tremors shook the ground, causing vases to topple from their plinths in the alcoves of the great tower, and smash on the ground. People were tossed from their straw stuffed mattresses onto the floor of their poor huts,

Children cried. Adults cursed. And in the rookery of the keep, the dragons and their djinn who had returned to their roost, trembled.

Deep underground, in a room bound on all sides by spelled silver cladding, a portal opened into another world, and through it stepped a man clad in the royal colours of the court of Camelot.

CHAPTER THIRTY-THREE

FANTASY BY SUSAN FAW

The Spirit Shield Saga

Seer of Souls

Soul Sanctuary

Soul Sacrifice

Soul Survivor

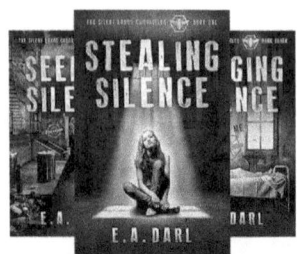

The Silent Lands Chronicles

Stealing Silence

Seeking Silence

Stinging Silence

Shadowed Silence

Sneaking Silence

The Heart Of The Citadel

Heart of Destiny

Heart of Tyr

Heart of Shadra

Heart of Bastion

Heart of Fjord

Heart of Tunise

Heart of Peca

Heart of Samos

Legends Of The Once And Future King

Bone Dragon

www.ingramcontent.com/pod-product-compliance
Lightning Source LLC
Chambersburg PA
CBHW050927030726
47503CB00007BB/2499